A
WELL-TIMED
MURDER

Also by Tracee de Hahn

Swiss Vendetta

A WELL-TIMED MURDER

TRACEE de HAHN

MINOTAUR BOOKS

NEW YORK

A WELL-TIMED MURDER. Copyright © 2018 by Tracee de Hahn. All rights reserved. Printed in the United States of America. For information, address St. Martin's Press, 175 Fifth Avenue, New York, N.Y. 10010.

www.minotaurbooks.com

The Library of Congress Cataloging-in-Publication Data
is available upon request.

ISBN 978-1-250-11001-5 (hardcover)
ISBN 978-1-250-11002-2 (ebook)

Our books may be purchased in bulk for promotional, educational, or business use. Please contact your local bookseller or the Macmillan Corporate and Premium Sales Department at 1-800-221-7945, extension 5442, or by email at MacmillanSpecialMarkets@macmillan.com.

First Edition: February 2018

10 9 8 7 6 5 4 3 2 1

For my parents

ACKNOWLEDGMENTS

Writing is a lonely endeavor, but I've never felt alone due to the support of my family, friends, readers, booksellers, and the entire mystery/thriller community.

My heartfelt thanks go to my parents, Lynn and Janet Leigh; my sisters, Amber Willis and Kathryn Balch; and my Hamman and Porta cousins who came out to support me in bookstores across the South. Also to Bette and Lance Morgan from Parma, Missouri, where I spent my first years, who traveled across more than one state line to see me in bookstores.

My husband, Henri de Hahn, and our constant travel companion Vacherin; they are the real Swiss inspiration.

My readers and encouragers who sustained me through plot changes and other anxieties: Ellen Braaten, Hannah Dennison, Kathi Good, Margaret Hamilton, Paul Haydon, Stacia Momburg, and Mindy Quigley. Thank you for the dinners, drinks, phone calls, and cups of tea.

Julia Smyth-Pinney, who spent several memorable days with

me in Switzerland and at Baselworld. Sorry we didn't leave with new timepieces!

Pierre and Danuta Junod for their hospitality and introduction to watchmaking. Daniel Bardy for the excellent fondue. Keep your fingers crossed for a French translation.

My fellow Miss Demeanors: D. A. Bartley, Susan Breen, Michele Dorsey, Alexia Gordon, Cate Holahan, and Robin Stuart. Love spending a moment of each day blogging with you.

Charles Todd for his encouragement and advice to a debut author.

Cassie Carter and Taylor, who represents all of our four-legged writing cheerleaders. Taylor, you are missed.

The Algonkian New York Pitch Conference where I met my marvelous agent, Paula Munier (thank you everyone at Talcott Notch Literary Services).

Everyone at St. Martin's Press, and I do mean everyone, from editors to marketing and publicity and cover art. Among this fantastic crew I'd like to mention a few in particular: my wonderful editor Elizabeth Lacks, who asks the right questions; publicist extraordinaire Hector DeJean; marketing guru Allison Zeigler; and Shailyn Tavella, who gave up her free evening to come out in support of *Swiss Vendetta* in New York.

Most important, all of the readers. Thank you.

Mine honour is my life; both grown in one;
Take honour from me, and my life is done.
—*RICHARD II*

A
WELL-TIMED
MURDER

One

There was a crowd but none of them mattered. Agnes Lüthi had eyes for only one man, the one she'd nicknamed the Roach. The one she'd only dreamt of finding in Switzerland.

She moved quickly despite her injured leg, focused on her destination, closing her umbrella when she reached the high canopy. A chain of buses discharged passengers in front of the Messe Basel Exhibition Halles, and they flowed past her toward the doors as if the world's premier watch and jewelry show might sell out of goods if they dallied. She had never before been to Baselworld, but from the look of the well-dressed crowd judged it was a fitting place to find this particular man.

She was within grasping distance of a door handle when Marcel Aubry appeared from behind a kiosk. He was cloaked in a long, belted raincoat and had a finger pressed to his ear, listening. Before she could speak, he grasped her wrist with his free hand and pulled her behind the advertising stand, out of sight of the glass front of the lobby.

"Slight change of plan," Aubry said, his voice low and hurried. "The Roach is headed this way." He frowned, listening to the voices in his earpiece.

Agnes moved closer to Aubry; it felt like stepping into a shadow. He was a big man, not exactly fat, but big enough to make her feel slim. She could hear the scratch of a voice broadcast from his earpiece, but not the words. Her pulse quickened. They'd worked together for years in Financial Crimes. Despite that, she'd never seen him run a field operation. This was an important arrest for him, one he'd not leave to others. She was thrilled to be included.

"Did you ever think you'd see us catch him?" Aubry said to her, still focused on the chatter in his ear.

"No, and I don't believe it yet today." She'd had the Roach in her grasp three times, only to have him scurry back into a crack at the last moment. All of Europe and half of Asia was looking for him. In addition to Swiss francs, he'd stolen millions of euros, yen, dollars, and pounds—all electronically. Despite his methods, she'd always believed that he occasionally appeared in person at a place he'd targeted. Now it looked as if her suspicions were proving true.

"This time he's definitely here," said Aubry. "Problem is, the place is littered with exits and there's a record crowd. Feels like half the world's come to Baselworld. Good for the economy, bad for us, since on-site security doesn't want a fuss disturbing their clientele." He nodded. "Anyway, I'm glad you're here to see it."

"I was nearby when you called. I left my mother-in-law at the Beyeler Museum like a bride at the altar. She may not forgive me." Agnes watched the crowd stream into the building, oblivious of the police operation. Aubry had orchestrated a smooth intervention despite having to move quickly.

"Your call was the best news I've had in weeks," she added. "A few days ago one of my kids accused me of missing the criminals."

Vincent—her oldest—had phrased it more bluntly: that she liked spending time with the bad guys more than with them. Before she could protest, her youngest son had added that at least she wasn't a criminal herself. They'd all laughed. It was true, she did miss work. Surely that wasn't a bad message for the boys? Their father had had a strong work ethic.

Aubry pulled his wrist up and spoke into a microphone, asking a question. He looked at her. "When are you officially back on the job?"

"Three days. Monday." She gave her wool jacket a downward tug and straightened the matching skirt. Her stint in hospital had melted a few kilos away. Nearly being killed wasn't the easiest diet, but it was no doubt effective. A few more kilos and she would consider thanking the man who had knifed her.

Aubry held up his hand, listening to chatter in his earpiece. "Any minute now," he whispered, as if they could be overheard. "He's heading to the lobby. It's perfect. Fewer civilians and more space gives us an advantage."

"He'll run." Agnes shifted weight off her bad leg. Critically, she eyed the long bank of doors. The building's sleek overhang soared across the street, sheltering trams, taxis, a restaurant, and a flower stall. She hoped Aubry really did have all exits covered. She had a vague notion that the five or six halls of the Messe Basel facility were connected by upper corridors and enclosed walkways. It was a large complex.

Aubry tapped his thigh impatiently. His gaze strayed to her leg. "How's life in Violent Crimes?"

A voice sputtered in his ear and Aubry listened, sparing her the need to answer. "He's on the move," Aubry said quietly.

Agnes tensed.

"Now," Aubry shouted, running to the doors and yanking one open.

Two men in suits moved from another angle and Agnes spotted their earpieces. The men broke into a half run, and a few bystanders gasped while others pulled out mobile phones set to record video. The officers pushed ahead toward the turnstiles leading to the show, and Agnes followed. Aubry put a hand to his earpiece and stopped her. He angled his head down and she could hear voices talking on top of one another. Someone yelled and Aubry flinched.

Suddenly, in the distance, car tires screeched. There was a loud thump and a scream, followed seconds later by other shouts. Agnes turned toward the noise and Aubry followed. They ran to the right side of the building, ignoring the drizzle. The side street was closed to all but exhibitors' vehicles, and Agnes pushed her way through the gathered crowd. What she saw stopped her in her tracks. Aubry, close behind, collided with her.

The street was dedicated to instruments of luxury and speed, and in the middle of the road a gleaming red Ferrari had struck a man. He lay in a shallow pool of rainwater a meter from the front bumper. Both car and man were broken. The hood of the car was dented and smeared with blood. The man's leg was angled midcalf, and the fabric of his pants was split by a bone. Blood spilled from the back of his head, pooling around his hair, mixing with rain and running in rivulets to the curb. Agnes recognized the man immediately. She put a hand to her mouth.

A second glance at the unique shape of his ears confirmed it: the Roach.

Aubry cursed under his breath and darted around her. Other officers were already there. A security guard leaned over the body; a quick check confirmed the obvious. The man was dead.

Agnes stepped back a pace, memories overlaying what was in front of her. Three weeks ago, a man had knelt beside *her*, spoken to *her*, and touched *her* neck for a pulse when she lay twisted on the floor with her leg and chest dripping blood. She remembered the blackness closing in, the numbness, the ringing in her ears. The memory bled into reality and she touched her side, feeling off-balance. She stumbled away, needing room to breathe.

Outside the press of the crowd, the scent of blood receded, the memories faded, and her pulse slowed. The rain had stopped and she leaned heavily on the tip of her furled umbrella. The Roach dead? He wasn't a murderer. This wasn't a fitting end to his crimes or to their investigation. There should have been an arrest. A trial. She glanced back in his direction. Officers were huddled over the body. She felt they'd been cheated out of the end. She'd wanted to interview him. To learn more about how he operated. Maybe even understand what motivated him. Why keep stealing when you've already made a fortune?

Her phone buzzed and she glanced at the screen. The feeling of uncertainty shifted when she read the caller ID. Julien Vallotton. He had saved her life, yet she'd ignored him in the past weeks, not ready to talk. Not trusting her judgment or her feelings.

This time the message was different.

She looked toward the dead man again. There were enough officers on-site to handle a situation far more complicated than this, and technically she was an observer to Aubry's operation. She pushed through the next layer of gathering crowd until she reached the building. There, she leaned against the cold black metal façade.

She reread the message: *Please call me. Urgent.*

She had seen Julien Vallotton only once since leaving hospital. Since then, he'd texted her twice. The first time to see if she was recovering. The second, to ask if she would like to go to dinner. She'd not replied the second time. How could she go to dinner with him? What would she tell her boys? Or her in-laws? With her husband dead only four months, what would she tell herself? She glanced at the message again. He wasn't the kind of man to say something was urgent as a ploy to prompt a response.

Baselworld security guards were dispersing the crowd, and Agnes could see past the dented Ferrari to its well-dressed driver. He was vomiting into a potted plant, and she hoped he would feel better once he realized he'd killed a master criminal and not a family man. She took another look at his car. Julien Vallotton had one like this. A Ferrari Pininfarina Sergio. What had he said, that it was one of only six in the world? Possibly the man was vomiting because he'd dented his hood.

She took a deep breath and called Vallotton. It only took one sentence to change the course of her day.

"We buried a friend yesterday. Police say it was an accident." He paused and his tone altered. "I think it was murder."

Two

Agnes held her phone tight against her ear and asked Julien Vallotton to repeat his words. An ambulance approached and she could barely hear him over the nasal *woohoo woohoo* of the siren. The noise reverberated between the exhibition halls, making her head hurt.

"I believe someone I know has been killed," he said, enunciating carefully.

The siren grew louder. She put a finger in one ear.

"The coroner says it was an accident. I—we—need someone who will listen to a different point of view. That's why I thought of you."

The crowd was dispersing, revealing a row of luxury automobiles backed in against the building. Lamborghini, Mercedes-Benz, late-model Rolls-Royce, vintage Rolls-Royce, Maserati, another Ferrari, several emblazoned with the logo of a luxury watchmaker or jeweler. Now that Aubry no longer needed her to interrogate the Roach, she had no reason to be at Baselworld. The alternative to listening to Vallotton was to return to the museum and her mother-in-law. She would rather help the cleanup crew than do that.

"Let's start with who died," she said.

Five minutes later, Agnes reached the center of Halle 1, where the glamorous Global Brands were displayed. The light changed. It brightened. She looked up from the Baselworld map she had been studying and laughed out loud. This was a different world from the gray drizzle outside. This was glamour and lights. The people who streamed into the exhibit had been transformed, stripped of their coats and umbrellas and turned into sophisticated butterflies. They laughed and greeted friends and admired window displays filled with watches that were gem studded or miracles of mechanical ingenuity or both. The air was heavy with a mixture of hushed noise and palpable giddiness, and Vallotton was here. Here with the dead man's daughter.

Heading toward the café where she had agreed to meet them, Agnes felt as if she were walking down the Bahnhofstrasse in Zürich. The individual pavilions were as large as houses and laid out like stores on a street: Chopard, Bulgari, Breguet, Blancpain, and dozens more in the distance.

Guy Chavanon, she said to herself, repeating the name of the man who had died. She hadn't recognized it even when Vallotton assured her that he was a well-known watchmaker.

Agnes passed the Patek Philippe showroom. The upper stories were built of luminous white glass, curved like a floating spaceship.

Hastening past early tulips blooming in raised long containers, she admired the Rolex pavilion to her left, tempted to take a photograph to show her sons, and instead committing details to memory. The building glowed green near the floor while the upper part was a contoured white structure, a geometric cloud. Farther on, Omega boasted a sophisticated white marble-and-etched-glass façade, while Tissot was a towering black grid. Agnes wondered if the show had a theme, thinking it should be money meets more money.

Carried along by the hum of the crowd, she felt the heart of Switzerland pulsing, transforming the raw materials of other countries into luxury items. Official theme of Baselworld or not, for six days money would definitely meet money here. Money would make more money here. It had been a fitting place to find the Roach, and for different reasons it was a fitting place to meet Julien Vallotton. Her own pulse rate increased.

At the end of the connecting passage, Halle 3, Stones & Pearls, was smaller and quieter. She glanced around appraisingly. The one-story showrooms were connected by standardized white, black, or gray façades. Overhead, large signs identified the brands. Immediately ahead, the sign above the café read as Julien Vallotton had described on the phone: THE HALL OF ELEMENTS. Elements meaning gold, diamonds, and their near relatives, Agnes presumed. No pedestrian fire and water for this crowd. Beneath the sign, she spotted Vallotton greeting a young woman. Even in a crowd of beautiful well-dressed people, he commanded attention: aristocratic bearing, dark, nearly black hair graying at the temples, arresting blue eyes. He wore a dark suit with a striped shirt and brightly patterned silk tie, and the cut of his suit was subtly better, and the shine of his shoes brighter, than anyone else's. Agnes hesitated. She'd avoided this meeting for weeks and now remembered exactly why. He approached before she could change her mind and leave.

"I didn't expect you'd agree to talk to Christine," he said after they had shaken hands.

Agnes's gaze flicked to the young woman at the café. The dead man's daughter. "Even after you learned I was already here?"

She relaxed now that they had passed any initial awkwardness. If only she could keep the conversation away from their personal life. *Her* personal life, she corrected. She shifted her gaze to the woman. She was young, maybe midtwenties, well dressed in a conservative dark suit. Her brown hair was pulled back in a low bun, and her makeup was tasteful. Her slightly irregular features would never be described as beautiful, or even pretty. She was attractive at best. Today, the rims of her eyes were slightly reddened, as if she had been crying.

"Full disclosure," Vallotton said. "Claiming murder was a statement longer on impact than fact, but I wanted your attention." His mouth was set in a grim line. He glanced at his watch and straightened a cuff under his jacket. "Christine's on a work break and doesn't have much time."

"If you stretched the truth, perhaps that's fortunate," Agnes said, surprised and disappointed. She stepped forward and extended her hand in greeting. "Mademoiselle Chavanon, I'm Inspector Agnes Lüthi."

The café bar was a long narrow oval, and Christine was seated at the rounded end. After shaking hands, Agnes sat on an empty stool and ordered an espresso from the waitress. "With an almond croissant, *s'il vous plaît,*" she added, seeing her favorite pastry in the case.

"Please call me Christine. I can't thank you enough. I

knew Monsieur Vallotton would know who to call." The young woman pulled an envelope from her purse, her hand shaking, and handed it to Agnes. "I found this under my doormat this morning."

The envelope was scuffed with dirt. Agnes withdrew a pristine sheet of paper, careful to touch only one edge. Two sentences were written in a distinctive man's script. *Be careful. We are being watched.* She glanced from Christine to Vallotton, noting his surprise. He'd told her that Guy Chavanon had died in circumstances that the police labeled accidental. A label Vallotton and the man's daughter didn't agree with. He certainly hadn't mentioned any threats. Agnes felt her adrenaline spike again.

"I haven't been home for two weeks," Christine's words tumbled out. Her voice quavered. "I was staying with a friend near the office because I was working so late getting ready for Baselworld, and after my father died"—tears streamed down her cheeks—"I couldn't face being there. Being so alone. I went back last night. I needed different clothes for today and I found the note this morning. My father must have put it under the mat before he died. It's his handwriting."

Her tears turned to sobs and Vallotton handed her a monogrammed handkerchief. Agnes studied the note for a moment, then returned it to the envelope and placed everything in one of the plastic evidence bags she kept handy. Slow and steady, she reminded herself. It was possible the local police had similar notes and had already discounted their importance. A worried victim didn't turn a death into a homicide, but thankfully, it also couldn't be ignored.

The waitress set the espresso and croissant on the counter. Agnes opened a packet of sugar and added it to the cup. Vallotton was speaking into Christine's ear, calming her. Agnes watched one of Aubry's men question a couple seated at the opposite end of the café. She wondered how many people had witnessed the Roach's final run. Behind the couple, she noticed a strikingly handsome man studying Christine. He was glowering, a term she'd never thought could apply to a real person, and it occurred to her that he objected to Christine's outburst. The atmosphere of the show was elegance and ease, and her tears were unwelcome.

"Why would your father leave a note when he could telephone or text?" Agnes asked Christine in an effort to stop the torrent of tears.

"He didn't like the telephone. He would always leave me notes. If I'd been home—" Christine started to cry again, and Agnes asked another question to keep her focused.

"I'm missing most of the details. Could you start from the beginning? When your father died?"

Christine sniffed. "It was a week ago tomorrow. They said he choked to death."

"Guy had a serious allergy to peanuts," Vallotton said, "and technically his death was anaphylactic shock. His airways closed, but not because of a physical obstruction like a piece of food caught in his windpipe."

Agnes glanced sharply at him. Choking? An allergic reaction? That *did* sound like accidental death.

Shifting away from her preconceptions and thinking of the multitude of ways peanuts could be slipped to someone without his knowledge, she asked Christine, "Were you there when it happened?"

"No, my father was at a reception at my half brother's boarding school, the Moutier Institut de Jeunes Gens, near Rossemaison. Do you know it? They called an ambulance. And the police." Christine twisted a paper napkin between her hands. The woman's soft voice was difficult to hear over the din of the crowd. A few meters away a television reporter was interviewing an Asian man who, judging by the size of his entourage, was famous. Agnes leaned forward to hear, and on the other side of Christine, Vallotton did the same.

"But they didn't investigate. Not really. Even though they didn't know how he came into contact with the peanuts, they said it was an accident. I know they are wrong. With my father's sensitivity, you still don't die from particles floating through the air. You have contact with the allergen. Real contact. And now this note. He was in danger and I didn't know it." Her words ended in a plaintive wail.

Agnes broke off a piece of almond croissant and took a bite, sampling the delicate filling and giving Christine a moment to compose herself.

"Christine," a man behind them said. He was of medium height with fine regular features and skin the color of light coffee beans. "I am not thinking you would be at work today. It is good to see you taking up life again." His French was good despite his strong Indian accent. Agnes had always liked the modern Indian style of dress, and the man's silk jacket was a marvel of tailoring with horizontal stripes in alternating shades of brown and gold accented by carved buttons down the front. A flat filigreed rectangle near his collar was inlaid with diamonds accented by a single dangling pearl. He clutched a sheaf of invoices, and she decided he was a jewelry dealer, probably with a showroom nearby.

"Monsieur Patel," Christine said tightly. "I'd like you to meet Inspector Lüthi, and you must remember Monsieur Vallotton from the funeral yesterday. They're here to speak with me about my father's death. His murder."

Narendra Patel stiffened slightly, then offered his hand to each in turn. Agnes thought that mention of murder was likely on a list somewhere of things not to drop into casual conversation, and she admired the man's decision to ignore it. Her mother-in-law would have pulled up a stool and asked for all the details.

"How are Leo and your mother?" Patel asked Christine.

"My *stepmother*? She's at home. Prostrate with grief. Leo is in shock. We all are."

Agnes heard her own voice in the girl's response. She'd been similarly angry with George's mother after his suicide. Sybille had collapsed while Agnes soldiered on, wishing she had the luxury of days spent in bed, heavily medicated in a darkened room. Mother versus wife. Stepmother versus daughter. Mourning was competitive.

"I am not surprised." Patel gestured with a flutter of his hand. "At the funeral yesterday, Madame had the appearance of collapse." He adjusted the top of his collarless Nehru jacket, fingering his pin. He glanced at Agnes as if registering her title for the first time. "There is a police investigation ongoing? That would be news of great distress."

Agnes suppressed a sigh of disappointment. Curiosity always won out over politeness. Even when someone's life was in free fall, people wanted more information; especially when they knew the details wouldn't be pleasant. This was her cue. "We're making inquiries related to the verdict of accidental death."

Christine leaned forward. "And I found—"

Agnes cut her off, not wanting to share information about the note until she had more details. "You were a friend of Monsieur Chavanon's?"

"We were the very oldest friends."

"Tell Inspector Lüthi what happened that day," said Christine.

Vallotton stood to allow Patel to take his stool.

"I am very sorry for you, Christine," Patel said, refusing the seat. "As I most carefully explained yesterday, you cannot bring your father . . . my good friend back. I was there and I know what I saw. What I told the police for their reporting. It was a tragedy, a great shocking. There are many difficult moments in life, and through wisdom we learn to accept them." He pressed a hand to his chest and nodded to each of them. "You will forgive my intrusion."

Christine glared as he walked away. "When he hears about the note, he will have to believe me. Someone killed my father."

"I'd rather you not tell anyone about the note right now," said Agnes.

"Okay, but Monsieur Patel will regret not believing me when he finds out. He said my father's death was all in line with *fate*." Christine sneered. "A bunch of nonsense about Lord Krishna and Father's soul going straight to heaven. He was apparently in such a happy frame of mind that death occurred at the very best moment. He's ensured a contented afterlife." Her eyes filled with tears and she pressed the handkerchief to them.

"I know my father wasn't perfect, but people are whispering that he was careless. Absentminded. Well, he was absentminded sometimes, but ten years from now they'll be saying he wasn't careless and it was suicide. Gossip feeds on a vacuum. They need to know that he was killed." Her shoulders convulsed with sobs and she mumbled excuses. She was gone before they could stop her.

Agnes hesitated, then decided a few minutes alone was what the young woman needed. Vallotton slid onto the stool next to her. He motioned for another round of coffees, and Agnes gave him a wry look.

"You called me before you knew about the note," she said. "What made you think Chavanon's reaction wasn't an accident?"

"At the reception after the burial, one of Guy's neighbors, a Monsieur Dupré, asked me if the police were investigating."

"You think he's the killer and is worried that we might be? Ah, that we should be so lucky." Agnes opened a sugar packet and doused her new espresso, toying with the small amaretto cookie on the saucer, deciding against eating it. Perhaps it was seeing the Roach die that had killed her appetite today. Everything tasted too sweet.

"Of course not. It was more like Dupré was anticipating it," Vallotton said. "He told me that Guy had been acting frightened."

"Did he report this to the police?"

Vallotton shook his head.

Agnes stirred her espresso. "Is that it? No specifics?"

"None, although I believe that the note Christine found proves the point. My conversation with Dupré started when I mentioned that I am Leo's godfather. We were cut short when someone walked up."

"Leo is Christine's half brother?"

"Yes. He's quite a few years younger than her. Dupré commented that it is a good thing Leo is away at school this year. That Guy had been acting erratically, avoiding his friends."

"That sounds like me these last weeks."

Vallotton glanced to her leg, and she wished she hadn't brought it up.

"Dupré also said that Guy was on the verge of a great invention. That's when we were interrupted."

Agnes penned Dupré's name in her small notebook. "Great invention," she repeated slowly. "Wonder what the odds are on that?"

"Guy was a smart man—" Vallotton broke off as Christine returned. She had freshened her makeup and looked in control of herself.

"I'm sorry, but I'm exhausted, and being here today, surrounded by everything Father loved, is harder than I expected. Finding the note—" She gulped again, tears welling.

"You suspected your father's death wasn't natural before you found the note," said Agnes. "There must have been a reason. Something he said, or someone who was angry with him?"

Christine didn't reply and Agnes tried another approach. "He was a watchmaker, correct?"

"Yes, my family own Perrault et Chavanon Frères." Christine straightened on her stool, making a concerted effort to control her emotions. "No matter what people say, he was such a thoughtful, gentle man. He loved watchmaking and the creation of beautiful masterpieces. It was his whole life."

"That sounds like some people wouldn't agree that he was thoughtful," said Agnes.

"He was often distracted. It could seem impolite, and he

could be vague. He was entirely focused on his work." Christine teared up again.

Vallotton handed her a fresh handkerchief.

"If I'm to help, I need more detail," Agnes prompted. "Something bothering him, a hint of trouble. You worked together. You would have overheard things."

There was an awkward silence. "I left over two years ago," Christine finally said. "It was a hard decision, but I needed to find my own way. I've been with Omega since then."

Agnes heard the hesitation in Christine's voice. Certainly not embarrassment over her new job. Omega was a worldwide leader in timepieces.

Nearby, a babble of foreign voices rose and fell as a large group assembled in front of a showroom. In the café, a man delivering pastries knocked over a tower of china cups and they shattered. Waitresses scrambled to sweep the floor.

Oblivious to everything around her, Christine reached to a nearby stack and selected a thin card emblazoned with advertising. She started to fold it, each turn precise. A small origami crane emerged. "Father was a genius." She glanced at Vallotton. "I don't care what Marie says, *we* know he was a genius. A visionary. There was always a new idea. He would take two notions and put them together in a way no one else could imagine. His memory was encyclopedic."

A great invention, the neighbor had told Vallotton. Agnes had met a few creative geniuses in her life and didn't find them the easiest people to be around. Sometimes she placed her father in that category. Certainly, his fellow chefs lauded him a genius. Her mother said he was impossible. He was lucky that she was willing to love the impossible.

"Marie is your stepmother? Your father's wife? Does she share your concerns about his death?"

"I don't know. She's been . . . busy with other things. She's not a bad person, but she doesn't understand the business. She doesn't feel about it like we do. To her it's *just* a business and not something more, not something special. Father dreamt of transforming the industry." Christine gave a little laugh.

"Had he made a great discovery? Is that why you were worried?" Agnes asked.

Christine set the origami bird on the café bar, balancing it carefully. "Being a genius doesn't mean you pop out an invention every year. It has to be the right idea and the right moment. His belief in the possibilities was what I admired."

Agnes heard the unspoken words—no, he hadn't invented anything. A dabbler? A man who didn't live up to expectations with a wife who wasn't supportive? "You enjoyed working alongside your father, yet you left the company?"

"I needed a wider range of experience." Christine's eyes flicked down, and Agnes doubted the vague answer contained the truth.

"Will Perrault et Chavanon remain in the family?"

"Marie would never sell."

"Sometimes businesses are broken up, either to generate capital or to make good on bequests."

"That won't happen. The company has always been more important than any one of us. No matter what, Marie can't sell. It's all that's left of our name."

"How involved is Madame Chavanon?" Agnes asked.

"She's in charge of the business end of things."

"Even though she"—Agnes glanced at her notes—"doesn't 'understand the business'?"

"It's the *soul* of what we do that she doesn't understand. Watches are who we are as a family. The science, the beauty. For over a hundred fifty years we've stood for craftsmanship. To Marie, it's *work*. Father would have died for it." Christine stumbled over her words. "I didn't mean . . ."

Vallotton slid a glass of water close and she took a sip.

Agnes rephrased her earlier question. "Had you noticed a change in your father recently? Was he afraid or secretive? I'm trying to pinpoint when his concern started. Something made him leave that note."

Christine fiddled with the paper crane, modifying its beak. "He had seemed more excited in the last months. I don't know how to describe it. Exhilarated?"

"Any explanation why?"

"I've been away a lot. For a while I was dating a man. Gianfranco Giberti. He was as beautiful as his name." Christine's smile was sweet, transforming her face. "Even my father, who liked him, said he was too beautiful." She patted her eyes carefully. "You asked about a great discovery. When Father talked about his inventions, I suspected he was trying to get me to come back and work for him. You know, make it seem exciting, better than Omega. He didn't understand that I'm not a child anymore. I need more than dreams."

"Yet you suspected homicide before you had evidence?"

"I couldn't believe he let himself be exposed to enough peanut to kill him." Christine gripped Agnes's arm. "You do believe me?"

"It's not a question of belief. My job is to follow facts. The evidence. The note is important." Agnes tapped her pen on her notebook to stop herself from adding that she knew how it felt to believe that there was more to be learned. When her husband died, she had listened to all of the facts and known there was more. She'd been right.

"I'll talk to your stepmother," she said.

"Is Marie here today with the Perrault et Chavanon booth?" Vallotton asked.

"No, Gisele and Ivo are taking care of it." Christine turned toward Agnes. "If you want to talk to someone who worked with my father, they do assembly and some marketing. But they won't know anything about the kind of special project you're interested in. He wouldn't have shared anything about a new design with them, not until he was ready to launch it."

"What about other employees?"

Christine added that, with the exception of a cleaning service, Gisele and Ivo were the company's only employees.

Agnes hid her surprise. "You're not at the company anymore. In your absence, if your father was excited about something, he might have talked to them."

"He was cautious. Everyone we know, everyone in town, is connected to the industry. He would never confide an idea to someone who might hint to a cousin or a neighbor who could then take it to their own company. He wouldn't even hint to me—his own daughter."

"But he did hint to you," said Vallotton.

"He only said that he was working on something revolutionary. . . ." Christine's voice trailed off.

"He used that word? *Revolutionary?*" Agnes asked.

"Does it matter?" Christine screwed up her face, as if reflecting, and Agnes could imagine the schoolgirl asked to come to the board and work a math problem. Focused, ready to try, but not as prepared as she should have been. "Yes, that's the word he used. But you had to know my father. That could be anything." She studied her nails, then sighed. "He was always on the verge of some great invention. He was the kind of man who talked about a smartphone before anyone else understood cellular technology. Everything interested him. Materials, technology, history, design, engineering."

Agnes glanced toward the nearby showrooms. The large group had moved on and she could see the window displays highlighting new products. What was revolutionary in the industry? Would someone kill for a design idea?

The waitress cleared their cups, chatting with Vallotton, and drawing Christine into their conversation about the extraordinary crowds at Baselworld this year. Agnes's phone vibrated and she checked the screen.

Vallotton noticed. "Do you need to go?"

"No, this is a message from André."

"How is Officer Petit?" Vallotton asked. "Happy to have left our local *gendarmerie* for the big city? He'll be missed in Ville-sur-Lac."

"Probably more tired than happy right now. He's still on leave. The baby is three weeks old and not sleeping. Petit comes back to work Monday, but judging by the texts he sends me at all hours, I think he wants to return now."

Vallotton laughed, but Agnes sympathized with Petit. She tilted the screen sideways to show Christine the latest image of her new partner's baby. While the young woman oohed and aahed, Agnes caught Vallotton's eye and nodded. She would investigate Guy Chavanon's death. She remembered an early lesson in police work. Preconceived notions should be avoided. The local police should have found the dead man's note. They had made a critical mistake and assumed that a severe allergic reaction had to be an accident. A week after the man died and she would have to start over. Maybe the widow knew what had frightened her husband. And maybe she knew what constituted a revolutionary design.

Three

"What do you expect to find on the surveillance footage?" Agnes asked Aubry. They were crammed shoulder to shoulder with other officers in the Messe Basel security control room. Aubry's men compared notes, while security personnel pulled the appropriate feeds for review. Too many of them were clustered in one space, and despite the air-conditioning, the room was hot. Aubry edged toward a small meeting room and Agnes followed him.

"My expectations here?" he said. "Between us, nothing. Officially, one of the witnesses swears she saw the Roach react to something or someone." Aubry demonstrated with an exaggerated movement of his head. "Near as we can tell, this was in the minutes before he ran."

Agnes suppressed a shiver at the memory of the Roach's fractured leg and head. Over Aubry's shoulder multiple camera views flashed onto the monitors. This was the kind of mind-numbing exercise that police officers dreaded. Dozens of cameras, thousands of faces, no one sure what they were looking for: Was there another person and a signal, or was the nod simply an everyday human gesture?

"You want to help?" Aubry asked, noting her gaze. "You can come back and work with us. You, me, Carnet. We did good work. You should be the one to wrap up this case. It's really your victory."

"I'm sure Carnet has found an excellent replacement for me. Besides, I've got a new case. The death of a watchmaker. I wouldn't have the time." For the first time that day, she laughed. "Time? A watchmaker? Get it?"

Aubry gave her a sardonic smile.

"You speak of Monsieur Chavanon?" A man in his late sixties, tall and immaculately dressed in a dark blue pin-striped suit, stood in the doorway. He had silver hair and an easy air of imperturbability. Agnes recognized Antoine Mercier, the president of the Federation of the Swiss Watch Industry. He was a vigorous defender of the laws regarding the sale or import of fake watches, but she'd never worked those cases and had never met him.

After introductions, Mercier repeated his question to Agnes.

"You knew Monsieur Chavanon?" she responded.

"Bien sûre." He studied her. "When the police speak of death, it suggests that it was not an accident."

Anxious to continue his investigation, Aubry motioned for Mercier to accompany him to the other room. For a moment, it appeared the man would insist they answer his questions about Chavanon, but he didn't. Instead, Mercier asked for her business card and told Agnes he would call her mobile the moment he was available.

After they left, Agnes chose a seat on the far side of the round table. She located the telephone number for the *gendarmerie* responsible for sending officers to the scene the day Guy Chavanon died. Waiting to be connected, she pictured the roads leading to Rossemaison. She had an excellent memory for patterns, and that extended to maps. Rossemaison was a small town off the main highway southwest of Basel. She had been there once, years before, with her husband on one of their few hiking adventures. George had missed the turn to a famous gorge and they had ended up at a smaller well-known ravine. She remembered that they'd parked in a glade and walked the final distance. Not much of a hike, more of a nature trail to an overlook. Her father had supplied a picnic basket from his restaurant, and they had hauled it near the edge of the rock face and eaten while listening to water fall to the stream below.

A man's voice over the telephone interrupted her reverie. Officer Jacques Boschung sounded a decade or so older than her thirty-eight years. His voice was deep and firm, and she could imagine him commanding the local officers with a deft hand. It was a no-nonsense voice and she quickly outlined her interest in Guy Chavanon's death, asking if he would share with her what he remembered.

"Work for Bardy, you say?" he asked.

Agnes paused a beat, unsure where this train of thought would lead. She hadn't called her boss yet. She was on leave through the weekend and didn't want him to reassign the case to another officer. Once she was immersed in the details, he was less likely to take it away. She also knew how Bardy felt about the Vallottons. If Julien Vallotton had called and asked for her help, Bardy wouldn't object to her offering it.

"We're a quiet community," Boschung continued. "Don't want trouble and don't have any. Your *chef de brigade* thinks you have to draw a net across the country. I heard Bardy speak once about this new division. Violent Crimes, he's calling it? Combating the modern criminal? Criminals stick to the city. We keep the peace, help people in trouble."

Agnes let him ramble for a minute. If Boschung was the original responding officer, he had a right to be defensive about her questions. She had also decided to not mention the note immediately, wanting to hear Boschung's version of events before clouding the issue.

"You were first on the scene when Guy Chavanon died?" she eventually broke in.

"Yes." Boschung's voice faded for a moment as he spoke to someone in the background. "The Institute called for an ambulance," he said, returning to their conversation. "I was nearby. I drive by when they have receptions or any gathering. There's never enough parking, and visitors pull over on the main road. Barely two lanes, and the ditches are close, so there's not much shoulder. Foreigners don't understand. If I catch them, I suggest double-parking on the property. I'd been by earlier and hustled a car along. I came back to see if there were more."

"The Moutier Institut de Jeunes Gens isn't a good neighbor?" This was a serious accusation in Switzerland, where courtesy was paramount to local harmony.

"That's not what I meant. But they have their opinion and needs, and we have ours in the village. It's up to me to help balance the two. We've got farmers driving through with trucks or on tractors. The roads have to stay clear and clean." Boschung seemed to realize he'd diverted from the topic. "Anyway, the receptionist, Madame Jomini, telephoned for an ambulance and I was near when the call came over the radio. The situation with Chavanon was clear from the moment I walked in. A half dozen people knew about the man's allergy, and the paramedics said the symptoms were a classic response. I know your team's trained to look for *violence*, but what I saw was an accident. Chavanon's friend . . . I've forgotten the name, Indian guy."

Agnes remembered the well-dressed man from earlier. "Monsieur Patel?"

"*Oui, c'est ça.* He said he'd witnessed an identical reaction when they were at university together. And the headmaster knew about the allergy. The chef knew, too, and was nearly hysterical that his food might be blamed. Bunch of people were upset, but we got the children away and calmed everyone. Later, the coroner confirmed the anaphylaxis. I did follow-through on that. You'll see it all in the report I just emailed you."

The outer door to the security booth slammed shut, as if pulled by wind, and Agnes flinched. "Did you find any peanut products at the school reception?"

"None, and we did look. We weren't looking to blame anyone, but there was the matter of an explanation." Boschung stopped abruptly, and Agnes could feel him wanting to retract the phrase. Looking into the other room, she watched the scrolling footage of the exhibit floor, tiny people moving at quadruple speed. She wouldn't say it to anyone, but she knew that her early insights into the Roach's methods were what set her career on an upward trajectory. Likely it was what recommended her to Bardy when he was assembling his team. A strange debt was owed to the dead man that she couldn't forget.

"Not that we needed an *explanation* about why he died,"

Boschung continued. "We knew what had happened, but we wanted to tidy up the report. It was all done correctly."

Agnes explained the note Christine Chavanon found. There was a moment of silence. She gave Boschung time to think through his reaction.

"*Mince*. Why didn't she—"

Agnes interrupted, explaining that the note was only discovered that morning.

"Still, makes us look like fools. We didn't even question . . . *mince alors*."

"You didn't find the source of the peanuts?"

Boschung's tone changed. He seemed to appreciate her matter-of-factness. "Yes and no. We tested Chavanon's plate and glass, really as a favor to the chef, who was out of his mind with worry. I've never heard such language, and in a school with children around. He insisted that he hadn't served anything forbidden. He was right. Nothing turned up."

"But you said no *and* yes. Meaning you did find evidence of the source?"

"There were over sixty people in the room. At least a half dozen confessed that they'd been around peanuts or believed they might have eaten something earlier in the day with nuts in it. People were staring at their hands like they'd brought the plague in with them. One man had visited his candy factory, where they were testing a new peanut nougat. Admitted he'd worn his suit jacket into the production room without pulling on a sterile overcoat. Of course, he was wearing that same jacket at the reception. I'd never thought about food that way, like a walking contagion. It was a miracle Chavanon hadn't died years ago walking through town."

Agnes knew that when you smelled food it was because of contact with airborne microscopic particles. Wasn't this the same? "Did anyone mention smelling peanuts?"

"No. Talk to the coroner. He'll agree with me. It looked like an accident. That's what he wrote on the death certificate." Boschung lowered his voice. "You saw Chavanon's note yourself?" When Agnes confirmed that she had, his tone changed. "Do you think we—"

She cut him off, not wanting to speculate. "I'll be in touch."

After ending the call, Agnes scrolled through email on her phone. Boschung had done as promised, and both the police and coroner's reports were in her in-box. She skimmed the documents, then tapped a new number on her phone screen. It took several transfers before she was connected to a man who answered with a curt "Aerni."

He sounded exactly as she pictured a coroner: hurried but precise. She quickly outlined the basics of the case.

"You can stop there," Aerni interrupted. "It was only a few days ago, I remember it well. Give me a moment to pull up my notes. I like to verify."

Agnes put her phone on speaker mode and laid it on the table so she could listen and simultaneously read the report, picturing the coroner doing the same. When she reached the identification photographs, she paused. Guy Chavanon had been a classically handsome man in the prime of life. She detected a little of Christine around the eyes and perhaps the mouth, but in the end the daughter was a pale reflection of the father.

"I stand by my original findings," Aerni finally said.

The connection had a slight echo, and Agnes wondered if he

was in the morgue. She didn't ask, not wanting to fix that image more clearly in her mind.

Aerni clicked his tongue against his teeth. "Appropriate treatment was administered—that doesn't always happen—but wasn't effective."

"Treatment before the ambulance arrived?"

"Yes, it's in the notes. Chavanon had an EpiPen with him and a friend knew about it and administered the dose. It's a shot to the thigh. All done quite correctly, it simply wasn't enough to counter his reaction. Not unusual in the severest cases."

Agnes skimmed through the notes she'd been sent. This was why Monsieur Patel was particularly upset. He had tried to save his friend to no avail.

"Anyway," continued Aerni, "the presenting symptoms were consistent with anaphylactic reaction producing shock. The deceased had a known allergy to peanut, therefore it was reasonable to assume this was a probable association with a known antigen."

"Officer Boschung mentioned people wandering around with peanut dust on their hands and coats. Was that a factor?"

"Understand that allergies are only predictable to a certain extent." The coroner launched into a lengthy explanation of the variables, including absorption, age, and other preexisting conditions.

"His stomach was empty?"

There was a pause. "Correct. With his history and the timeline of his reactions in the past, coupled with the severity of the episode, I expect the first symptom presented almost immediately following ingestion."

"Meaning a short time before he died?"

Aerni hesitated again, as if reading. "Yes, a very short time." He described the symptoms in exhaustive detail: tightness of the throat, dizziness, chest pain, shock. Agnes listened carefully. Aerni's words were clinical and precise, yet based on a mixture of probability and fact. Coroners were human; they had to interpret. Aerni didn't know how Chavanon came into contact with peanut, only that it had killed him.

"If he didn't have anything in his stomach, is it realistic that one of the other guests had enough peanut product on them that Chavanon died from it?" She thought of the man who had toured the nougat factory before coming to the reception. "Was it possible he shook hands with someone who had peanut oil on their hands, then rubbed his eyes or touched his nose and had a reaction?"

"No, with an extreme concentration he might have irritated his eyes this way. But most of us would have discomfort with a foreign product in our eyes. That's not how his anaphylaxis was triggered." Aerni paused. "You are correct that this was not a stray particle or casual contact."

Agnes told him about the note. She felt Aerni weighing his next words.

"Inspector, the man had a history of severe allergic reaction, these reactions are unpredictable, and he died in a room full of people and food in close quarters. Officer Boschung had no alternative findings and I knew the cause of death. I was comfortable calling it an accident."

She saw the opening. "The note is new evidence. Perhaps someone used knowledge of the allergy to deliberately introduce peanuts."

"The cause of death is unquestionable." Aerni clicked his teeth again. "I can guarantee the cause of death was anaphylaxis-induced heart failure. However, what caused the cause . . . that's for you to determine."

"The difference between falling on a knife and having someone stab you? Both thrust, both sever an artery, but only one is murder?"

Aerni took his phone off speaker. "You think this was foul play?"

"I don't know, but I'm not done yet." It would be a perfect crime. Killing someone with a poison only deadly to them.

After thanking the coroner, she hung up and texted Christine Chavanon. *Who knew about your father's allergy?*

The reply came almost immediately.

Everyone.

Four

Agnes crossed the threshold into the room.

Antoine Mercier didn't rise; instead he slid Agnes's business card onto a nearby tabletop. "When we were introduced earlier, you didn't mention that you are with Violent Crimes."

She nearly sighed, disappointed that Mercier's earlier charm had so quickly vanished. However, she wasn't surprised. In her experience, charm was a patina that when rubbed the wrong way revealed a band of unpolished steel.

The president of the Federation of the Swiss Watch Industry had telephoned to meet her. Now she recognized it was a summons. It was in Mercier's body language and in the place he'd chosen. The room resembled an intimate living space with three pairs of low leather chairs grouped around sleek steel-and-wood tables. The atmosphere was calm and expensive and clearly intended as the backdrop to finalize the sale of luxury watches.

To rebalance the equilibrium in her favor Agnes extended her hand, forcing Mercier to stand or risk being rude. Once that ritual was complete, she walked to the chair opposite his and sat, placing her handbag on the floor and removing her notebook. The chair looked more comfortable than it was. Designed for a taller occupant, she had to sit forward awkwardly to avoid sliding down against the sloped back. Clearly luxury watch companies imagined all their clients were heroically proportioned tall men.

As if on cue, a tall employee entered the room carrying a tray laden with crystal glasses, small bottles of San Pellegrino, and a split of chilled champagne. He set it on the coffee table, and Agnes poured herself a glass of water. After taking a sip she looked around, her eyes landing on the watchmaker's logo inlaid in the wall: BAUME & MERCIER GENÈVE.

"Are you with the company?"

"No, I'm not, and the name is coincidence." Mercier had the grace to look embarrassed, and Agnes knew he had chosen the location to remind her that this was his territory, and not hers. He'd probably hoped she'd assume there was a family connection.

"If I had less experience, I'd think you were worried." She took another sip of the water. "I like this lime-flavored one."

Mercier leaned forward, elbows on knees, and fingertips together. Agnes noted the move from aggression to concern. She wondered where men—and women—picked up these standard poses.

"It was an unsettling affair today. Not Chavanon, but the man who died here." Mercier pushed a small button, and the uniformed young man reappeared as if he'd been waiting for a summons. "Inspector, a coffee? Or something else? Something to eat? They'll bring whatever you want."

She shook her head, reminded of Château Vallotton and Julien. This was how he lived.

She waited while Mercier explained exactly how he wanted his espresso made, down to the type of bean and the temperature of the water. When they were alone again, he was once more the relaxed, charming ambassador for Swiss products.

"Hearing Guy's name in the context of the police was a surprise," Mercier said. "His funeral was only yesterday. A very small family affair, which I didn't attend although, of course, it was at the forefront of my mind."

Agnes had a sudden image of Mercier diving into a private chapel tucked away in an exhibit hall, perhaps a room set up so people could pray before spending vast amounts of money. What would they pray for? Would they give thanks that they had so much money?

"I've been in the industry my entire life," he continued, "as was my father and his father before me. Guy comes—came—from the same tradition. It was a tragedy that he died so unexpectedly. Sad news for everyone. So many of the smaller old companies, the traditional backbone of what we call Swiss Made, are dying out."

"You believe Perrault et Chavanon will close?" Christine Chavanon had been certain the company wouldn't be broken up or sold. Perhaps there was no struggle between heirs, only a stepmother who didn't *understand* the work and might be anxious to get out of it altogether? Madame Chavanon could settle the estate with a sale.

Mercier shook his head. "I didn't mean to insinuate anything, but Guy was innovative, and that's what's needed today. When I heard about the accident . . ." His voice trailed off.

Agnes ignored his obvious play for details. "You mentioned

Monsieur Chavanon's innovative spirit. Had you heard about any major advancements in his work?"

The door to the room opened and the espresso was delivered on a tray accompanied by a selection of Lindt chocolates. Mercier added sugar to his cup and drank before answering her.

"A major advancement? What an interesting idea, Inspector. Could you be more precise about the nature of this development?"

"I was only adding to what you said, about Monsieur Chavanon being innovative."

"I meant it, but not in a specific way."

"If you were predicting a major advancement, what might that be? Generally, I mean."

Mercier reached for a chocolate, offering one to Agnes. She contented herself with a sip of lime-flavored water, wondering why she'd lied earlier about liking it. She would have preferred an espresso if she hadn't already had enough caffeine today to consider popping the cork on the nearby champagne bottle for balance.

"Most are refinements in the process of manufacture, in miniaturization of components, of use and content of metals. Things of that nature." Mercier extended his arm to expose his wrist. "The one I'm wearing today was created by Richard Mille. He sponsors a Formula One racing team and created this with them in mind. It's the world's lightest split-seconds chronograph. Only forty grams total weight. Remarkable engineering." He shrugged. "There are advancements to suit all types. Perhaps you have seen one of the e-straps? Attachable to any watch, it allows the connoisseur of analogical design to make the device . . . *intelligent*."

Agnes noted the barely disguised sneer. She leaned forward

to examine Mercier's watch. "Would you call this design revolutionary?"

"If I was paid to write advertising copy, perhaps. But no. In the purest sense of the word, the last revolutionary advancement was the advent of quartz in the 1970s." His face went rigid. "Not our best moment."

"Surely advancements are a positive thing, even intelligent watches?"

Mercier looked as if he'd eaten something sour. "Up to the advent of quartz movement, watches were mechanical, full stop. With their introduction, all of mechanical craftsmanship was made obsolete." He dropped his hand like a guillotine. "By 1981 the crisis was a death knell. Cheap and accurate was in demand. Interest declined in the *grand complications;* instead, it was all digital displays and integrated circuits." He shivered. "Literally and figuratively that tiny sliver of mineral quartz powered the watches and powered the industry. Unfortunately, it powered design and manufacturing away from us to Japan, then elsewhere around the world. It has taken over forty years to truly recover."

He gave her a gentle smile. "But that is in the past. You've seen the crowds here today. We've reasserted ourselves with laws protecting Swiss Made. With rising populations and emerging markets, high-end watches—the kind that we are known for— have a bright future."

"Would you be surprised to learn that Monsieur Chavanon was working on something revolutionary?"

"Yes." The words echoed with finality. Agnes gave Mercier time to expand on the idea, but he didn't.

"You'd not heard anything specific about Perrault et Cha-

vanon, their situation as a company, or about Monsieur Chavanon in the time before his death?"

"These are very concerning questions, Inspector Lüthi. You
are suggesting foul play."

"Would it surprise you?"

Mercier glanced at her sharply, dark eyes gleaming. "We are
a competitive industry. We have learned how to keep our secrets,
how to protect our techniques and products. Our Swiss know-how,
our pride and our identity. Guy was part of this community, and
he was also . . ." Mercier placed a finger to his lips briefly, reflecting. "Not a renegade, but independent minded. He was part of a
long continuum of tradition, and at the same time, he was forward
thinking. I would laugh at his wit and only later would I consider
that he was serious and perhaps didn't see situations entirely as I
did. As we do."

There was a knock on the door and a woman stepped in.
"Monsieur Mercier, your press conference is starting. The others
are waiting."

He stood and Agnes followed him. On the ground floor,
television lights glared outside the pavilion. A huddle of digni-
taries was waiting, and she thanked Mercier. He shook her
hand more warmly than he had at the start of their conversation.

"I spoke with Guy recently," he said, as if the memory had
sprung to mind at that moment. "If I had to characterize his
mood, it was exultant. It appeared the future was bright."

"When was this?"

Mercier hesitated. "A few months ago. At a restaurant in
Genève."

A handler gestured impatiently for Mercier and he stepped

into place. More lights flashed on and someone did a final sound check.

"Inspector," Mercier said, suddenly turning again to Agnes. "Remember Copernicus. I hope not to hear the word *revolutionary* again."

With that, he turned to the camera and began to speak.

Five

Standing under the enormous expanse of the cover over the plaza outside Halle 1, Agnes replayed Mercier's final words. She disliked people who confused cryptic with clever. What had he meant about Copernicus? He was an astronomer, that much she remembered. Famous for saying that the sun and not the earth was at the center of the cosmic order.

Absently, she thumbed through the copy of the Baselworld *Daily News* she'd plucked from a stack by the lobby door. The magazine-newspaper hybrid was filled with photographs of happy people and glamorous product. The articles were laced with words such as *epic, technology par excellence,* and *dazzling.* Scanning the pages she wished Guy Chavanon's wife would answer the telephone. Agnes had already called the Chavanon residence three times with no response, although that wasn't surprising the day after a funeral. She knew all too well that it was difficult to listen to condolence after condolence. She would wait another day before turning up at Marie Chavanon's door unannounced.

Halfway through the *Daily News,* Agnes stopped. She recognized two men in a large color photograph. On the left was Antoine Mercier, smiling broadly, holding up a watch for the camera. The other man was the kind of handsome that looked airbrushed even in real life, and she had seen him earlier in real life. She scanned the article. Gianfranco Giberti was being interviewed about the advance in the photo-realistic moon phase on the Omega Speedmaster.

Agnes read the name again and verified that it referred to the man in the photograph before slapping the newspaper shut. This was Christine Chavanon's former boyfriend? Christine hadn't exaggerated when she'd said he was beautiful. Agnes had a hard time imagining the two of them together. Christine was too hesitant, too *blurred.* Giberti was sharp as cut crystal. Why had he watched them so intently earlier? Why not come forward with condolences or slip away if he wanted to avoid his former girlfriend?

She glanced at the article again. Giberti ran the research division of Omega. That was interesting. Christine had hinted that her father liked her boyfriend; now Agnes wondered if that affection extended to shared confidences. Confidences about innovations and research. Confidences about revolutionary ideas. She amended *confidences* to *hints.* What if Giberti had listened to the hints more carefully than Christine did? It was possible to take the tiniest notion of an idea and develop it. With Guy Chavanon out of the way, there was no one to say that Giberti hadn't come up with the idea on his own. From her experience in Financial Crimes Agnes knew all too well what people were willing to do to advance their careers. Industrial espionage and

theft of intellectual property were more commonplace than anyone admitted.

Mulling the implications, Agnes walked toward the narrow
street where the Roach had died. Police tape still blocked the
entrance, and a few officers were idling around the damaged
Ferrari. She doubted they were doing anything productive.
Likely they were on a break. She speculated that the cost of
replacing the damaged hood was equivalent to replacing her entire Peugeot. One of the officers recognized her and she waved
at his greeting before stepping off the curb.

After winding her way through the trams on Clarastrasse,
she headed to the Palace pavilion and the Perrault et Chavanon
Frères booth. The Palace, where the International Brands were
showcased, was by far the smallest of the five buildings: A miniature, one-story structure vaguely reminiscent of the "palaces"
constructed by architects for eighteenth-century follies. Given
the steel-framed exterior, Agnes half expected a plant-filled con-
servatory appropriate for ladies in long skirts wearing white
gloves. Instead, her first impression of the interior was of white
and modern and intimate.

She made her way down the central hallway, weighing what
she saw against the Global Brands in Halle 1. Since *global* and
international were nearly synonymous, the organizers must have
wanted to emphasize a distinction. To her eyes, the quality of
the watches was equal, therefore the scale of manufacturing
must be different. She paused at a booth. A watch was on display
in a tall cabinet. "A unique piece," the description read, detailing
specifications about the movements and materials. The mechanism of the watch was partially visible through cutouts on the

face, and a small mirror on the bottom of the display reflected the back side. The reverse casing was covered with highly detailed engraving. Agnes found the watch in the catalog she'd picked up upon entering the booth. They literally meant unique. This was the only one of its kind.

Her instinct was confirmed. The booths in this pavilion might not represent the manufacturing power or have the wide-spread name recognition of Omega or Rolex or Blancpain, but that didn't mean the quality was lesser; in fact, she wondered if the quality might be higher. Unique pieces. Custom designs. She wished Vallotton were with her; he understood custom-made products better than anyone else she knew.

"Inspector Lüthi?" She heard a voice and for a moment thought she'd imagined it was Vallotton. When he entered the booth, she was caught off guard more by having been thinking of him than by the actual sight of him.

"I thought you left," she said.

"Without seeing the entire show? I saw you crossing the street and managed to catch up." He removed his calfskin gloves and slipped them into his coat pocket. Together they walked down the light-filled central aisle.

"There they are." Vallotton pointed to the end of the short wing of the pavilion. PERRAULT ET CHAVANON FRÈRES, 1841 read the sign.

"Very different from Halle 1," Agnes commented, remember-ing her meeting with Antoine Mercier. The Baume & Mercier pavilion had a grand showroom on the first level and private rooms upstairs, each space beautifully appointed. This was little more than a temporary shop, separated from its neighbors by impermanent walls covered by decorated panels. It didn't look cheap, and the companies clearly went to a lot of trouble to brand their booths, but they couldn't achieve the appearance of permanence and sheer luxury she'd experienced in the other building.

"What do you know about Perrault et Chavanon?" she asked.

"They were originally gunsmiths. Not unusual because of the precision involved in the workmanship. The family were French Huguenots who fled persecution. They set up workshops in small groups and—"

She shot Vallotton a dry look. "I'm more interested in the current situation, not the history."

"Then I'm embarrassed to say I don't know much."

"You're Leo Chavanon's godfather, you must know something."

"I send gifts for holidays and visit him at school. He's too young to need me for more right now. My father was closer to the family, and to Guy. They live outside La Chaux-de-Fonds, up a hill to the northwest of the town, and the factory is beside their house. Typical for an old company." Vallotton launched into a detailed description of the family home, apparently designed by a famous architect.

Agnes gestured for him to move on to what interested her. "Christine said there are only two employees, not counting her stepmother."

"That was surprising. The factory building is large." Vallotton flashed her a grin. "Not overwhelming you with details, am I?"

She nodded toward the booth where they'd met. "Back there, the label in one of the cases said a unique piece. Is that the kind of work Perrault et Chavanon do?"

"No, Philippe Dufour is a living legend and often makes only one watch a year. I suppose he has a helper or apprentice occasionally, but he works alone. It's unbelievable, the attention he pays to every detail. The way he polishes metal is practically spiritual."

Agnes shuddered to think of the cost of a truly unique time-piece, particularly one that a craftsman spent an entire year fabricating. She suspected that passion for the products ran high, and passion meant behavior contrary to reason. Vallotton extended his arm, exposing his wrist. "This one of Dufour's was my father's."

Agnes looked from the watch to Vallotton's face.

"Don't looked so shocked," he said. "It's not made of radioactive material."

"If it's a collector's piece, why are you wearing it?" She reached for his wrist.

"To tell time, mainly."

She studied the watch face, conscious that she was holding his arm. Carefully she let go. "How can you walk about wearing something so valuable? What if you lose it?"

Vallotton laughed. "Is your job more hazardous than I realize? Are watches routinely wrested from your wrist?"

"Of course not, but things do happen."

"How many watches have you lost?"

"Three, maybe four?"

Vallotton looked horrified.

She held out her arm. "They get left on the beach or in hotels. I replace them."

He glanced at the navy-and-green plastic around her wrist. "Then that's a good pick for you."

"You don't approve of Swatch?" She looked at it fondly. "My youngest son picked this one out. Paid for it himself. It was a Christmas gift."

"Peter?"

"Yes." She was surprised he remembered the name.

"I approve of it and them. Don't look so shocked. If everyone was like Dufour, there wouldn't be enough watches to go around. Hayek had a clear vision after quartz nearly doomed the country. Without him—without Swatch—the watch industry might have faltered irretrievably."

Agnes remembered a background dossier she'd read once at work. "The Swatch Group owns many of the big brands, don't they? Including Omega." She scrolled through her memory. Which others? "Harry Winston? Breguet, Blancpain. A dozen more?"

"Sounds about right."

She pulled her sleeve over her watch. Hard enough being a small company, but competing against larger ones bundled together under a benevolent parent? Extremely competitive. She wondered again at the gaps in Christine Chavanon's knowledge. It was possible Guy Chavanon had developed a transformative product. Something that would assure his company's future. It was equally likely that he was experiencing the pressure of inexorable decline. Would a desperate man do something out of character—deal with people he'd normally shun? That would be an explanation for his recent behavior if the neighbor's account was to be trusted and could justify the fear he'd expressed in the note. She'd arrested too many decent people who had taken a small turn in their financial dealings, an "only this once" decision made in a moment of desperation that had ended badly.

With that in mind, Agnes examined the front of the Perrault et Chavanon booth. It was crowded, and it took her a moment to identify the employees Christine had described. The man, Ivo, iPad in hand, looked to be in his thirties. Handsome in a boyish way, he was huddled with a pair of foreign-looking gentlemen. His colleague, Gisele, was fielding questions left and right, her eyes darting everywhere.

Agnes stepped forward while Vallotton moved in the opposite direction to study a pair of watches with convincing intensity.

"I'm Gisele LeRoy," the woman said in response to Agnes's introduction. Up close, her eyes were the color of a summer sky. Her clothes were more relaxed than the dark suit worn by Christine Chavanon, and her short blonde hair created a halo around her head. Light shimmering on and between the individual strands caused Agnes to look for its source.

They were standing by a display case that held a dozen models in a range of styles. There were no heavy chronographs, or specialty sporting watches promising accuracy to astounding depths of the ocean for voyagers to that final frontier. The *complications* were simple ones: perpetual calendar, phases of the moon. Gisele opened the case and ran her hand across the faces, as if reading braille on the glass. At last, her hand stopped and she selected a watch, holding it out to Agnes. The face was white with tiny flecks of color scattered as if paint had dropped on a canvas. The case was thin and gold, and the band was subtle. A soft barely tan leather. A lady's watch, not too delicate, but feminine.

Agnes held it to her wrist. "It's lovely," she said, meaning it.

"Would you like it?" Julien Vallotton said, appearing beside her elbow. Hastily, Agnes returned the timepiece to Gisele, shaking her head emphatically. Vallotton moved off to study a case of men's watches.

Gisele looked between the two of them. "It would make a nice gift?" she suggested before returning the watch to the case and locking it.

Agnes shifted the conversation back to the reason she was here. "Was there anything particular that you remember about the days leading up to your employer's death?"

"I wasn't at work the week before Monsieur Chavanon died. Since I'm here for eight straight days at Baselworld, they give me time off before the show. Ivo takes his time off afterward. You should talk with him." Gisele motioned for her colleague to join them.

"I'll miss Monsieur Chavanon," she added. "I liked it when he walked around and talked to us, even though he was distracting. His mind was off in a hundred different directions." She motioned again to Ivo. "Have you been to the factory? Make sure you see the collection. Ask Christine to show you."

"Not Madame Chavanon?"

Gisele made a face. "She doesn't know that much. She's all-business. I don't think she really cares about watches. We could make surgical equipment for all it matters to her. She's not even from La Chaux-de-Fonds. She's from Lausanne."

Agnes could hear her mother-in-law saying something similar: my daughter-in-law's parents aren't from here, they're American. Years, decades—in Agnes's case, an entire life—didn't make a difference. Being from somewhere in Switzerland wasn't taken lightly.

When Ivo broke away from the clients he was helping, Gisele crossed the showroom floor to take his place. Agnes introduced herself. Ivo smiled warmly, although the expression didn't reach his eyes. He asked that they go to the nearby café bar. They didn't speak on the way there, and when they sat down, he had a lengthy conversation with the waiter about the hot drinks on offer before deciding on a cappuccino. Agnes ordered one as well, sensing that Ivo was nervous.

Once the drinks arrived, he spoke rapidly. "I was the last one to see him alive."

"You were at the Institute the day Monsieur Chavanon died?" Agnes leaned forward, startled.

"No, I mean I was the last one of us to talk to him. From the company. Or the family."

Agnes sat her cup down too hard; it banged the saucer.

"I came in that weekend to start packing for the show. I'm in charge of displays and we were making a few changes."

"Monsieur Chavanon was there?"

"He wasn't in the factory when I arrived. He saw my car and came in. He was like that. Always wanted to see what we were doing."

"He kept a sharp eye on everything?"

"Not like checking on us. He was simply interested." Ivo moved his cup to the side. He looked away. Agnes waited, watching him replay those last words and actions in his mind. The last memory. Routine conversation, routine actions cemented forever as the end. A hurried goodbye that should have been "I love you."

"On Monday," Ivo continued, "when Madame Chavanon told us . . . when she said what had happened, I told her that I'd seen him on Saturday and that he had been so happy." Ivo looked directly at Agnes. "I don't know why I said that. It just came out. As if it was better that he felt good before he died. He was nice man. A generous boss. A visionary."

"No one is disagreeing with that."

"That Saturday I had finished checking the panels we bring to the show, making sure none were damaged, and I was working on the cases. Madame Chavanon had decided to make some adjustments—updating the interiors slightly—and I was nearly finished."

Ivo rubbed his palms across the top of his thighs as if they were sweaty. Agnes motioned to the waitress and asked for a bottle of San Pellegrino and two glasses.

"He was angry," Ivo said. "He asked why I'd torn up the cases. He said that we had a reputation to uphold and now they looked like backdrops for cheap imports. I didn't know what he meant or why he said it. They looked nice to me, good-quality wood. I was so stunned that I didn't argue. I just stood there. And he left. Practically ran out."

"Do you think he was angry before he came in to see you?"

Ivo reflected. "He was always preoccupied, and he was that day, until he caught sight of the cases and blew up."

"This wasn't usual behavior?"

"No. Monsieur Chavanon was mild mannered. Almost absentminded, although that's not right. He was focused on whatever he was working on." Ivo smiled at the memory. "He was a gentle man."

"He didn't say anything else that might indicate why he was so angry? Where had he been before you saw him?"

Ivo shook his head. "I don't know. I was pretty mad myself. I walked out and left everything laid out in a mess. I barely remembered to lock the door." He poured a glass of water from the bottle and drank it down. "I didn't lie to Madame to avoid what he'd said about the cabinets. I wasn't thinking clearly and wanted to say something nice."

"Do you know where Monsieur Chavanon went after he left you?"

"No, but he drove off in a hurry."

"What time was that?" A note in the police report said that Guy Chavanon came directly from his house to the school reception. Marie Chavanon was shopping in Bern and had left the house hours before. Christine was at a friend's house.

"One thirty. I only know because when Madame Chavanon told us he'd died, I realized that was about the time I arrived home, and it had been an hour since I'd seen him. I was fixing myself a sandwich, angry, not knowing that right then he was dying."

After a few more questions Agnes stood and thanked Ivo. He returned to work and she took a sip of the fizzy water and visualized the road between La Chaux-de-Fonds and Rossemaison. Guy Chavanon had been pronounced dead at two thirty. It was unlikely he would have ingested peanut product in his own home, and the timeline was wrong anyway. The coroner said the reaction occurred within minutes of contact. What had happened in that hour?

She spotted Vallotton in a booth across the aisle. He disentangled himself from the saleswoman and met her in the center of the pavilion.

"Too much mother-of-pearl." He motioned over his shoulder. "Aimed at the Asian market, I suppose. Funny what one finds here. I liked the watch you were looking at, though."

She ignored his comment and slipped into the stream of people heading for the exit. Among the throng moving in the other direction, Agnes spotted Narendra Patel. She looked over her shoulder in time to see him enter the Chavanon booth. The sight of him reminded her of what she wanted to tell Aubry. One of the images in the video she'd seen in the control room had triggered a memory. A face in the crowd. The thought was interrupted by the sound of her name called out over the general hum. She didn't need to see this face in the crowd to recognize the voice. Her mother-in-law's tone was designed to carry across fields.

"How did you find me?" Agnes asked. Fortunately, Sybille was too focused on Vallotton to hear the accusation in her tone.

"This place is enormous," Sybille said. "I barely got through that big exhibition when I gave up and asked for you at security. That nice Monsieur Aubry found you on the surveillance cameras. Do you know I saw a watch at Patek Philippe, called Sky Moon something, that cost over a million francs? I can't imagine even an American paying that kind of money. Imagine what over a million dollars would buy! And a watch? It tells time just like mine." She extended her wrist.

"It does a bit more than that," said Vallotton. "The back has sidereal time and a sky chart that traces the stars and the phases and the orbit of the moon, and the usual things like a perpetual calendar. Some of the parts are microscopic. Plus, it has an engraved platinum case that's a work of art." Sybille looked at him wide-eyed, and he continued as if talking to a fellow connoisseur. Agnes bit her lip to conceal a grin. "Did you see their platinum World Time model? Practical if you travel a lot, and easy to use." He paused dramatically. "Should be, for a cost of around four million francs."

Both Agnes and Sybille stared at him.

"Well, no matter what they can do, they're still expensive." Sybille extended her hand in greeting. "We've met briefly, when you came to my home."

Agnes was about to remind her that it was *their* home when Vallotton stepped into the breach with a greeting and small talk. Before Sybille could quiz him too deeply about what he and Agnes were doing together, Agnes asked about Sybille's morning at the museum, even though she knew this was entering troubled waters.

"Interesting," said Sybille. "Educational. Probably not as interesting as your day. Whatever it was that took you away and kept you here." She looked around as if expecting to find murder and mayhem in every corner.

"They caught a man I'd been hunting for five years," Agnes said.

"I don't understand why Financial Crimes needed your help when you are no longer with them. You're not even back at work yet." Sybille seemed to remember Vallotton's presence and smiled. "Is this where they caught him? Right here?"

They exited the building and Agnes was tempted to point across the street to the spot where the Roach had died and describe it in vibrant detail. Wasn't that what Sybille wanted?

"No," Agnes said, instead. "I'm here making inquiries about a different case."

"Such an odd way to spend the afternoon, particularly when we had plans. How could this be better than time spent with your family?"

"The boys are skiing, they haven't missed me today."

Sybille was not to be outdone. "If you hadn't been injured,

you could be there with them. Such a dangerous job. Monsieur Vallotton, you must agree?"

"I think it's an admirable vocation. Not many people make such a difference in the lives around them."

Sybille shifted subjects as easily as an ice-skater changed direction. "Agnes, it's a shame you had to leave the museum before seeing the exhibit. You'll have to go back."

"I doubt I'll have time. A man died and I'll spend the weekend tracking down details."

"There was an entire wall about your father."

"Daddy, in a museum?" Agnes halted.

"Yes, didn't I tell you before we left this morning?"

Agnes knew she hadn't.

"The exhibit was about food and history. You must remember how the photographers flocked to your father when he was starting out. Some of them became famous. There were even a few photographs with you in them. When he received his first Michelin star." Sybille smiled at Vallotton. "Bill was the first American to have a Michelin star in Switzerland. He was famous."

"I know the restaurant, of course," said Vallotton. "But I didn't know that bit of the history."

"I can't believe they had photographs of him on display," said Agnes. "Of course, I'll make a point to go see it."

"Let me take you," said Vallotton. "Now that Madame Lüthi has spoken in such glowing terms, I wouldn't dream of missing it either."

Sybille's mouth opened and closed. Agnes had never seen her mother-in-law speechless and found the experience exhilarating.

Six

Marie Chavanon watched the setting sun move across the façade of her late husband's factory. Unlike their home, which was lauded for its modernity, the factory was built in a style loosely imitating a château, with a high sloped roof, and windows and doors surrounded by stone lintels. At odds with this suggestion of a historic building, the exterior walls were decorated with art nouveau murals. When she had first visited, she thought the buildings and the family delightfully eccentric; years later she was ready to label them crazy.

In the opposite direction, down the steep hill, sat the grim gray town of La Chaux-de-Fonds. She quickly drew her eye away, wondering what UNESCO saw that she didn't. World Heritage Site, indeed. The whole place was nothing more than a well-laid-out and regularized factory town. She slapped a dish towel onto the countertop. All well and good a hundred years ago when their ridiculous house was built and the town accounted for 60 percent of all Swiss exports. A factory town to support the world's insatiable appetite for the luxury of Swiss watches. She knew that era was over, even if the townspeople didn't realize it.

The sun shifted steadily, and she wondered if her husband had ever stood on the floor of his factory, gazing out the high windows, and had these same thoughts. Guy professed to look toward the future, but she didn't believe him. All those hours surveilling activity at the factory, as his father and grandfather and their forebears had done? He had to admit that in his case it was not to check that all was well with the stream of workers coming and going, but to remember what had been. To remember what time and change and bad decisions had lost. How could it all be about the future with such a past?

Since his death, she wished she had asked more questions, at the same time knowing that she wouldn't have done anything differently. Guy was proud of his heritage as the descendant of one of the earliest and finest watchmaking families. Despite living in the house where he was born and raised, working in the same factory where his ancestors oversaw the rise of a great dynasty, where generations had designed and consulted and imagined precision timepieces that were also masterpieces of art and elegance, he had been obsessed with the future. Obsessed.

The sun dropped farther, and Marie turned her attention inside. There was too much food left over from the funeral reception the day before. She'd sent everyone away before it was eaten, no longer able to tolerate people in her home. Feeling them wondering. Judging. She glanced around the kitchen and out to the hall and living room, remembering what it had looked like when she'd first visited the older Chavanons. A newly engaged young woman, she had been thrilled to meet Guy's parents and to see and admire the fine house and its pedigree. To live in a house designed by Le Corbusier was beyond her imagination. She would be part of a legacy.

At first, she was shocked by the stark interiors, but was too timid to say anything. Even now, all these years later, it was impossible to pass judgment on such a famous architect. After all, until she met Guy, she'd only ever lived in her quaint neighborhood in Lausanne. A city girl surrounded by apartments, not a girl who dreamt of a villa.

Her first visit was nearly twenty years ago, and the house was even sparer now than then. A house for a modern couple, Marie said to the neighbors who noted the changes. The past could be overwhelming, she claimed. Now she looked around, wondering what was left to sell before she couldn't make excuses.

"You shouldn't go tomorrow," a man's voice said. Marie started. Stephan Dupré was through the side door and into the kitchen before she noticed he'd crossed the lawn. He was a lean tall man, his face angular. All of him was angular, as if distilled to pure energy draped over skeleton. At fifty, he was handsome in the way of men whose charisma blurred any need for classical features, and she could never see him without thinking of Guy. Stephan was a doer while her classically handsome husband was a dreamer.

"I don't have a choice," she said. "I have to pay the bills. Leo depends on me."

Dupré dropped a pile of papers on the table, then veered to the other window, as if appreciating the view he'd seen a thousand times before.

"I brought your mail up." He stepped to the phone and turned the ringer back on.

Marie glanced through the stack and selected a large envelope labeled with the Institute's logo. Inside were photographs.
She smiled. They were similar to the one Leo had texted to her
three weeks ago. Although his shot hadn't been the best—a ski
glove blocked a corner of the frame and the boys' faces were
halfway covered by caps and scarves—the sheer joy in their eyes
had reminded Marie why her son lived fifty kilometers away.
These formal shots from the school photographer were clearer
and would make their way into a frame, but they didn't capture
the joy of the selfies.

"Leo's gone?" Dupré said. "I thought you were taking him
tomorrow."

"I was delaying. He'll be happier with his friends at school,
and Narendra drove us. He's checking on Gisele and Ivo for me."
Tears formed in her eyes. "Guy always took Leo to school. I
thought it would seem less lonely than him going alone with his
poor old mother."

"You're not old."

"Don't say that." Marie set the photographs down. "He needs
to get back in his routine, and he can't stay here alone. I should
have been at Baselworld today."

Dupré took a step closer. "Gisele and Ivo can take care of
your booth. They did the setup without you, and the first two
days have gone well, haven't they?"

She swung to face him. "They don't know our merchandise
like I do. They can't make larger deals on my behalf."

"Do you have merchandise for larger deals?"

She moved as if to put a fist on his chest, but stopped short.
"Yes, I have merchandise."

"You know what I mean."

She drove her hands into her pockets, crossed the room, and turned on a lamp.

"I don't know why you go to Baselworld anymore," he said. "You didn't want to go this year. You told me you didn't, and now you don't have to."

"It's different now. Guy's family has had a booth since the show began. A hundred years. I can't quit the week he died." Her voice softened. "The fee was paid. Next year, I'll see."

"Will there be a next year?"

"I don't know what you mean."

"Did Guy reveal his world-changing idea? Do you have that? Is that what you're counting on to pay the bills?"

Marie pressed her temples. "Stop it. He's only been buried one day."

"Have you been in his workshop? Seen what he left you?"

"You need to leave.

"Do you even have a key?"

She bit her lip.

"Because I do."

Seven

Agnes was disoriented. Low morning sunlight streamed through the windows, hitting the papered walls and illuminating a set of framed family photographs. She slipped a hand out from under the duvet and rubbed her eyes. Slowly the objects around her came into focus: jewelry box on the dresser, George's robe laid over the back of an armchair. She eased her head onto the pillow again. This was her own bed. Her own bed in her own house. That's what was wrong.

She hadn't slept here since George died. Last night, when she reached the driveway, she had bypassed her in-laws and turned in next door, entering the house she and George had shared. It wasn't habit; that had been broken months ago. It was something else. A different need. She'd spoken with Aubry again before leaving Baselworld, hoping that what she'd remembered would help his investigation. Afterward, Vallotton had walked her to her car. If honest with herself, that was the reason she had slept in her own bed.

She closed her eyes. It wasn't the same. The old familiar sounds were absent. The boys were away skiing, and George was never coming back. The house was empty. No, not empty; it felt abandoned, which she supposed it was.

She swung her legs out from under the covers, and a streak of pain shot down her right side from hip to ankle. She lay back, gritting her teeth, starting her relaxation exercises. Three weeks ago, she hadn't known what a femoral nerve was; now she felt as if it were her closest companion. The doctor had said he didn't know if the pain in her leg would ever ease. Apparently, nerve damage was part science and part mystery. At least this time she could identify the cause. She had walked more yesterday than in all the days since her injury.

The pain subsided. Her stomach growled and she remembered that there was not a morsel of food in the house. Not even coffee. Sybille had seen to that, citing a desire to avoid attracting rodents to the pantry.

She sat up, carefully this time, checking the bedside clock. She'd arranged to meet Christine Chavanon at the family's property this morning. She would also speak with Guy Chavanon's wife. Depending on what Marie Chavanon said, the priorities would become clear. Hopefully she would know enough to call Bardy. Then she could enlist officers from the local *gendarmerie* to ask questions around the neighborhood. If Chavanon thought he was being watched, someone might have seen something. Neighbors in Switzerland were notoriously eagle-eyed.

Thankful she hadn't moved all her clothes next door, Agnes dressed and headed to her car, planning to stop at a highway restaurant for coffee and a croissant. One foot on the front porch and she knew the plan was flawed.

Sybille was in the front garden of her own home, stationed near the hedge separating the two properties. She'd brought her gardening shears as a prop and was waving them as if planning an attack on the climbing roses. Agnes wondered how long she'd been there. Probably since dawn.

"I didn't know you'd slept next door," Sybille said cheerily despite the blatant falsehood.

A Saint Bernard nosed his way past her, attempting to force his large body through the shrubbery to reach Agnes. When they were younger, her boys made the dog wear one of the iconic barrels on his collar every time they walked him to the village. In case they needed rescuing, they'd explained. Sometimes she thought Brandon missed the prestige of the small barrel. Agnes reached over the hedge to pat the top of his head.

"I thought you would enjoy an evening to yourself," she said. "I wanted to check on the house and must have fallen asleep."

"A house changes when it's empty." Sybille aimed the shears toward the front door.

At the gesture Agnes wanted to shout, *En garde*. Instead she said, "I was thinking of moving back in. There's no reason not to." She knew there was every reason not to, but something about Sybille made her act like a fifteen-year-old, arguing a point simply to show that she had her own opinion. When Sybille didn't respond, Agnes had a moment of panic. What if Sybille didn't object? She couldn't leave her boys alone in the house after school, much less when work kept her late. That was the reason they'd continued to sleep at George's parents' house after the initial shock of his death wore off.

"You should rent it to someone," Sybille said, studying the two-story stucco structure with an appraising eye. "There's not enough housing with the population growing so quickly, and you'd make a nice income. You're not going to move back in. Not when you need me to look after the boys."

The houses were twenty meters and two hundred years apart, something that reverberated through their lives. Agnes wondered if her in-laws knew how much she'd loved their home from the first moment she set eyes on it. George's parents lived in a picture-perfect three-story chalet with balconies running on the upper floors and flowers cut into the old-fashioned wood shutters. The wood was darkened with age, and a feeling of permanence was in every detail. It was a stark contrast to the house they had built for their son as a wedding gift. At the time, Agnes had been so thrilled that they would have a home to call their own, particularly one large enough to welcome the children they'd imagined, that she'd not objected to the proximity to her new in-laws. Nor had she objected to the modern design. It was well built and comfortable. In that moment, she knew that she wouldn't rent it out. It was still theirs. Hers and George's.

"Your roses were lovely last summer," she said to Sybille. "When they return from skiing, I'll ask the boys to give the vines a thorough pruning and clear away the winter deadwood."

"Leaving the house empty is like looking for ghosts. It needs new life. It would help the boys move on."

Sybille waved the shears dangerously close to Agnes, who took them and snipped the stems that protruded over her side of the hedge. She was surprised when Sybille didn't object to her inexpert cutting.

"Have they said something?" Agnes tossed the stems into the wicker basket, catching her thumb on a thorn. It bled and she sucked it clean.

"They don't need to. The house is a reminder of their father. It's waiting for him. It's a mausoleum."

This was unexpected. Agnes had thought Sybille would want her son's home kept as a tribute. Then she remembered the feel of her own sheets that morning. The silence of her own home. It didn't have to feel abandoned.

"The boys will grow up, they won't always need—"

"Attention?" Sybille scoffed. "They'll never outgrow that. Not until the day they die."

The word hung in the air like an accusation.

"The kind of attention changes," said Agnes. "Eventually they'll want to feel independent."

"Coming home to a warm welcome and hot meal is something no one should outgrow."

Agnes found a tissue in her pocket and wound it around her bleeding thumb. She was suddenly weary, and it was more than the strain of a first day back at work. Her thoughts drifted to Julien Vallotton.

Sybille gave her a knowing smile. "Go on, get to your work. I'll check that you've locked up properly."

Agnes handed the shears back. Then she remembered. "Sybille, I won't be home for dinner tonight." She hesitated, but it had to be said. "I'm having dinner at Château Vallotton."

The Chavanon property sat on several acres halfway up a forested hillside overlooking the city of La Chaux-de-Fonds. Although the factory was also there, the wooded neighborhood felt affluent and residential. Agnes decided that most of the homes were built after the Chavanons were well established.

She pulled into the Perrault et Chavanon parking lot and got out of her car, looking around. The entire property had an abandoned air. Not abandoned, she corrected herself, since the grounds stretching between the factory, the house, and the two smaller structures were immaculately kept. Lonely. A dusting of snow capped the higher elevations, and the fresh cool air was tinged with the fragrance of evergreens, but it did little to enliven the atmosphere.

The factory was exactly as Julien Vallotton had described it. The steep slate roof was shingled in a pattern of muted colors; the windows and doors had elaborate stone surrounds, and the entire edifice resembled an overblown one-story château. A statement building for a proud family. The house was closer to the main road than to the factory and had its own driveway with parking on the far side. The modern white blocky structure was three stories tall, topped by an old-fashioned pitched roof. Wide terraces wrapped three sides, reminiscent of walkways around a ship, and Agnes wondered what dynamics led a family to juxtapose a modern residence so near a falsely antique factory. Perhaps a generational divide?

Farther across the broad sloping lawn were two other buildings; small traditional houses, cottages by comparison to the main residence. She knew one was Christine Chavanon's. The buildings were one story, neatly kept, and, for the moment, silent.

She checked her watch. They'd set a time to meet and she was early. Although closed for the weekend, the factory was an intriguing building and she walked closer. Unfortunately, little was to be learned from the exterior. The main door was locked and the windows were too high off the ground to see through. She searched the surrounding lawn for any useful debris or ornament to step on, but found nothing. Imposing and silent, the building looked like a place that death had recently visited. A funeral wreath wouldn't have been a surprise, and the view down the hill toward town didn't help the atmosphere. The city was too distant to see in detail, and the general impression was gray.

"*Allô! Bonjour*, Inspector!" a woman's voice called. Christine Chavanon approached from across the lawn. "I was up all night," she said when they were near enough to speak.

It was sunny, but a sharp wind blew across the lawn, and Agnes shifted so her back was to it. Maybe it was time to consider exchanging her skirts for slacks. Christine appeared impervious to the weather. Her eyes were bright with excitement. Or from lack of sleep, Agnes corrected.

"Have you remembered something?" Agnes asked.

Christine looked shocked. "Of course not. I simply couldn't sleep."

Agnes doubted that. She'd had her share of sleepless nights, and what kept her awake were the thoughts. Swirling, illogical fears and concerns and threads of blame and anxiety. She also remembered denying it.

"Who lives in the other cottage?"

"That's a nice name for them. They were built for the factory managers a long time ago. My father used the other one as his workshop."

"I'd like to see inside."

Christine turned in the opposite direction. "Let's start with the factory."

Agnes followed the younger woman around the corner of the building to a small door.

Christine entered a code in a digital keypad. "We put this in about five years ago."

The entry was large enough to hold thirty or forty people at close quarters. Metal racks for time cards were affixed to the wall, and a large white-faced clock hung over the double doors leading to the main factory. Another door led to an inner glass-walled room where the manager would have an unobstructed view of everything on this level. The room had a disused atmosphere, like a museum vignette.

They passed beneath the clock. The main floor of the factory was large, and the windows let in an enormous amount of natural light. Despite this, the room reminded Agnes of a movie set. Real, but not real, at the same time. "Nothing unusual happened here before or after your father's death?"

"If you mean a burglary, Gisele and Ivo would have noticed. I can't imagine what anyone would want. They don't keep much gold anymore; it's all lesser metals and they're locked in the big safe."

Agnes wondered why someone had added an elaborate lock with diminished numbers of employees to monitor. She walked to the middle of the room. Without financial reports she had little sense of the scale of success among watchmakers. Julien Vallotton had implied that Dufour, working alone, was the epitome of success. A living legend. Omega and others with their thousands of employees were also successful. Was there a middle ground? Was Perrault et Chavanon a business on the uptick, or in a slow and inexorable decline? Did someone hope Guy Chavanon's death would speed the descent or prevent it?

"We need to talk about your father's note and who he thought was watching him."

"I told you it didn't make any sense to me." Christine looked around the large room as if seeing it through a visitor's eyes. "At the height of production, fifty or seventy-five years ago, there would have been a hundred people working here every day."

Several of the tall desks were modern, with white tops and high-powered lamps attached to the upper corners. Two had powerful illuminated magnifying glasses affixed to one side. The fronts of the desks were padded so employees could brace their arms to steady them. Neat boxes of tools sat on flat surfaces and on adjacent rolling storage units. Freestanding cabinets with drawers, cubbyholes, and shelves dotted the area. Agnes peered into a drawer.

"Component parts." Christine pulled a long flat box from a shelf. It held hundreds of tiny orange watch faces. She frowned, making her plain face decidedly unattractive. "This is Marie's doing. They're not marked with our logo. They'll be distributed under the name of the retailer who buys them." She slammed the boxes down, then seemed to think better of it and adjusted them carefully on the shelves. "I'm being unfair, it's what everyone does now. They have to, to survive."

Which meant rivals, no matter what Christine said, thought Agnes, reminded of Antoine Mercier. He'd felt Guy Chavanon was innovative. He'd also mentioned Copernicus. A revolutionary. All at once, she understood what Mercier meant. Copernicus was the astronomer who changed the order of all things: the sun was now at the center of the universe. It was a *solar* system. More important, people had died defending his beliefs. Were Mercier's words a threat or a warning?

"You mean survival by selling a less expensive product?" she asked. A series of completed watches were laid out. They looked nice to her. Fresh and fun. Perfect for someone who would never buy a timepiece that cost as much as a car or a yacht. She recognized several models from the displays at Baselworld and remembered the one Gisele had shown her. She should have asked the price.

"It's not the cost as much as it represents the end of craftsmanship," said Christine. "Or at least the kind of craftsmanship that we always stood for. The kind I'd always hoped to continue. A century ago, when you said Perrault et Chavanon, people knew what to expect. They could imagine the watch. The heavy case, the mechanical movement. Now, we dabble in everything. To me, it means we're about nothing."

Christine opened a cabinet, revealing large cubbyholes holding tools, and selected one made of brass. It was the width of two hands with four parts that could be drawn together by turning the large screws. She demonstrated how it worked. "Tools like this are obsolete in a modern factory." She set it back in the cupboard and shut the doors. "We kept these because my grandfather insisted new employees know how to use traditional tools. They did watch repair as training. You have to thoroughly know a watch to repair it." She slipped her hands into the pockets of her heavy sweater and visibly relaxed as she told what was likely a familiar story.

"My grandfather's great-grandfather opened the doors to the company in 1841. A remarkable era. Swiss watches accounted for over half the world's production." Christine looked around. "When my grandfather was here, the whole town was part of the operation. And not just our factory. All of the factories in La Chaux-de-Fonds and across the valley. They were filled with craftsmen, and others, mainly women, did smaller bits and sent their work to the factory with their husbands or delivery boys. Everyone had a role. All across the city, everyone took pride in what was done."

"Isn't that a romantic notion?" Agnes pictured Guy Chavanon wandering the floor, holding court. It would be distracting to anyone engaged in close, meticulous work. And overhead, Madame Chavanon would look down from her office. Watching. She wondered if Guy Chavanon kept records of his inventions in the factory or if they were in his workshop.

"Karl Marx wrote in *Capital* that La Chaux-de-Fonds should be considered as a same manufacture. He meant that we were individual workshops all pulling toward a common goal. I don't think he was a very romantic person. There was an incredible sense of unity and purpose."

Agnes set down the tweezers she had been examining. "Is that why you went to work for Omega? Don't they practically control Bienne?"

"They employ a lot of people and we're spread out in quite a few buildings, but it's not the same. It's not as"—Christine searched for a word—"communal."

Agnes shifted topics. "I read the interview with Gianfranco Giberti in yesterday's *Daily News*. It must be difficult working for the same company now that you're no longer a couple."

Christine stiffened. "We're in separate divisions. He's research and I'm design. We don't see each other at work, ever."

"Did he and your father spend time together? Without you, I mean. It would be natural, they're both watchmakers."

"My father wouldn't have had anything to talk about with Gianfranco, certainly not work. He said he was nice looking, that's all."

Agnes walked toward the more distant workstations. Here the veil of time descended. The tables were constructed of thick wood planks, and the tops glowed with a patina of age and use. It felt as if the workers had left off a moment ago; however, she suspected these desks had been empty for years, if not decades. She didn't need to imagine the past; this was the past.

"Could I see upstairs?"

The walls of the owner's office were paneled in wood carved in traditional scenes, and the desk and chair fit the décor. Large, heavy. Masculine. The rest of the room was less a part of the whole; particularly the bookcases filled with modern notebooks. Agnes removed one and found the usual array of company correspondence. Orders, invoices, bills paid. Letters of agreement and of dispute. Glancing through the material, she expected a sense of coming home. This was her expertise in Financial Crimes. Track the money. Today it felt hollow and she returned the notebook to the shelf. There wasn't a computer, but she supposed that Marie Chavanon might use a laptop and keep it with her.

Christine moved toward a carved wall panel. It concealed a cabinet and she pulled out a notebook very different from those on the exposed bookshelves.

"Our design books." She laid one on the desk. It was slightly larger than a traditional notebook, and the pages were not all the same texture or color. It was created to hold a collection of individual pages, not the other way around.

"When I was little, my grandfather let me sit up here and look through the archives. I thought it was a treat. Later, I realized they were thankful I was so easily entertained." She selected another book and laid it beside the first, glancing at the spine.

"Gisele mentioned a collection of watches," Agnes said.

"Yes, about thirty examples of advances over the last few hundred years." Christine crossed the room. "A few are our models, but most aren't. We should lend them to a museum." She whipped away a cloth covering a glass case. The shelves were empty.

"That bitch." She slammed her fist on top of the cabinet. Her hand crashed through the glass and she screamed. Her expression transformed from rage to shock to embarrassment. Blood ran down her arm.

Agnes ran forward. "Don't move." She pulled a leather glove from her pocket and used it to break pieces of glass from the wood frame. Carefully Christine eased her hand from between the remaining shards. She was pale and shaky. The long slice across her forearm bled profusely. Agnes found a clean handkerchief and used it to stanch the flow, then she pulled a small chair near and urged Christine to sit while she examined the cut more thoroughly.

"You need a doctor." Agnes pressed her handkerchief back in place, holding it firmly.

"Use my scarf."

The silk was perfect for binding a wound, and Agnes fixed a knot. Blood stained the blue patterned fabric, turning the flowers a grotesque violet. Christine propped her other arm against the wall and leaned her head against it. Her lips were white.

"I didn't mean to break the glass, it just fell away."

"An unlucky tap." Agnes cast a doubtful look at the cabinet.

The glass was thick and anchored firmly in the wood structure. Christine had been angry. Her blow was forceful.

Five minutes passed. Christine breathed in and out slowly. When she finally opened her eyes and surveyed the empty cabinet, she sounded more angry than injured.

"Typical. Marie probably took the collection to the house and boxed everything up. She doesn't care about our heritage. She's part of what's wrong. That's why father didn't work here anymore."

Eight

They stood beside Agnes's car. The conversation had reached an impasse. Agnes insisted Christine go to the hospital for stitches. Christine resolutely refused.

"You have to talk to Marie," Christine said, blood leaching through the bandage on her arm. "I want to see her reaction when you show her the note and say my father was killed."

"Need help?" a man's voice called out across the lawn.

Agnes turned. He was closer to Guy Chavanon's generation than her own. Well dressed in casual clothing, his shirt collar was open underneath a moss-green V-necked sweater. Above it, his lightly lined face was handsome and confident. She noticed a flicker of anxiety disturb Christine's already pained expression, but the man was upon them before Agnes could question her.

"What happened?" the man said.

"A little accident." Christine grasped her arm as if shielding the injury from view. "Inspector Lüthi was kind enough to offer me a ride to the doctor." Agnes noted the change in plan.

A shadow passed over the man's face, and Agnes wondered if it was caused by her title or Christine's injuries.

"I don't think we've met. Stephan Dupré."

Agnes recognized the name. At least the man hadn't lied to Vallotton about being a neighbor, although judging by Christine's reaction he wasn't a favorite one.

"A police inspector?" Dupré said casually, explaining that he lived on the far side of the Chavanon property, past the cottages. He took Christine's arm, gently lifting the knotted scarf to peek underneath. "I was trained for volunteer rescue, did it for years." He frowned. "This is more than a little accident. Is this why you're here, Inspector?"

It was definitely her title that disturbed him, Agnes decided. No one would think that the police were called out because of a cut, especially someone who trained for volunteer rescue. "I happened to be there when Christine cut herself."

Dupré took another look at Christine's injury. "You didn't try to hurt yourself, did you?"

Christine snatched her arm away, wincing at the movement. "I broke a piece of glass. It was an accident."

Dupré turned to Agnes. "Marie's not here. She went into town."

Christine sucked air in between her teeth.

"I happened to see her drive away," Dupré added.

"Do you know when she'll return?" said Agnes. "She was expecting me. Late yesterday I spoke on the telephone to a man who promised to tell her I was coming." Agnes paused. "Was that you?"

Dupré ran a hand across his forehead. The elegant gesture

managed to convey dismay and a confidence that all would be forgiven. "Caught. I answered the phone when I dropped the mail off at her house, and it seemed like the natural thing, to say Marie would see you, but—" He repeated the wiping gesture. "I forgot to tell her. Stupid, but we've been so upset about Guy. Not thinking clearly at all."

Agnes couldn't pinpoint the nature of the lie. Did he forget, or did he change his mind about telling Madame Chavanon, or had she refused to receive her visitor and he was too polite to blame her?

"I was going to look you up today, anyway," she said.

"A bit odd, the police being interested now, a week later," said Dupré. "Did something change?"

Christine opened the passenger door and sat in the car sideways with her feet on the ground. She motioned for Agnes to take her time.

Agnes eyed the other woman through the windshield. Christine leaned her head against the seat and closed her eyes. Her color had returned, which was a good sign, and the bleeding had stopped. A short delay wouldn't cause any harm.

Agnes turned to Dupré. "At the funeral you gave Julien Vallotton the impression that you weren't surprised Monsieur Chavanon died."

Christine opened her eyes, listening intently now.

"You mentioned that he was nervous and acting unlike himself. Or did Monsieur Vallotton mislead me?" Faced with Dupré's blank expression, she threw in that last bit, suspecting he wouldn't lie about a conversation with one of the Vallottons.

Dupré shrugged easily. "Yes, I said those things. I was upset.

I overreacted. Guy died so suddenly it made me imagine he wasn't himself. I think I preferred that to the explanation that he didn't want to see me."

"How well did you know Monsieur Chavanon?"

"We've been friends since childhood. Grew up here on the same street."

"And the part about him being followed?"

Dupré glanced around as if an explanation would walk across the lawn. "Guy may have said that he saw a car he didn't recognize. I—" Dupré rubbed his head. "Look, I know who Julien Vallotton is, and I'm ashamed to admit I was pleased to meet him. I said some things I shouldn't have, made more of a story to keep his interest. I didn't think he would tell the police. I didn't think it mattered. Hell, we were at a reception following a funeral. People say things. Guy died from eating peanuts."

"He didn't eat them," Christine called from inside the car.

"He died from the peanuts," Dupré said loudly. "I always told him to be more careful. Don't know if I could have lived with that hanging over me my whole life."

"I suppose people adjust to their own burdens," said Agnes.

Christine's eyes were closed but she spoke again. "It wasn't his fault. He didn't eat a handful of nuts."

"He hadn't been himself, that wasn't entirely a fabrication," Dupré said, angling closer to Agnes and away from the open car door and Christine. "But that doesn't have anything to do with the way he died."

"Would it surprise you to learn that he left a note saying he was being watched?"

"That's absurd. Leave a note? Why not tell someone? He would tell me or Marie. The workshop is where he spent most of his time, and if he was worried, he'd tell me so I could keep an eye out." Dupré turned to look toward the house. "He didn't say anything to Marie."

Agnes wasn't sure if that was a question or a statement.

"Have you been inside the workshop?" Dupré asked.

"No, we were on our way when Christine was injured."

"Inspector," Christine called out. "I realized we have to wait for Marie. My father changed the lock and I don't have the new key."

"I have one," said Dupré.

"Father gave you a key?"

Agnes glanced to Dupré to judge his reaction. Satisfaction?

"About three months ago." Dupré smiled broadly at them both. "I don't keep it with me. It'll only take five minutes to retrieve it from my house."

Christine nodded. "We'll wait."

After Dupré left, Agnes slipped into the driver's seat of her car. "You haven't been inside your father's workshop since he died?"

"I haven't gone in his workshop since I joined Omega. I couldn't risk seeing anything they might want. Intellectual property and all that."

"Sounds like you thought your father might be inventing something important. What about the factory? We were just there."

Christine shot a disdainful look at the larger structure. "Omega doesn't care about that work. There's nothing innovative there. It's all superficial design. And now that's all the company will have. No, I wouldn't have risked my father thinking I'd seen something in his workshop—even something he didn't fully develop—in case it turned up later at Omega."

"Do you know if your stepmother has been in?"

Christine made a disgusted noise. "Marie never went there when Father was alive. It can't mean much to her now. It's different for me. I used to work there with him. Nearly every day we had coffee together near his fireplace." Christine smiled. "He had old-fashioned habits."

"Your father was an engineer, wasn't he? He went to the EPFL?"

"Yes. He knew how to build a watch, he knew about metals and balance, and so many other things. He taught me everything I know." Christine fingered the scarf wrapping her arm. "I don't use much of it anymore, the design part I studied at school, but the other, it's part of my past now, I guess."

"Did your father keep a notebook like the ones you showed me upstairs?"

"Stephan's back."

"I'll meet him. It will only take a few minutes," said Agnes.

"I'm going with you."

"What about Omega and intellectual property?"

"I'll have two witnesses to say that I only stepped inside, hardly time to steal design secrets. Not that I think there are any."

As they approached the cottage, Agnes noticed that the hedge created a pathway to the door. It should have been the entrance to a secret garden. She glimpsed the small porch and noted that the windows on either side were shuttered. It was a darker place than Christine's cottage with its white curtains and gleaming windows.

"I told Marie she'd need to come in and clear everything

out," said Dupré, jerking his head toward the path. "Offered to help, but she's too upset. It'll have to wait."

"It's only been a week," said Agnes. "Madame Chavanon may need more time before she disturbs the place her husband worked."

Dupré pulled a single key from his pocket. "I've never used it, but there's no reason to think it won't fit the lock. Guy always gave me one for emergencies. Guess he figured I'd rush over and put a fire out if I had to." He handed it to Agnes. "We'll let the police do the honors. That way Marie can't get too angry. She's protective of the place."

Agnes took the key and walked the narrow path to the porch. Upon closer inspection, the shrubs were large but well maintained, with the tops gently rounded. They created a path directly to the steps. Dupré followed her closely. When she reached the porch, she stopped, blocking his view. "When was the last time someone was here?" she called over her shoulder.

"Not since Guy died," Dupré said. "Why?"

"Stay back." The door wasn't locked. It wasn't even closed. There was a slight gap between it and the frame. She placed her toe at the bottom of the door and nudged it open. It barely moved.

"What the devil?" Dupré said behind her.

Agnes motioned for him to back away. "Is anyone here?" she said as a final warning, not expecting a reply. She pushed the door again, this time more forcefully, and it swung open.

What she saw stunned her.

Nine

Guy Chavanon's workshop had been ransacked. Agnes stepped inside, moving cautiously. Paper was scattered on the floor. Boxes were overturned, the contents heaped in piles. Tools, clocks, scraps of metal, and miscellany lay in tumbled heaps. She flipped a light switch on. The walls of the original living room were covered with large pieces of paper. The exterior shutters were closed, and the interiors of the windows were also papered over. Every centimeter was covered with scribbles. Equations. Diagrams. Notes. Agnes hadn't seen anything like it since her last mathematics lecture in university. In the center of the room, four long tables were shoved together and covered with paper and boxes of mechanical parts.

Fresh air shifted. Agnes crossed to the back wall where a windowpane had shattered on the floor. The opening was large enough for a person to crawl through. Leaving it, she quickly moved to the next room. Originally the bedroom, it was lined by tables. Piles of unbound sheets of paper lay scattered on the floor. The bathroom was next. There, the empty cabinets were open. That left the kitchen. She called out again, although she knew the cottage was empty. There was something palpable about an empty building.

"We shouldn't be here," Christine Chavanon said from the front porch.

She looked ill, whereas Dupré looked dazed. "My God, everything I told Vallotton was true." He started forward and Agnes motioned for him to stay outside.

She knelt to study the area around the shattered glass. There was no moisture on the floor or wall, and the glass was dry. It had rained the day before in Basel, but not at her home near Lausanne. She would have to check the local weather to establish a timeline for when the break-in occurred.

"It looks like the studio of a madman." Dupré gestured to the covered walls and mounds of paper.

Agnes didn't disagree.

"My father was a genius," Christine objected. "He had a genius's way of working. That's why he wanted a room apart from the main factory. People didn't understand how his mind operated. He needed the freedom to process ideas and—" She started to cry.

Dupré ignored her. "It wasn't like this the last time I was here."

"When was that?" Agnes asked, wanting to comfort Christine, but needing information first.

"Maybe a year ago?"

"Why did you stop visiting?"

"There wasn't a reason." Dupré peered in through the open doorway. "Or at least I didn't think there was."

"Christine, when were you here last?" Agnes stepped closer to the door.

"When I left the family business. Nearly three years ago."

"Your arm is bleeding again," said Agnes.

Christine placed a hand firmly on the bandage, not seeming to care. She stared in disbelief at the heavily marked paper covering the walls.

Agnes stood in the doorway of the former living room, examining the kitchen. It had been transformed into a cross between a lab and a metal shop. Dupré kept talking, his anxiety palpable.

"I write travel books. I'm often gone for weeks, even months, at a time, and I spent a lot of time in Asia recently. When I returned, I figured Guy had fallen into other habits. I knew that once he'd finished whatever was occupying him, he'd be anxious to sit with me again."

"That had happened before?" Agnes studied the formulas on the walls. Some elements were familiar to her. Those looked accurate. Messy, but correct. Others were beyond her base of knowledge, straying from pure math into chemistry. This looked beyond the mechanics of watchmaking, even beyond the calculations needed for metallurgy. On the porch, Christine was bent over at the waist, as if she was going to be sick. Agnes tried to decide, were these the writings of a well-educated yet unstable mind or the calculations of a genius?

She crossed to the broken window, careful not to touch anything, and leaned near to study the exterior of the building. Whoever entered had to slide behind the tall hedge and then climb up to the window. There wasn't room for a ladder, which meant that an intruder would have to hoist himself by his hands and perhaps feet, scrabbling up the wall and breaking the glass, then jumping inside. Difficult, but not impossible for a grown man or a tall woman.

"Certainly, I tried to see him," Dupré answered. "I'd knocked once or twice and he called out that he was busy. That wasn't unusual. If he was working with metals, he couldn't be disturbed and interrupt the play of heat and timing."

Agnes returned to the former kitchen to inspect the piece of equipment fixed to the floor in place of a stove. Judging by the thick exterior, it was a small forge. She opened the door and peered in. There were a few tiny fragments of what looked like paper. She frowned. The nature of Guy Chavanon's work was difficult to judge. It wasn't at all what she had expected, even disregarding the chaos. She crossed to the entrance.

Dupré blocked the doorway. "A couple of times he hollered out that I'd be better off taking a drink up at the house."

"Marie is a *very* welcoming hostess," said Christine. She was upright again. Pale but focused.

"Yes, she is," Dupré said sharply. "Your stepmother has always been an excellent hostess. I don't see a reason to take that tone about it. Your father was very proud of her."

He flushed and Agnes eyed him speculatively. "Can either of you tell if something has been removed?" she asked.

Christine stood at the threshold, shaking her head. "There's no way to know."

Dupré shrugged.

"Inspector," Christine said, "you've asked why I left three years ago. We weren't surviving. I needed a job in case my father closed the company. That's why I didn't want to come inside earlier. I wanted to remember the good times, the past."

"But the business didn't close," said Agnes.

"Not yet. I estimated he had about three years of capital left. I needed more than dreams of the next great innovation. I needed to be assured of a salary."

"He had a new investor," said Dupré.

Christine looked up, surprised. "For what?"

"I don't know."

"You said you were exaggerating when you spoke with Monsieur Vallotton at the funeral?" Agnes said.

"About not being surprised that Guy died, but I was serious about the other. He hadn't been himself. He mentioned the money to me maybe six months ago."

"He didn't say anything to me. Marie never told me." Christine's tone was accusatory. Agnes saw the disillusionment of a child understanding that the parent has a three-dimensional life beyond her.

"He only hinted to me after a few drinks, made me swear I'd not tell a soul. I didn't. After that he grew distant."

"I had no idea," said Christine. "He didn't mention who or what?"

"No, only that it was big and Perrault et Chavanon would last through this century."

"Then everything is fine. Marie can continue." Christine's voice faltered, and Agnes wondered if the young woman now regretted leaving her father's company. If she had stayed, she could have led the business into the future. Now her decision was made. She worked for a global brand. Had that made her a traitor in their eyes?

"I'm going to call the local *gendarmerie*," Agnes said. "They'll secure the building and gather any evidence."

"I need to see a doctor. My arm is bleeding again."

"Marie won't believe this." Dupré waved an arm around. "But she should be grateful. What if she'd left it for weeks? The place would freeze up, animals might wander in. Mice would eat all this junk she'll want to save."

"Junk? This"—Christine gestured wildly—"this is a testament to my father's genius. It's . . . he was right and I didn't listen. He was working on something important."

Agnes ushered them off the porch. "I didn't see a safe. Is there one, or somewhere he would have kept his important documents?"

"The only safe is in the factory." Christine leaned against a porch column as if faint.

"Guy would have been more likely to bury his notes than put them in a safe," added Dupré. "He always did things his own way."

"An idea important enough to steal," said Christine softly.

"Or kill for," said Dupré.

Christine gasped and clutched her injured arm. "But he was already dead when they broke in."

"Are you sure?" said Agnes. "Monsieur Dupré, you said that you didn't think anyone had been here since Monsieur Chavanon died. We don't know when he last entered. Someone could have broken in after he left and before he died."

Christine opened her mouth to speak, then shut it.

Dupré spoke for her. "Who would have thought Guy was really onto something."

Ten

A distant clock struck one and Agnes glanced skyward, easing her foot off the gas pedal. Guy Chavanon's workshop was a processing nightmare. That was the pronouncement of the local officer who'd arrived at the scene in response to her call. Only when she'd offered to bring in reinforcements had the man backed down, assuring her that his team was up to the task.

Agnes had taken the man at his word and decided she wasn't needed. Marie Chavanon wasn't responding to phone calls, and Christine had agreed to let Stephan Dupré take her to the hospital for stitches. It was time to go to the school where Guy Chavanon died.

By the time she arrived, the morning sun had disappeared behind clouds, and the countryside near Rossemaison was wrapped in a dark gloom. In the distance, snow blanketed the higher elevations. She slowed her car. According to Christine Chavanon's directions, she would reach the Moutier Institut de Jeunes Gens a few kilometers before the village.

It was a pretty drive with woods on both sides. Tree branches formed a partial canopy overhead. As she rounded the final bend, the Institute came into view, and Agnes pulled her car into a parking space off the circular drive. The towering chalet reminded her of George's family home. The chalet belonging to her in-laws wasn't half as large as the one in front of her, but both were elegant in that rustic traditional way beloved by Swiss and tourists alike.

A discreet sign instructed visitors to enter, and the front door opened into a medium-size room. The floor, walls, and ceiling were all burnished wood, and the atmosphere was inviting. There were a few small tables and groups of brightly upholstered comfortable chairs. The tables held artfully arranged brochures and magazines featuring the Institute and life in Switzerland, while the walls were covered with photographs of enthusiastic students and instructors dating back over a hundred years. Agnes noted that the boarding school was all-male. Evidently the Institute was either old-fashioned or deeply traditional.

She walked down the broad corridor that cut through the middle of the building until a small area opened up, fronted by a desk. A middle-aged woman jumped to her feet. Agnes glanced at the placard. She'd spoken with Madame Jomini earlier. Agnes presented her credentials and waited while the receptionist slipped into the inner office.

The woman who emerged with Madame Jomini was tall, well dressed, and unstintingly headmistress. In a cool and unwelcoming tone she gave her name as Helene Fontenay. She angled forward unnaturally as if there was a problem with her hips, with her wrists pressed against forearm crutches. Otherwise, she was lean and elegant with shoulder-length light brown hair pinned back on both sides with small metal clips. She wore little makeup: pale lipstick and a light application of mascara. The result emphasized her clear skin and gray eyes. Upon a second glance, Agnes decided that the headmistress was younger than her stern demeanor let on, probably in her early thirties.

To set the tone of an informal discussion, Agnes complimented the beauty of the chalet. When Madame Fontenay didn't reply, Agnes moved past her into the office, uninvited.

That room told the history of the school. In it, were elements of the past and visible nods to the current leadership. The center was occupied by an enormous partner's desk. It was surrounded by seating areas with chairs, a sofa, and appropriate tables, all contriving to lend an atmosphere more suited to a sitting room than a place to work. The furniture was a mix of antique and modern designs, and Agnes suspected that the modern pieces were chosen by Madame Fontenay; they seemed a fair reflection of her cold personal style.

Agnes removed her coat and laid it across a hassock. "Should we wait on the headmaster to discuss Monsieur Chavanon's death?" She claimed a cushioned chair in front of the desk, tucking her skirt under her and setting her handbag on the floor.

Helene Fontenay sighed audibly and crossed the room. Agnes was surprised by how swiftly the woman moved, despite her crutches.

"This is unnecessary," the headmistress said, ignoring her desk and sitting in a hard-backed chair across from Agnes. "We don't need to wait on my husband. And I don't know why you're here with questions. It was a terrible day and we've put it behind us."

"Were you there when Monsieur Chavanon died?"

Helene touched the row of small pearl buttons that closed her pale yellow sweater. "Not in the room. But I spoke with the police. They spoke with everyone. Having you here only disrupts our routine and frightens the boys."

"I have three sons of an age to attend your school. I don't think they frighten that easily."

"Monsieur Chavanon's son will be upset. The funeral was only two days ago. Your visit will fuel talk about his father's death."

"Madame Fontenay, I think that the boys are going to talk about what happened no matter what we do. Leo will probably want to talk about it with his friends. I know my boys would."

Agnes remembered telling them that their father had died. The shock and tears and denial. The anger. Eventually they said that they understood, although she knew they didn't. She could barely understand, and they couldn't conceive of permanence the way she did. Later she'd overheard them talking together, and with their friends, and was convinced that was where the healing began.

She continued, "Leo Chavanon lives in La Chaux-de-Fonds, an easy driving distance, yet he boards. Are your students required to board?"

"I don't know why you are asking these questions."

"Interest, right now. Is there something that concerns you? Something you'd rather I not inquire about?"

Madame Fontenay pressed her lips together. A minute passed. The only sound was the ticktock of a large cuckoo clock high on a far wall.

"We have eighty pupils," Madame Fontenay said. "All boys and all in residence. The older ones are in the newer dormitory, the younger in this building."

"And the teachers and the staff? They live here?"

"Of course not. My husband and I do, but none of the others." Madame Fontenay motioned to a door at the far end of the room. "The stair to our apartment is there. Completely private. The faculty rotate sleeping on the premises. One each on the dormitory floor of the chalet and in the new building."

Agnes wondered why a woman who needed crutches would want to walk up the stairs between her office and apartment. Surely they could have accommodated private quarters on the ground floor of such a large building. "How many faculty?"

"Sixteen teachers and the same number in other jobs: secretaries, housekeeping, gardeners, a chef and his assistant. There are small villages on either side of us and most live there, or on local family farms."

"Have the staff said anything about the day Monsieur Chavanon died?"

"There is nothing to say." Madame Fontenay smoothed the front of her sweater again.

"Nothing at all? No gossip about what happened?" Agnes smoothed her own wool skirt. "In my experience people like to talk about a shocking event. It helps them make sense of what they've seen."

"Rumors," said Madame Fontenay. "Falsehoods, figments of imagination, and folly." She took a deep breath and her voice calmed. "Rumors are to be expected in a closed community like this one. We know how to deal with it. We may be new to the Institute, but we know how to run a school. We know our job."

"What is our job, darling?" A tall red-haired man stepped into the room, glowing with health and enthusiasm.

Madame Fontenay introduced her husband to Agnes. In contrast to his wife, Bernard Fontenay gripped Agnes's hand warmly.

"Delighted. Delighted. Madame Jomini found me and said you were here. Darling, I'm famished. Do you think a snack might be arranged?"

Agnes expected the headmistress to ring for staff, but Madame Fontenay nodded tersely and left. She allowed the office door to bang shut behind her.

"Horrible thing, Chavanon dying." Bernard Fontenay unwound a scarf from around his neck and dropped it onto a side table.

"I imagine it was a shock to the students who were there. To everyone really. You didn't have any reason to wonder if it was more than an accident?"

"No." He looked at her wide-eyed. "Surely you don't think it was purposeful? How could it be? I thought these were routine questions. This sounds like you are opening an investigation."

"I would like to talk to everyone who was here that day. I'm making sure we haven't overlooked anything important."

Fontenay took a seat opposite her, his long legs filling the space between them. "Better you than the locals, keeps it on an elevated plain. Most of the teachers and the students attended the reception, or planned to. They weren't all there when Monsieur Chavanon collapsed, and once he did, we closed off the dining room and no one else entered. As you can imagine, the reception was over at that point. Of course, the parents—" He looked concerned. "You won't need to talk with them, will you? We have to be careful of the school's reputation, you understand."

"How many were here?"

"We had planned to hand out the ski awards, and it was a large gathering. It was a busy day and afterwards with the confusion . . ." He shrugged.

"Did they RSVP?"

"What? Oh, yes. I hadn't thought of that. Madame Jomini will have a list of who responded. Hard to know who had actually arrived. Of course, Monsieur Chavanon was there. He had a friend with him. Monsieur Patel, an Indian gentleman. I didn't see them before—" Fontenay wrung his hands. "Before it was over. I don't know who among the others Chavanon knew. Many of the parents are nodding acquaintances, a few are friendlier, and several are intimately connected. Extended family, even. The dining room was full, and there were six or seven more sets of parents outside on the lawn when it happened, watching their sons show off their soccer skills. It was cold, but they can't be forced to stay inside."

"You were in the room when Monsieur Chavanon died?"

"You know who would have the best recollection? Monsieur Navarro. Jorge Navarro is always first to arrive, plus he has an excellent memory. Talk to him and you'll have a better idea to start from." He stood abruptly, propelled by restless energy.

Agnes slipped her notebook into her handbag. "Your wife mentioned rumors. She said that they're to be expected, but she didn't mention what they were precisely."

"The usual nonsense was what she meant. The boys are imaginative. I remember being at school and trying to scare the younger forms. We invented a ghost who lived on the dormitory floor. It all seems so silly now. No levelheaded adult would believe half of what we said."

Agnes found it interesting that he thought of the students

while his wife indicated the staff. Perhaps a representation of their natural division of duties? Clearly they both had heard rumors they didn't want to discuss.

"Madame Fontenay was troubled by my presence. I think she'd rather I not speak with anyone."

"Helene? She'll be happy it's dealt with."

"I had the opposite impression. She clearly thinks my presence—any police presence—is problematic."

"She doesn't like disruption in routine, but she'll cooperate."

He sat down again and leaned forward, clasping his hands together as if in prayer. "I shouldn't make light of the situation. Helene wouldn't like it. You see, I'm Swiss. Taught at Oxford after taking my degree, but I wanted to do more than teach. Actually, I wanted to return here. To this landscape." He gestured broadly as if the walls of the room couldn't block his connection with the countryside. "I thought it would be good for Helene after the accident. We put together the money and bought into the Institute nearly three years ago. It's our life."

He rubbed the knuckles of one hand with the other. They looked like the hands of an academic. The skin was nearly perfect. Fontenay was a man who dealt with the world through his head, not his hands. And now his world, their entire investment, their livelihood, was resting on maintaining an illusion of complete calm and safety at the Institute, something so deeply Swiss that, even after a lifetime, Agnes had a difficult time understanding it.

Fontenay rose to stand near the door. "Come along. Let's put this to rest."

Eleven

Bernard Fontenay suggested they begin their tour outside so Agnes would have a sense of the scale of the Institute before diving in, as he put it, to the details of the buildings. He was clearly proud of the establishment. As they walked, he pointed toward various buildings ringing the central lawn.

"The dormitory for the older boys is the nearest building on the right. Beyond that is a classroom building. You can't see it from here, but farther out is our indoor pool. Across the lawn is the newest academic facility, where all the science labs are."

Agnes thought the dormitory resembled a modern apartment building in her village. The narrow two-story structure was neatly stuccoed. Pleasant but nondescript, especially when compared to the majesty of the old chalet. On the other hand, the classroom buildings were interesting. Each was two stories high and built of beautifully smooth concrete punctuated by large windows.

Fontenay led the way to the kitchen garden. It was to one

side of the chalet, protected from the wind by a high stone wall. The gate was open, and inside a gravel path crunched delightfully underfoot. Most of the plants were winter brown, a few were evergreens, and some were wrapped in burlap. Shrubs, Agnes supposed. She looked around appreciatively. A garden of this size took commitment and hard work.

Fontenay waved to catch the attention of the man standing at the far end. "Navarro has a good memory and can fill in details."

When she caught sight of him, Agnes's first thought was of the headmistress. What did Helene Fontenay think about this rumpled, dusty man? The knees of Navarro's trousers were damp with earth, and his overcoat was not much cleaner. He wore a battered felt hat. His eyes twinkled pleasantly, though, and despite his short stature he had a presence.

She extended her hand in greeting. Navarro wiped his hand on his trousers before accepting. She felt a dusting of mud work from his palm to hers.

Fontenay made the introductions. "Navarro, the inspector is here to question us." He paused. "About Chavanon. They sent someone from outside the village."

Navarro looked hard at Fontenay. The headmaster shoved his hands into the pockets of his overcoat, hunching his shoulders. "Not quite spring yet, Navarro. You may want to come inside to talk. I'll leave you to it. Helene will have my snack ready, don't want to ignore her."

Navarro didn't move to go indoors and Agnes didn't insist. She was warmly dressed and they were protected from the worst of the wind.

"The death of Monsieur Chavanon," Navarro said, rocking

back on his heels. "Leo's father, poor boy." His warm Spanish accent softened his words.

"You were in the room when he died?"

"Who else have you talked to here?" Navarro reached into the depths of his pocket and retrieved a cigarette and lighter.

"Only the Fontenays." Agnes watched him light up. She had broken the habit while in hospital, but hadn't been around a smoker in the weeks since then.

"And now me?" Navarro clicked his lighter and the flame ignited. "Why? I didn't have anything to do with it. Everyone says it was nuts. His symptoms were classic anaphylaxis. It has nothing to do with this garden."

"Not many people would recognize anaphylaxis." She inhaled slightly. Appreciatively. Tasting the smoke.

"Did someone in the village tell you that I grow poisonous plants? Was it Boschung? Is that why they called you in?"

"No, Monsieur Fontenay told me that you are from the Canary Islands and are an expert on exotic plants, and that you teach botany in addition to chemistry." She glanced around the dormant vegetation. "Are the plants why you recognized anaphylaxis?"

Navarro took another puff of his cigarette, then dropped it to the ground, crushing it under his heel. "There are no peanuts in this garden."

Agnes realized that, like her, he was an intermittent smoker. A calming habit, not a consistent one. He was willing to waste half a cigarette. She inhaled a last stray tendril of smoke and tried to remember what peanut plants looked like. A ground vine? Was it even possible to grow them in this cold a climate?

"Poisonous plants are an unusual hobby at a school around young boys," she said.

"It's research."

"Of course." A large classic tabby with white paws and chest leaped from a branch onto the wall, looking at them from its perch.

"These villainous plants hold within them the secrets that may save a life." Navarro had a rich, well-modulated voice and Agnes thought he'd do well onstage. She also wondered if his imperfect French wasn't part of his persona. Her initial impression of a musty scientist had evolved. He was sharp. Sharp enough to guard his words.

Agnes followed him as he moved to the next bed. Overhead the cat kept pace as if interested in their conversation.

"Although my research is related to the slow shutdown of the body that we find with the classic poisons like hemlock; that's why I've read about anaphylaxis." He shoved twigs toward her.

Agnes took the clippings. "You're not worried about keeping the poisons here, at the school?"

He scoffed. "Houseplants can be poisonous; we trust people not to eat them. Household cleaning products have been fed by mothers to their babies to kill them."

"Are the students allowed in the garden?"

"You think they're smart enough to create a peanut substitute from what they'd find here?" Navarro glanced around as if appraising the possibilities. "If they did, then they deserve their diploma now." He withdrew a knife and dug among the roots.

Agnes knelt beside him to hear better. Balancing the clippings on one knee, she turned up the collar of her coat.

"Atropa belladonna." He handed dead leaves to her. "Better known as nightshade."

She stood, uncomfortable. "That one I *have* heard of."

He laughed. "See? Got your interest. If the boys think they are studying something dangerous, their ears perk up."

"Nerve-racking for parents."

"I've learned to judge my audience. At the reception I was telling Monsieur Patel about the distillation of—" Abruptly, Navarro stopped digging. "You're here about that day and not about my garden. Did they find out how Monsieur Chavanon came into contact with the peanuts?"

"No. That's why I'm here. The headmaster tells me you are an acute observer."

Navarro moved to another plant, then snipped more twigs and handed them to her. She dropped them into the wicker basket, thinking of Sybille. She would appreciate this place. The sun peeked through the clouds and Agnes turned her face to it, enjoying the warmth. On the top of the wall, the cat did the same, then a boy walked past and the cat jumped down.

"I'm afraid there's not much about a parent reception that interests me. Therefore I did not observe carefully and can draw no conclusions."

"This isn't a science experiment, monsieur. I can sort fact from impression."

Navarro stood and grasped the handle of the basket, gesturing for Agnes to follow him. "I was distracted. I registered Monsieur Chavanon subconsciously, but I didn't greet him. We don't talk shop at the receptions. It's all pleasant and hello and everything is wonderful."

Agnes wondered if he was quoting Monsieur and Madame

Fontenay. It was likely they gave specific instructions about interacting with their guests, who were, after all, footing the hefty tuition and fees. "Nothing stands out?"

Navarro led her from the garden toward the chalet. "It was the usual suspects. Normally I have a glass of wine with my colleagues, then ease into talking to the parents. I'm not much at small talk."

"Earlier, you said that you recognized anaphylaxis?"

Navarro coughed apologetically into his hand. "When it was over. Not right then. It was—" He stopped and set the basket of clippings down. "This is what I remember. I could see Chavanon through the crowd in front of me. At first I thought he was choking. You see, choking is more common and he was gasping for air." Navarro raised his hand to his neck, touching beneath his chin. "He had his hands on his throat, staggering. I remember that he grazed a chair, then he drew back, like someone had attached strings to his shoulders and ankles and were pulling them together." Navarro picked the basket up again. He shook his shoulders. A gesture partway between a shiver and an attempt to loosen the muscles.

"I thought he was having a seizure. It was an impossible movement, unnatural. He knocked over a table, then fell onto the buffet. The sound was terrible. The crash and the food and plates scattering. Until then, I felt like we were all frozen. The noise woke us up."

They had reached the rear entrance to the chalet. Nearby, a handrail marked the top edge of the retaining wall. Below, the basement level opened onto the ground. The landscaping was artfully done, and the main lawn divided to gently slope down to the sliding glass doors below. The students were on break and a group kicked a soccer ball among them. It reached the slope and accelerated downward. Across the lawn, sunlight glinted off the classroom windows.

"Who was near Monsieur Chavanon when he fell ill?" Agnes asked.

"I don't know. It was too crowded and people were moving around all the time. When I first glanced up, he was standing alone."

"Completely alone?" Agnes leaned over the handrail. She could see down into the dining room where the reception had taken place.

"Seemed to be. Alone in a crowd, if you know what I mean. He was looking out the windows toward the lawn. There was a group outside playing soccer, like today. Maybe they caught his eye. I halfway remember some cheering." Navarro paused. "I wasn't staring at him. It's possible someone was speaking with him and backed away when they realized he was in distress. That would be natural, I think. I don't know what happened after that."

"You must remember something."

"I've tried to forget." He sighed when she waited for him to continue. "A woman screamed that someone was choking, and Chavanon's friend ran into the room, saw him, and called for a doctor. He ran out to get the EpiPen. It must have been in Chavanon's coat pocket, and Patel knew where it was. I ran for the school nurse. Later someone told me that Patel stuck the EpiPen in Chavanon's leg, but the medicine didn't help. The paramedics said that the serious cases might need two or three doses."

This coincided with what the coroner and Boschung described. The antidote failing. Chaos. People eating and drinking. It had to be in the minutes before this that Chavanon ate something deadly. Boschung had assured her it wasn't in his wineglass and he didn't have a plate of food. Was it possible that Aerni was wrong and Chavanon had eaten something before arriving and vomited it up? She knew the coroner would say no based on the stomach contents and the intensity of the reaction. After hearing Navarro's description, this sounded right. The symptoms came on suddenly and violently. Immediately. The question was, immediately after what?

Navarro opened the door to the chalet and motioned for Agnes to enter.

"Our nurse, Madame Butty, arrived a few minutes before the paramedics. They pronounced Chavanon dead. It was remarkably sudden. Monsieur Patel was so distraught the paramedics thought he was having a heart attack. Leo was hysterical. A few of the women were crying."

Standing in the calm atmosphere of the wide back hall of the chalet, Agnes could imagine the shocking events of that deadly day. She heard Madame Jomini answer the school telephone. Farther away she heard the clack of Helene Fontenay's crutches. They had returned to normal. Or had they?

After thanking Navarro, Agnes headed downstairs to see the dining room where Guy Chavanon had died. Where he had been poisoned.

The original storage basement had been carefully renovated to accommodate the changing needs of the school. The dining room was light and airy, and one entire wall was filled with sliding glass doors that opened onto the lower level of the lawn. The window curtains were a bold red-and-white stripe with a border of perfectly square white-on-red crosses. Tiny embroidered Swiss flags. Cheers drifted in from the soccer game. In the next room, balls cracked on a pool table.

The dining room was large enough to seat the student body alongside the faculty at long tables for eight. The tables and chairs matched the light blond wood of the floors and walls. The furniture was configured for meals, but it was easy to visualize the tables removed for a reception: parents wandering onto the lawn and others arriving from the interior hallway. Organized chaos.

Behind Agnes, a man cleared his throat and she turned. He wore a white chef's jacket and toque over black-and-white-checked pants.

"Chef Jean," he announced in a raspy deep voice. He was of average height, with broad shoulders and thick arms that suggested years of pounding, chopping, stirring, and kneading.

Agnes offered her hand and introduced herself.

"I heard you were here from the police and it worries me, this discussion of the death of Monsieur Chavanon. Last week they did not trust my word. I can assure you that I take the preparation of the food and the storage of ingredients most seriously. We have two students with allergies, and peanut products are never served here."

No one else had mentioned students or guests with the same allergy. Agnes motioned for the chef to join her at a dining table.

"To blame me, my food, is ridiculous when there is dust all around us." The chef gestured across the room. "If light falls at the correct angle, we see that the air is full of particles, floating by in clean air. When the aroma from a kitchen travels, that is particles in the air. If you can smell it, then it is present physically. Monsieur Chavanon had such a severe reaction that it might have taken only the tiniest particle. A particle traveling with him or with one of the other guests. Perhaps he picked up something on his jacket and brought it to the Institute. I do not know. I do know that it did not come from my kitchen."

"Were the students with allergies at the reception?"

The chef calmed himself and reflected. "Both Koulsy and Rudolph were here. They are at an age to never miss a meal, and we serve quite good food at the receptions."

"Even with Monsieur Chavanon's sensitivity, the allergens were either ingested or placed directly on a mucous membrane. The eyes, nose, mouth." Agnes paused to let the chef digest this information. Death was not caused by a tiny invisible particle brought in on Chavanon's jacket. "Were you in the room?"

"*Non*. Normally I would circulate, but my fool of an assistant dropped a tray of canapés and we were in a rush to replace them."

Agnes glanced around, noting air ducts near the ceiling. Someone would have remarked on peanut dust piped into the air, and the two students would have also fallen ill.

The chef noticed her attention. "Those are exhaust for the kitchen and dining room. We push the air outside to keep the smell of food out of the rest of the building. It is a modern system, put in when they renovated the kitchen a year ago. The chalet is still heated with radiators."

Upon arriving, Agnes had noticed that a few upstairs windows were open despite the chill. It was the same at her house. To cool a particular room one opened a window; it was the only way to quickly balance the heat during the winter. She wondered where else Monsieur Chavanon had traveled in the building. Had he come into contact with forbidden food in a student's room?

"You've been very helpful, Chef. I may have more questions later."

He asked a passing student to escort her up the stairs to the headmaster's office. She recognized the boy. He had walked by the garden earlier. It was her first close look at the school uniforms, and they were as old-fashioned as they had appeared in the lobby photographs. Costumes more than uniforms, the white-collared shirts were fastened at the neck with a piece of black fabric somewhere between a string tie and a scarf. The trousers were wool, pleated at the front, and were better suited to a Dickensian play than they were to actual play. The jackets were fitted with two small pockets at the front and a narrow collar. The ensemble was certainly more formal than anything her own sons would have tolerated.

"Tommy. Tommy Scaglia." The boy extended his hand. He looked about thirteen and had short dark hair and bright black eyes. His American accent cut through the French vowels like a chain saw. "Good to see you here. 'Bout time."

"Why do you say that?" Agnes asked.

He led her toward an enclosed stair. "Heard Madame Fontenay say the police were here. Good thing. My dad will be relieved. There's funny stuff going on." Tommy slowed to match her pace.

"Do you mean Monsieur Chavanon's death?"

"No, they shoved us out of there pretty quick. He was looking better, and suddenly people were screaming and he went all pale and sweaty, clutching his throat. I heard that he bent over backwards until his head almost touched his heels, but I missed it." Tommy scrunched his eyes as if remembering. "I thought Leo would throw up. We had to go to our rooms and they wouldn't let us out until the ambulance took him away. Then we had dinner in the lounge upstairs. Afraid we'd be traumatized if we went back in the dining room too soon, I guess. Don't know what Leo thought. I didn't see him afterwards and his dad's friend drove him home."

They reached the landing and turned onto the main floor. Tommy stopped. "That's not what worries me. There's a lot of strange stuff happening here. Threats, weird lights at night. I think someone should take it seriously."

"Do the Fontenays know about this?" Agnes glanced down the hall. Monsieur Fontenay was walking in their direction.

"Oh yeah, they know. But they don't care. It's getting scary and I think my parents may take me home."

Twelve

Tommy Scaglia ducked down the stairs as the headmaster approached.

"Have you spoken with everyone you needed to, Inspector?" Bernard Fontenay said, leading Agnes toward his office.

"I've made a start. One of the students—"

Just ahead a door flung open, and Helene Fontenay emerged. A young boy and older woman were framed behind her. The headmaster darted past Agnes and placed a hand on the woman's shoulders before briefly hugging her.

"*Madame Chavanon, bienvenue, mes hommages,*" Fontenay said. "I'm sorry I didn't see you yesterday. I would have been here to greet you if I'd known." He ruffled the boy's hair. "Leo has settled in well."

Leo Chavanon was slight, and his pale blue eyes and white-blond hair made him appear fragile. He swayed toward his mother to give her a hug, then stiffened as if remembering he was at school and should act grown-up. Marie Chavanon knelt and pulled him to her, whispering something in his ear. Behind her, Narendra Patel emerged from the office carrying a small suitcase. He took the boy's hand and led him toward the stairs to the dormitory floors. Patel looked tired, but Madame Chavanon was clearly exhausted.

Nearby, Madame Jomini placed a bouquet of flowers on the reception desk, smiling at the card on the counter. Agnes moved away; the scent of lilies was overpowering.

"Narendra was right. Leo needs to be here, among his friends," Agnes overheard Marie Chavanon say. "I'm no company for him right now. I have too many preoccupations. But I needed to see him again, and we brought things from home he forgot yesterday." She started to cry quietly and the Fontenays soothed her.

Patel watched the stairs long after Leo disappeared from view. He carried himself stiffly, reminding Agnes of the men at her husband's funeral and the reception afterward, and every time she saw them over the next weeks. It took a long time for people to know how to react after a sudden death. They wanted to help, then regretted being around the grief stricken. She approached Patel.

"You are the friend of Mademoiselle Christine?" he said before she could speak. "I recognize you from the café yesterday. She and Marie are much affected." He tapped his temple. "The brain can only handle so much of the grievings. It was the most terrible of accidents." He laid a hand on his chest. "I am hoping you are not encouraging her. What she said about Guy dying was rubbish."

"You were here the day Monsieur Chavanon died," said Agnes. "Would you share your impression of what happened?"

Patel's facial expression didn't change, but Agnes saw the

shock beneath the surface; the slight tightening of the muscles under his skin. This was a decided difference from financial crimes. People who lost money were often angry. Belligerent even, with occasional white-hot rage or resigned disbelief. This was a different kind of emotion. More restrained yet more deeply felt.

"What do you remember?" she repeated.

Patel flushed and drew nearer until they were nose to nose. "Why all these questions? The police that day were satisfied and you can't bring Guy back. Think of the trauma to Marie. To Leo. What is your purpose?"

Agnes stepped back, faintly alarmed by his quiet fury. "The coroner's report leaves room for questions. I'd think a close friend would want answers."

Patel took a few deep rapid breaths. He seemed to collect himself. "What I remember from that day is that my friend is gone. I nearly died from my shock. This, what you do"—he pressed his fingertips together, then released them quickly in an outward motion—"is ripping the heart out again. It is unhealthy for the family. He is gone and our friendship is gone forever. Every word you say reopens the wound."

"I lost someone recently. I understand how hard it is."

"It was his fault, no one else's," Patel added in a calmer tone. "His actions. His reactions, I should say. It is an unfillable gap in our lives."

"The police have an obligation to ask questions."

Bernard Fontenay interrupted, "Inspector, you haven't met Madame Chavanon."

Marie Chavanon wiped her tears away, her back straight with effort. Agnes remembered that brief condolences were preferable to falsely effusive ones. The combination of the words "investigation of his death" and "break-in at the workshop" drew an immediate reaction from Marie.

"You should have called me."

Agnes explained that she had, repeatedly.

"I don't look at my phone when I'm with my son. How inappropriate. He deserves my full attention."

"We can talk here or—"

"I have to leave immediately. I can't believe the police are searching my home and I'm not there."

"They're not searching, they're documenting. And only in the workshop. Your stepdaughter gave permission."

Marie Chavanon shot Agnes a dour look. "I must tell Leo that I'm leaving."

Motioning for Patel to join her, she stalked off without a backward glance, Bernard Fontenay in her wake.

In the silence that followed, Agnes turned to the headmistress. "I'm surprised Antoine Mercier sent flowers to Leo at the school." She gestured to the florist's card on the counter.

"They're not only for Leo," said Helene. "They're for all of us. Monsieur Mercier realizes how difficult it is for everyone here."

"I've never heard of sending flowers to"—Agnes hesitated—"the place someone died."

"Monsieur Mercier knows us well. He was here only last week." Helene shook her head sadly. "It was the day before Monsieur Chavanon died."

"Does he have a child here?"

"No, he came to talk to the students, we have people in from time to time. Antoine spoke to one of the upper-form classes."

Agnes found it interesting that Mercier hadn't mentioned his connection to the school. Wasn't it natural to mention that you had only the day before been at the place a man died? Mercier had been anxious to appear sympathetic; now it seemed he had taken trouble to distance himself.

"When we spoke earlier, you didn't mention the other problems you're having," Agnes said.

Helene drew her lips into a tight line and walked into the office. "We deal with our concerns internally. Attention grabbing is what this is."

She made her way to a chair and Agnes sat opposite her. Waiting for Helene to continue, Agnes studied the part of the room visible over the headmistress's shoulder. The wall was dense with paintings and photographs. Several were too small to make out any detail at this distance, but the larger ones were darkened with age and looked as if they had been hanging on the wall since the chalet was constructed.

Madame Fontenay's crutch scraped the wood floor as she shifted. "He only came to me this morning. Did he tell you that?"

Agnes murmured inaudibly and pretended to consult her notebook. Tommy Scaglia was going to be in trouble later.

"His father is in government overseas and is under some pressure. Death threats," Helene added.

Agnes sat up straighter. Immediately, she felt a twinge of guilt. A sad state of affairs to find death threats exciting. "Threats to the boy?"

"No, Koulsy thinks he's at risk of kidnapping. That is who you are talking about?"

Not Tommy after all, Agnes realized, but this was what he meant by threats. She nodded as if agreeing.

Madame Fontenay continued, "It's absurd, of course, but

there you have it. Once they get an idea in their minds, they won't . . . let . . . go." She twisted the edge of her sweater sleeve into a knot.

"Koulsy also has an allergy to peanuts?" Agnes said, concerned by the coincidence.

"Yes, but that had nothing to do with . . . we take great care to protect—" Helene Fontenay stopped as if realizing that great care hadn't saved Guy Chavanon. "This kidnapping idea is fanciful. I don't know why he said something to the police without consulting us. I don't think anything that supports their fantasies is helpful, although my husband will likely disagree. Just as he disagreed with me about allowing you to interfere. He doesn't understand how important *mental* discipline is. It is mental discipline that stands behind the success of everything: academic success and physical success. It is our motto: *Mens sana in corpore sano*. You needn't be involved. Koulsy is a boy looking for attention, and Monsieur Chavanon died as the result of an accident."

"They shared the same allergy." When Madame Fontenay didn't respond, Agnes added, "Can you positively rule out the threat of kidnapping?"

The headmistress shifted uncomfortably. "His family connection makes it impossible to completely ignore. On the other hand, he is of the age to suddenly crave attention. I've checked with his teachers and he's doing well in the classroom. Sometimes the boys create tales when they are behind in their schoolwork. A diversion of sorts. Tommy Scaglia was a master of this until he settled in."

That, Agnes could well believe. She'd heard her share of

tales of woe when really it was homework that had been left undone. "What's the boy's full name?" she asked, pen on paper of her notebook.

"Koulsy Haroun."

Agnes didn't need to ask how to spell it. The elder Haroun had recently been in the international news and she recognized his name. It was a miracle he hadn't been assassinated. In fact, he and his cronies should be assassinated for the damage they'd brought to their country, part of a widespread pattern of violence across Africa. She tapped her pen against her notebook to focus her attention. Was it possible Koulsy Haroun had been the target when Guy Chavanon died? Revenge? A warning to the father?

She heard Marie Chavanon's voice in the corridor. "Tell the inspector that Monsieur Patel will drive me home. Madame Lüthi can follow or not, it's as she likes."

Agnes sighed. Life almost never let one do as one liked.

Thirteen

Marie Chavanon's anger burrowed into Agnes's back with the bite of a sharp stick. Their relationship had disintegrated.

"You don't need to stay and watch," Agnes said from the steps of the porch. Marie stood on the threshold of her husband's workshop, darting glances inside, following every move made by the police officers documenting the interior. "They're professionals; they know what to do."

She'd not had a real conversation with Marie despite managing to arrive at the Chavanon property ahead of her. The woman had run from the car, leaving a grim Patel in the driver's seat, and headed straight for the workshop, where the police were still working, apparently intent on doing the thorough job they'd promised. Now Marie stood silently in the open doorway, her slight frame rigid. Anger rolled off her.

"It's ruined. They've ruined it. Picking through everything."

"Someone was here before us," said Agnes. "You saw the

broken window and the door wasn't closed." She heard a spray of gravel. Patel leaving.

"How do you know someone did this?" Marie demanded. "Perhaps Guy left it this way?"

"The note he left indicates—"

Marie turned on Agnes, fury in every crease of her face. "You believe everything you read, Inspector? I don't understand why you can't lock it up and leave everything alone. I wanted time before I went through Guy's things. There is nothing here to steal. Nothing of real value. Only memories."

Agnes didn't repeat the possible connection between the break-in and Guy Chavanon's death. Marie Chavanon didn't need words. She needed time and distance. Something she wouldn't get right now.

"They'll lock the workshop tonight after they finish," Agnes said. "We've already replaced the windowpane to keep rain and animals out. Tomorrow they'll bring photographs for you to look through. You may notice something you didn't today."

"I don't need to see them. I won't look at them."

"We want to be sure that nothing is missing. Or you may notice something out of the ordinary. Both Christine and Monsieur Dupré mentioned that your husband was on the verge of an important invention, for want of a better term. What can you tell me about that?"

"Invention? Guy? You can see for yourself. He couldn't focus on one idea long enough to invent anything." Marie glanced inside the cottage. "Paper and more paper. All ideas. All nothing." She spoke so forcefully one of the officers glanced up.

"Monsieur Dupré and Christine didn't remember the workshop being so . . . full. Monsieur Dupré remembers it as more organized. Would you agree?"

"What should I say, Inspector? Guy was chasing dreams that would never be realized, descending into a spiral of delusion." After a final glance inside she shoved past Agnes and ran across the lawn. She reached the steps leading to a side patio of the house and steadied herself on the thick iron railing.

Agnes caught up with her. Clouds covered the sky and an early dusk was falling. Lights were on in the house. Time was passing too quickly.

"Guy died as a result of his allergies," Marie spat, not turning to look at Agnes. "He wasn't well, but that has nothing to do with his death. Your inquiry into what he had become in his last months—this past year—will make us the topic of speculation. My son, his son, deserves more than that. Please think of Leo. Memories are all he has left."

Without a backward glance, Marie entered the house, leaving Agnes alone on the lawn.

Marie Chavanon poured herself a glass of wine and drank it down swiftly. Only then did she take her coat off. Stephan Dupré closed the shades on the front windows, knowing they were illuminated by the interior light and visible across the neighborhood.

"Inspector Lüthi wasn't a stranger," he said. "Christine called her."

Marie started, as if she hadn't seen him. She lifted the bottle to pour herself another glass. Instead she poured one for Dupré.

Stephan took the glass like the peace offering it was. "I happened upon them. I walked over looking for you. I thought you might have changed your mind and left the show in the more than capable hands of Gisele. I wanted to talk about what you said yesterday."

"You should forget what I said, forget everything I've said since . . ."

"Since you told me you love me? Do I erase everything these last months?"

She crossed the dining room, turning the lights off as she left. A long salon ran the length of the back of the house. The old-fashioned room, pleasing to sit in during the day, was lined with doors opening to the veranda. Marie clicked a lock open and stepped outside. A few minutes ago she had been cold, now the house was claustrophobic. She gripped the metal railing of the veranda, thankful it faced away from the other houses in the neighborhood. It was enough that Christine was across the lawn, watching the main house, fuming. Righteous anger, Marie thought, at how her father's inadequacies were revealed. His pathetic papers pawed over and photographed, exposing him as the failure Marie had known he was. He was the one who'd destroyed the family honor, not her. And not Christine. He couldn't live up to the past.

"I didn't go to Baselworld," she said. "I had to see Leo."

Dupré touched her shoulder. "I shouldn't have snapped. But this is what we wanted. You wanted to be free of Guy."

Marie moaned softly.

"Don't let guilt stand in the way of our happiness. Yours, mine, and Leo's."

"What of Christine's happiness?"

"You've said it before. She has her own guilt. She knew Guy was troubled and was too busy to care until he was dead and it was too late. It's only been a week. She'll settle down—"

"Settle down? You think that's what we need to do? The women need to settle? He's dead, Stephan. He's not coming back." Marie had wanted to leave the workshop abandoned until the contents decayed to dust.

"I didn't mean it to sound that way."

"What way then?"

"I understand that he's dead. Guy was my first playmate, my oldest friend, and I'll miss him." Dupré raised a hand. "Wait. You know that I liked him."

"You have a nice way of showing it."

"That's not fair. What happened between you and me was unexpected."

"Happened. Past tense."

"I meant the start. We're not past tense. And Guy had turned in upon himself. He was always intense, and these last years, mainly this last year, he was circling around himself, cutting us out. You know that's true."

"He left a note saying he was afraid."

Dupré gripped the back of a wrought iron chair, his knuckles white with strain. "Maybe he was crazy and none of it was true."

"He was a genius."

"Likely." Dupré sighed. "I always thought so. Crazy ideas, a million ideas."

"You told Inspector Lüthi he was on the verge of a great invention. Why would you say that, Stephan? Why create this trouble for me?"

"It was before we saw the workshop. It was casual conversation."

"Don't lie. You thought he created something and I didn't tell you. That I was on the verge of a great fortune."

Marie flipped a switch. The outside lights blinked on, and soft light cascaded up the white façade of the house, illuminating the terrace. "He had good ideas." She spoke softly.

"Yes, he did."

"But it wasn't enough."

They were both silent.

"Was it?" Dupré asked.

She reached for his hand. "I owe him respect, at least. I won't talk about the end. His death."

"You're going to have to. Someone broke in. Christine was already upset, stirring up this notion of Guy being killed, and now the inspector thinks she has proof. After this evening, she is probably convinced Guy was murdered, and the inside of his studio is God knows what. Although I can't imagine anything was stolen. It was all papers. It was nonsense." Dupré hesitated. "At least I think it was."

In the distance the porch light of the far cottage clicked off, plunging that section of lawn into shadow. Every light in the workshop still blazed, like silent alarms.

Marie released Stephan's hand and crossed her arms in front of her chest. The cold catching up to her. "I don't think Leo should go inside. Not like it is. I wanted him to go in. I'd told him that we would sit in the workshop and light a candle for his father. But we can't now. He'll know it's not right. It will trouble him. Neither of us have been in there for . . ." She paused as if counting backward. "Since last summer."

"I should leave." Dupré started toward the edge of the terrace. When he stepped onto the grass, he stopped. "She's not going to leave it alone. Christine, I mean. Guy was always so careful. This afternoon, Christine called him paranoid and I can't disagree. Especially now. He was certainly obsessive. These last years he was careful, not like when we were kids. I couldn't believe that he'd died that way."

"It was an accident."

Dupré didn't respond.

"Are you accusing me of something?" she said.

"No."

"But now you think Guy was a genius and he was killed for his idea?" Marie gave a wild laugh. "Is this how you hope to bring him back? By building up a hollow legacy? Guy is dead. There is nothing to be done and I have to think about the future. I have to find a way to keep the company going for Leo. Fiction and dreams won't help. I learned that long ago from my husband."

Dupré returned to put his arms around her. "Then talk to Christine. She's never been able to let anything go. After today she thinks he had a big idea and it was stolen. I could see it in her eyes."

Marie relaxed against Dupré. "I've forgotten how hard this is for her. I'll talk to her tomorrow and help her understand."

Fourteen

Agnes nosed her car down the long steep lane. The last—and only—time she'd been at Château Vallotton was to investigate a murder. Her reception, everything about the circumstances that day, were unique, so she didn't know what to expect this evening.

The gravel circle at the base of the cliff was well-groomed, and she pulled to the point nearest the massive walls of the old fortress. She parked her car and looked up through the windshield. The weather had cleared, and by craning her neck she could see all the way up to the covered parapet. In the darkness between château and cliff, the bright lights illuminating the lakeside façades created a sharp edge on both sides, accenting the darkness around her. The façade facing the cliff was bleak. The near wall was punctuated with slit windows originally intended for arrows. Light shone through here and there, but it wasn't welcoming. She eyed the entrance. The gaping hole was large enough to drive a car through or, she realized, a horde of men-at-arms on horses.

Delaying a few more minutes, she listened to the voice mail she'd received while driving. It was Bardy. She replayed it twice, alert to all nuances of his voice, before slipping her phone into her jacket pocket, where she would feel it buzz in an emergency. It was dark and her boys were certainly off the ski slopes and at the cabin with their grandfather. Coats and gloves would be draped over warm radiators, with a fire blazing on the living-room hearth and fondue melting in a pot on the stove. There would be good-natured arguments over what size to cut the bread for dipping, and whether potatoes were better. She considered calling to say hello; a glance at the car clock told her she was already late. The cocktail hour was mercifully over; however, if she delayed any longer, she would be inexcusably late for dinner.

Stepping out of the car, she saw movement in the shadows ahead. Julien Vallotton was standing in the passageway that cut through the fortress to the central courtyard. He waved and she sighed. There was no longer any way to avoid this evening.

She passed under the château's outer wall, unable to resist glancing overhead. The threat of an iron portcullis dropping every time you entered or left your home seemed some sort of metaphor the family had decided to accept. Beyond it, Vallotton was backlit. Fruit trees and clipped shrubs in the courtyard cast long shadows around him, like fingers. He wished her a good evening, and she shrugged off her gloves and coat. He took them without comment, even though they were still outdoors and the night was crisp.

"I apologize, I'm late."

Vallotton was dressed in a smoking jacket, which, in her household, wouldn't have been categorized as informal. She was wearing the same wool jacket and skirt she'd worn all day. It was one of her favorites, with a thread of blue running among the gray. The blouse was new, but it wasn't at all dressy.

The door to the château opened and a uniformed maid stepped out. She took Agnes's coat from Vallotton, then stepped back inside, closing the door. Agnes didn't recognize the girl from her previous visit.

"I came straight from work," she said, cold now and wishing she'd kept her coat on, feeling foolish.

"You look perfect. We're glad you could come on such short notice."

"No, Monsieur Vallotton, thank you for inviting me."

"I've told you before. It's Julien. I think we could dispense with formality, don't you?" He stepped near and lightly gripped her by both shoulders, kissing her three times on alternating cheeks. The local habit was so ingrained that Agnes returned the gesture without thinking. He smelled like leather and old books. She felt her face flush and blamed it on the cold.

He stepped away and pushed the heavy door open, ushering her inside. The entrance hall was familiar, and she glanced up at the enormous iron chandelier, slightly surprised the candles were lit. Then she noted that there only a few electric lights. The hall was nearly as gloomy as it had been the last time she was here, when power was out across the entire region. The adjacent corridor was also deeply shadowed. Two steps inside the thick walls felt like a journey of two hundred years. She followed Vallotton and amended that to a thousand years.

She expected Vallotton to turn toward the dining room, where she had eaten with the family during the investigation into the murder on their property, but he headed in the opposite direction. She followed, heels clattering on the flagstones. She had a faint memory of this corridor, but then she'd walked every meter of the château at some point in the inquiry. Vallotton reached a final turn and she recognized the carved double doors leading to the banquet hall. She had been here only once on her previous visit. An auspicious once.

"No bad memories here, I think?"

"As long as the power doesn't go out again," she joked. Once inside, she nearly laughed: the banquet hall was lit entirely by candles. Silver candelabras dotted the center of a dining table, and fat candles on shoulder-high stands lined the perimeter of the room. There were six ancient but well-oiled suits of armor and a table that could easily seat forty. Tonight, the table was set for nine, and the place settings were clumped together at one end.

This was a life so far from hers that it felt like stepping into a lavish stage set.

"Inspector Lüthi," said Julien's aunt, moving from the shadows. The elderly woman was wearing a floor-length gown of silvery-blue pleated silk. Around her neck was an elaborate, old-fashioned diamond necklace that nearly covered her chest in a web of stones. Some of the diamonds were as large as a fingernail.

"*Madame la marquise*. It was kind of you to include me." Agnes hesitated over the greeting, thinking a curtsy wouldn't be out of line. The woman's necklace evoked images of long-dead czarinas and genuflecting aristocrats. Before Agnes could say more, there were voices and the sound of running feet.

"Our true hostess for the evening," said the marquise.

A small girl ran in followed by an enormous Great Dane.

"Mimi," said Agnes, delighted to see the child. Suddenly the marquise's necklace and elaborate gown made sense. The girl was wearing a perfectly charming and appropriate dress. But on her head was a tiara. And not a child-size one. A ruby-and-diamond crown fit for a princess. It flashed in the candlelight to full effect. Mimi put her hand to her head and grinned. A series of jeweled bracelets flashed from her wrists. The dog sat quietly beside her, wearing a diamond choker. Agnes remembered Winston and thought he appreciated the dose of glamour. Either that, or he had more important issues on his mind and didn't care. His head reached above Agnes's waist and she patted it, hoping he remembered her, for she certainly remembered what he'd done for them.

Mimi launched into a lengthy and detailed explanation of everything that had happened in the weeks since she'd seen Agnes. Before she finished, five adults entered. The women were dressed in cocktail attire, and the men wore suits or smoking jackets. The jewelry transformed an ordinary dinner into something fantastical.

Julien Vallotton ran through the names of the guests for Agnes, skipping her work title. She shook hands and offered greetings. One of the women stroked a heavy triple strand of pearls and diamonds that hung nearly to her waist and said, "It's too bad you weren't here earlier when the jewels were being handed out. I felt like I was in Aladdin's cave." She glanced around. "The girl is sweet and is impossible to refuse. I should have claimed a tiara as well. Would have been a treat."

One of the men touched a large sapphire broach affixed to his lapel. "Meant for a woman but I didn't want to disappoint."

The group moved to the table, and Vallotton fitted his hand beneath Agnes's elbow, guiding her to the chair beside his. "Mimi normally takes her dinner earlier. Your visit is a special occasion for her, and somehow the whole affair turned into her version of what a grown-up evening should be." He looked fondly down the table at the little girl. She was chattering amiably with the adults to her left and right. "She's doing remarkably well after what happened. We indulge her. There's no harm in it."

Agnes enjoyed herself more than she would have thought possible. The other diners were houseguests of the Vallottons, all from London, and all clamoring for Julien Vallotton to return to that city as quickly as possible. She liked that they didn't know about her work or her past or anything at all about her. She was a friend of the family's to them. Not a recently widowed police inspector. They were well dressed, wealthy, she supposed, and utterly charming.

Dinner was served at a leisurely pace by a nearly invisible staff. Knowing Sybille would insist on details, Agnes paid close attention to the menu: *confit de foie gras de canard* and smoked salmon press with toasted sesame, pan-fried scallops with pumpkin ravioli and a tartuffon emulsion, and, following a lemon sorbet, the final course of pigeon with mushroom and bitter shoots. She slipped the place card into her handbag as a memento.

The meal ended late, with Mimi sound asleep in her chair, head tipped awkwardly to the side, tiara askew. The girl's nanny came in to retrieve her as the plates of chocolate meringue tart were being cleared.

Soon after, the marquise rose. "Madame Lüthi, would you do me the favor of accompanying me to my sitting room?"

"We'll be in the blue salon," said Vallotton.

Agnes walked beside the marquise, close at first, in case the woman needed help, then at a more comfortable distance, realizing that the escort was for conversation and not assistance.

The marquise asked a polite question about Agnes's recovery, then dismissed the subject. "You have returned to your calling. Julien mentioned that you are investigating Guy Chavanon's death. An irregular death, I take it?"

"Possibly." Bardy's phone message replayed in her head: *Monsieur Mercier has called to . . . um . . .* There had been a long pause and she'd held her breath, hoping she hadn't made a series of decisions that would end her time with Bardy's team. *To complain about your inquiries.* The second pause had been so long she had known it was bad news. Then Bardy had cleared his throat. *Looks like you're back at work.*

Looking at the marquise, Agnes amended her answer: "Likely an unnatural death."

"Is one of the family responsible? Isn't that who you usually suspect?"

"There is a chance Chavanon wasn't the intended victim. Two students at the school where he died had the same allergy. One of them has awkward family connections."

"Aren't most family connections awkward? It's merely a matter of degrees."

"Most people hesitate to implicate the family."

"As if pretending is kinder," said the marquise. "The dilemma of the ages. A solution to one problem is the beginning of another."

They reached a broad stair, and the marquise gathered her long skirt in one hand. "You have an interesting profession, Inspector, examining the darkest emotions of humanity. Death is the ultimate problem. The ultimate test of who we are. When I was a girl, I wanted to be an archaeologist, which is a form of fascination with death. Perhaps if I was young today, I would want to follow in your footsteps. Association with death makes one feel alive."

Electric lights beckoned from the top of the stairs. Agnes remembered the first time she had climbed these stairs to meet the marquise. She had been nervous. Justifiably nervous, she thought.

"I have lived a full life and seen many things," said the marquise. "There has been great joy and infinite despair. We remember the highs and lows, don't we? During your career, you will likely come across all of the seven deadly sins. A range beyond what I have witnessed."

"Certainly the full spectrum of life."

With each step, the marquise's necklace reflected constellations of light across the stairs and walls. "Targets of greed and envy." The marquise touched her jewels. "Pride, greed, lust, envy, gluttony, sloth. I have forgotten the seventh sin."

"Wrath, I believe," said Agnes.

They reached the top of the stairs and turned into the marquise's sitting room. Fires blazed on both hearths and several lamps were illuminated. The marquise settled on a chair in the center of the room and indicated that Agnes should join her on its twin. Agnes remembered these chairs. The frames were solid silver and they glinted in the warm low light.

"Which of the deadly sins do you think will be at the root of Monsieur Chavanon's death?" the marquise asked.

"It's too early to say. Gluttony and sloth seem unlikely, though."

A servant entered with a tray of liqueurs. The marquise took a small sherry and Agnes joined her. They both took a sip. Agnes felt sinfully civilized. She anticipated Sybille's questions about the evening, knowing the answers would live up to expectation.

"If gluttony and sloth are unlikely, you are left with lust, pride, greed, envy, and wrath." The marquise laced the fingers of one hand through the heavy cords of her necklace. "Those may be the deadly sins, but I think there are other reasons to kill."

"I'm sure there are."

"Honor should be on your list, Inspector. It's worth killing for."

"Can't honor be linked to pride?"

"You think pride and honor are intertwined?" The marquise closed her eyes briefly, and Agnes remembered how the woman's husband had died. The Marquis de Tornay was a French war hero. He had died for honor. Agnes watched the muscles of the marquise's face shift and wondered, or was it pride that killed him?

"Pride is a strong emotion," Agnes said. "But I agree with you that pride and honor are not the same." She took another sip of sherry. "I think honor isn't on the list because it's not a sin, even if it moves people to kill."

"A police inspector who doesn't believe killing is a sin?"

"I don't believe self-defense is a sin, so, no, not always."

The darkness of the room lent an exceptional quality to the atmosphere. It was the atmosphere of shared confidences and of the ability to think deeply without the influence of modern impatience. Agnes felt her mind wander through the possibilities: poison in food or drink, through contact, by injection.

Poison administered to the wrong person. Not an accident, though.

"Inspector, has your pride recovered?"

"My pride? I don't know what you mean."

"It was your burden the last time you were here. I feel you are lighter now."

"I was grieving. My husband had died only a few months before. I suppose I am lighter now that more time has passed."

"What was at the root of your grief?"

Agnes sat her glass down too hard, sloshing the liquid. "How my sons and I missed George."

The marquise fingered her necklace, and Agnes had the odd sense that the woman drew some special power or awareness from her jewels.

"Emotions are complicated when someone dies suddenly," said the marquise. "All these decades later, anger is what I remember most in the days following my husband's death. Anger at what I had been forced to do. Anger at him for endangering us all. Anger at a world at war. When I fired that shot, I told myself it was to protect others, myself included. Later, I realized I also fired in anger. Passionate anger."

Tears stung Agnes's eyes. She hadn't longed for George during those days at Château Vallotton. Her grief was not centered on missing him. She was angry at him. She was angry at the lies she still told on his behalf. The lies she maintained to protect his parents. And why? Was it really to protect her sons until they were old enough to understand their father's decision? Or was it pride? Her own pride, and not his.

The marquise took a sip of sherry and set her empty glass on a side table. "I was a very young woman when my husband died—much younger than you are now—and I wore my pride like a cloak." She looked at Agnes pointedly. "It hardened until I could barely remove it."

"Your husband was a hero, and he died during a war. My situation is entirely different. My husband was depressed. It is too common a problem, and he took his own life."

The marquise nodded. "Pride."

Agnes wasn't certain if the marquise was referring to her or to George.

Her phone buzzed through the pocket of her suit coat. She slipped her hand in to silence it, but the marquise waved her off. "You are responsible for your children; please check your phone. I live enough in the modern world to accept this."

Agnes stood and pulled the phone out before the call disconnected. The number wasn't one of her sons'. It was Inspector Boschung from the Rossemaison *gendarmerie.*

"We've got a bloody shed here," he announced without preamble, adding, as if she'd already objected, "Do you want to come or not?"

"To Rossemaison?"

Julien Vallotton entered the room, mobile phone in hand.

"The Institute," Boschung continued impatiently. "Whole inside's coated in blood. Are you coming or not?"

"Yes, I'll be there shortly. Thank you for calling me."

"Don't thank me. Thank him."

She looked at Vallotton, who nodded. Clearly the *him.*

Fifteen

The only sound as they crossed the lawn was the slight brush of leather soles on grass. The moon was barely visible through the clouds, and only the occasional flash of light indicated their destination. Agnes relied on the light from Julien Vallotton's mobile phone to find her footing. Vallotton was intent upon his task and she stifled a smile, thankful she'd not dressed for dinner. He managed to look at ease despite his evening clothes. She would have felt ridiculous.

"It's not my fault Boschung called me first," Vallotton said, picking up the conversation where they'd left off.

Agnes nearly laughed at the irritation in his voice. They'd already had this near argument during the drive from the château to the Institute. Vallotton had insisted on driving, saying that she'd had three glasses of champagne to his one, and she'd not had a counterpoint to that argument. Plus, she hadn't wanted to admit that her leg could only take so much walking and driving two days in a row. Better to rest while he drove, and his car was faster and more comfortable.

She stumbled. They had reached the end of the smooth lawn behind the Institute; broken ground indicated the start of the surrounding fields.

Vallotton gestured with his light. "The shed is behind that hedge."

Agnes located a heavy stone embedded in the ground and scraped the worst of the mud from her shoes. She heard male voices.

"Why are you on the board of directors here?" she asked, delaying. Pain snapped up and down her thigh like the crackle of lightning. She expected it to pass as quickly. "Didn't you go to school at Le Rosey in Rolle?"

"My family owns the land that the Institute sits on—"

She resisted saying, *Of course.*

"—and my great-grandfather set the place up for his old tutor. A member of the family always sits on the board of directors."

Agnes tightened the belt of her coat, motioning him forward. There was a gap between two sections of hedge, and Vallotton trained his light on the opening. She looked over her shoulder toward the chalet. A few lights were on and it looked like a constellation in a dark universe.

Bloody shed, Boschung had said on the telephone. She had shivered with excitement. After all, she was part of a Violent Crimes team, and not just any team, but Bardy's team! Her shoe went sideways into a hole and she sighed. Dinner at Château Vallotton had been a perfect evening; it should have ended there.

"First you bring me to look into Chavanon's death, and now

this," she said in a low voice. "You won't be welcome at the school much longer."

"The properties on both sides of the Institute belong to us. We lease them out for pasture, and I like to know what's happening if there's trouble. Villages love gossip and I don't like things to fester."

Agnes almost snapped that it wasn't up to him to decide what festered or didn't fester, but she stopped herself. It might be up to him. If the Vallottons owned the land that the Institute sat on, as well as farms to both sides, they might also own a good part of the neighboring village. She refused to ask him if they did, wondering if there was a part of Switzerland that Julien Vallotton didn't call his own.

"I talked to Bardy while you were getting the car," she said. "He thinks I'm a magnet for trouble." They'd agreed that she would tread carefully with Boschung. Bardy liked to stay on good terms with their law enforcement colleagues. Civilians—such as Mercier—Bardy didn't care as much about.

She ducked through the gap.

Despite the bright handheld lights and the small cluster of men surrounding it, the shed was as unpretentious as it sounded. Constructed from heavy timber, it was three meters by five, windowless, and topped with a traditional slate roof. An older man in a police jacket, who she presumed was Jacques Boschung, stood alongside Bernard Fontenay and another man she didn't recognize. Two men in police jackets with reflective striping were taking photographs of the interior of the shed. The dark outline of a large structure marked the far side of the field. In the distance were scattered lights.

"Bad business," said Boschung, after introducing himself.

"We're a quiet place and now this." He was of medium height, stocky, and wore his hair cut short in a military style. His eyes were crinkled at the edges from years of squinting into the sun. He was older than he sounded on the telephone, and Agnes judged his age at nearly sixty.

She walked to the open door, and the local officers stepped aside. The faint, unmistakable metallic odor of blood wafted out. She directed her phone light around the interior. The source of the smell was evident. Near-black, rust-colored liquid had pooled on a large block of wood and formed sticky patches on the nearby ground. Five great sprays of dark reddish brown marked the far wall. They were violent. Repetitive and aggressive. She stepped back, slightly shaken, not sure what she had expected. She took a few steady breaths and focused. Boschung hadn't exaggerated. The interior of the shed was covered in blood.

"Hamel"—Boschung motioned to the man standing beside Fontenay—"found it and called me in right away."

"Monsieur Hamel is our handyman and groundskeeper," said Fontenay, good manners helping him overcome his distress. "This will bring the police. They'll be everywhere. They'll want to see everything."

Agnes resisted reminding him that she and Boschung were the police. The man was clearly unnerved. Even in the darkness he looked strained.

By contrast, Monsieur Hamel exuded quiet authority. He wore a traditional dark blue wool jacket with capped sleeves. The throat of his shirt was closed with a string tie clasped with edelweiss. The flower was also embroidered on the lapels of his jacket. He was the personification of a kinder, gentler era. Agnes shifted her phone light slightly so she could better see his face. His features were immobile.

"Tell me what happened," she said.

His account was succinct. He'd been on a routine inspection of the property and had only to take a whiff before he'd known something was wrong in the shed. Agnes nodded sympathetically.

It started to drizzle and she pulled a brimmed wool hat from her handbag and shoved it over her head. The rain brought out farm smells. Cow dung, earth, the scent of smoke. She glanced around, surprised no lights were on in neighboring farms. In Switzerland, there were always near neighbors. To the south, tiny pinpricks of light dotted the Prévôté Valley as far as the eye could see. To the north was complete darkness where the hills rose.

"You call this building a shed, but it must have a use," she said. The men had moved closer to the structure to shelter under the eaves. "Someone accesses it."

"Not really. Not anymore," said Hamel. "Used to be storage for the farm, but the equipment's all up at the big barn now."

"Is that the dark shape across the field? Why are there no lights?"

"That's the house and barn that belongs to the farm, but no one's living there. The family that works this field lives another farm over. It's theirs entirely and they lease the land here for the extra grazing."

Agnes took another look in all directions. One of the officers pulled Boschung aside for a question. Slightly up the hill she saw a light, or lights, bobbing. "What's that?" she asked Fontenay. "I don't remember a road in that direction. Does someone live in the forest?"

"No, it's likely someone crossing the edge of the field to visit a neighbor."

"Boschung may want to question them."

"They've not been out walking for an hour. I wouldn't worry them."

Agnes wondered if Fontenay was in shock. He looked stricken, yet sounded uninterested in answers. She gestured, nodding her head slightly toward the headmaster. Vallotton understood.

"We'll return to the Institute," he said, including Hamel in his suggestion. "Unless you need us?"

"Go ahead," Agnes said, adding in a low murmur as he passed, "Have Fontenay see the school nurse."

With the group thinned to only the professionals, Agnes stepped again into the open doorway. One of Boschung's men handed her a strong flashlight, and she moved the beam around the space. The ground inside the shed was hard-packed earth. The walls were rough timber, grayed with age. Bits of debris had accumulated in the corners, and a pile of old lumber leaned up against one wall. There was no sign of human habitation or use. Except for the blood, and that wasn't accidental.

She studied the center of the room, crouching for a better angle. A great deal of what she presumed was blood was on the stump and surrounding floor, and the pooled areas looked sticky. Recently, the nights had been cold, but not freezing. However, blood dried quickly, unless there was a lot of it. This wasn't several days old. Yesterday, maybe? In the right conditions, two days at the most. Fake currency she could spot at a glance, but she didn't have enough experience with blood to date it more precisely.

No footprints were visible on the hard-packed earth. She

moved the light back and forth to catch nuances of what she was seeing, stopping to study the back wall. The streaks of maroon-black fanned out as they neared the low ceiling. The part of her brain that had earlier screamed disaster was calmer now. More details were revealed with a stronger light.

"Are those feathers?" she asked the nearest officer.

"Yes, madame, I mean, Inspector. Probably part of a ritual."

Agnes wished people wouldn't watch so much television. "Have you ever seen anything like this before?"

"No, Inspector, we're a calm community. Haven't had an un-natural death in at least twenty years."

She didn't tell him that she had only come to Rossemaison because of a suspected homicide.

The spray on the back wall was smudged in places, and squinting, she wondered if a hand had been dragged across it. With no single palm or fingerprint visible, the size of the hand was difficult to judge. Something was off about the entire scene. It felt staged. Of course a ritual would look staged, that was the point of it.

She knelt and aimed the beam along the ground. "You still don't have an unnatural death here, unless you forgot to men-tion a body."

"All this blood, what else could it be?" the officer said.

"Anyone reported missing recently?"

"No, we're all accounted for in the village."

Boschung joined them. "We can give way, your team can take over."

"I think you've done an admirable job," said Agnes.

"Aren't you the specialists?" said Boschung.

"Rituals," the other officer repeated, nodding sagely.

"I think your officers will conduct a thorough investigation and go from there," said Agnes.

"We've never had doings like this, not in all my years," Boschung replied.

Agnes was about to express disbelief when there was a noise nearby. A familiar man's voice called out and a light shone through the hedge. She stifled a smile when a head poked through. She'd told André Petit that he didn't need to come, although she knew that he would. He was eager to return to work, and to prove himself. Blood in an abandoned village shed was too much for him to ignore. He was proud to be joining Violent Crimes. She motioned him forward.

"Officer Petit will lend you every assistance," she said to Boschung. Before he could argue, she spoke briefly to Petit, then left her beaming associate asking a dozen questions in rapid succession.

It was still drizzling when she neared the chalet. The groundskeeper was waiting on the back patio, and Agnes joined him under the shelter of the roof.

"Boschung grew up next farm over," Hamel said. "Always hated the farm life. It's good that he found a job in town. He'll take care of us."

"Did he attend school here?" Her coat dripped water in a puddle and she carefully removed her hat. Her short hair was damp and flattened against her head.

Hamel laughed. "Where would he get the money for this place?"

Point well taken, she thought. "You've been at the Institute a long time?"

"Started when I was a boy, did everything by hand back

then, the grass cutting, the trimming. There were more of us. All from the village. When the head gardener retired, I replaced him. Bit young for it, but I proved myself." Hamel smiled at the memory.

"You're in charge of everything on the property? Gardens and buildings?"

"Not Monsieur Navarro's plot of land. I stay clear of that poison nonsense. Otherwise, yes. That's why I do my route. Walk the perimeter, check all the buildings with an eye toward preventive maintenance."

Agnes glanced around. "But the shed isn't on school property? Isn't the school boundary the rectangle of structures? The lawns and terraces are all within that."

Hamel snorted. "I walk the larger perimeter since the Vallottons own farms on each side. Won't do to let things go by the wayside. My grandfather and my father worked for their family, and we've kept up the tradition. Take care of them, and they'll take care of you. Old Monsieur Vallotton paid to send my middle boy to school for music. I'd never heard of such a thing, but he had a voice like an angel. Lives in Vienna now, sings with the opera, been all over the world."

"However, you work directly for the Fontenays?"

Hamel swung around to face Agnes full on. "Monsieur Fontenay's full of grand ideas, a lot of talk about education and the philosophy behind everything. Nonsense really, when what you're supposed to do is tell kids how to listen and learn. How to behave. He's not got her spine. She likes things just so. Strict. She's not a coddler, that's for sure."

Hamel narrowed his eyes. "You arrived with Monsieur Vallotton." She nodded and Hamel rocked back on his heels. He wagged his chin toward the door. "I've seen it all, hundreds of boys passing through here over the years. The things they'll get up to would scare most parents; course that's why they're sent here. My wife calls it the 'patina of security.'"

Agnes couldn't disagree. On the other hand, these boys came from all over the world. They weren't a typical cross section of a village or even a city. She said as much to Hamel.

He frowned. "Don't think the ones from bad places bring the trouble. Raised three boys and a girl myself, and in my experience, even the good ones are a handful when they're passing through the stages of growing up. So many together in a big bunch takes the right kind of person to keep an eye on everyone. On everything."

"You don't think the Fontenays are the right kind?"

"It's a good place to work." Hamel seemed to regret saying as much as he had. He wiped his forehead.

"Is there anything else that's troubled you lately?"

He drew air in between his teeth. "You're a smart one. Nothing like today. Nothing to hang your hat on, or I would have told them before. It's hard to know sometimes what's an accident or natural and what's malicious. There've been things."

Agnes pulled out her notebook.

He eyed it. "It's only been these last weeks, since that big storm. Had a window—no, two windowpanes out. Not broken, but laying out of their putty like it dried up overnight. And I've seen some lights on at odd times."

"Lights?"

"People walking where they shouldn't be."

She remembered the ones she'd seen earlier. The ones that

hadn't troubled Fontenay. "People walking on the property? Trespassing?"

"Not quite trespassing. Walking on the edge of the fields, near the forest where they shouldn't be. There are wild boars there and it's dangerous. No reason for someone to stir up trouble that way. That's why I was doing my rounds so late this time. Hoping to catch them at it. Guess the joke's on me."

"Do you live here?" According to Madame Fontenay, two teachers were always on duty at night, in addition to the head-master and mistress. Everyone else lived away from the campus.

"They don't call it 'here.' I'm up the hill a bit. We lease from the Vallottons. My family's always done since my grandfather built the house. He helped build the chalet, slept up the hill to oversee construction."

"You have a good view of the property?"

Hamel grinned. "Good enough to see lights."

This didn't sound like much to Agnes, but she dutifully made notes. "Anything else?"

"There was that arrow in the wall."

Sixteen

An awkward silence spread through the headmaster's office. Despite a fire blazing on the hearth, the room felt cold. Only a few lamps were on, and beyond their glow the room was a mass of shadow and darkness. The Fontenays sat on opposite ends of a long sofa, emanating fear and anger in alternating currents. Agnes was perched on the front edge of a cushioned armchair, wishing she had dry shoes to change into. She eased Bernard Fontenay's jacket nearer the armrest, then leaned back.

"If this gets out . . . When this gets out . . ." Bernard choked back a gulp of brandy, slamming the empty glass on the table.

"Is there trouble between the Institute and the village that might play out this way?" Agnes asked.

"With bloodshed?" Bernard was aghast.

"And the arrow shot into the chalet by the boys' rooms. Which no one mentioned to me until tonight."

"You need to talk to Koulsy Haroun and see if he knows

anything," said Helene Fontenay. Her face was sliced in half by a dark shadow, reinforcing the chill in her voice.

"You think he's responsible?"

"There are no complaints about us in the village," Bernard interrupted.

"There must be the usual grumblings," said Agnes, eyeing Helene. She had leaned farther into the shadows, and Agnes wished she could see the woman's face. Monsieur Fontenay's was a mask of nerves and anguish, as was his voice. Madame Fontenay was angry, but her reaction was controlled. A white-hot stillness enveloped her.

"We're part of the village, but not precisely part of village life," Bernard said. "The boys walk over and buy treats and spend money in the shops and probably cause minor trouble."

"Madame Fontenay, is this why you mentioned Koulsy? Has he caused trouble there?"

Bernard answered, "No, Koulsy isn't a troublemaker."

"But someone else is?"

"That's not what I meant."

"We've not had any complaints," said Helene.

"Do you go into the village often?"

"We're too busy here," said Bernard, "and there's nothing to shop for. Helene goes to Bern for clothes and other items."

Agnes remembered the village above Julien Vallotton's home. Ville-sur-Lac was tiny, with little of interest to the family, yet the marquise made a point of occasionally taking coffee in the *confiserie* or visiting the tiny *brocanterie*. Some might view it as noblesse oblige, but Agnes knew it was a mark of support and respect important to maintaining the old traditions. The Fontenays didn't have those ties here.

Bernard Fontenay bolted to his feet and crossed to the door leading to the private upstairs apartment. Helene Fontenay slid his empty glass across the end table away from her. As she did, she moved into the light. Her expression was grim.

"Madame Fontenay, you mentioned Koulsy."

"He's at an age to want attention, that's all I meant. That's what I told you earlier. If we were aware of something specific, we would have said. You don't want me to speculate, do you, Inspector?"

Agnes wondered what Helene had started to say before her husband interrupted. It was late, too late to talk to the boy tonight. Agnes stood. "I'll be in touch tomorrow. There'll be more questions."

"Do you think Monsieur Vallotton will support Bernard if trouble comes?" Helene asked abruptly.

"He's spoken highly of both of you to me. He certainly loves this school."

"But would he stand by him? Is he loyal?"

"I think he can be trusted to stand by what he thinks is right." Vallotton had stepped out of the office when Agnes returned from the shed. It had shifted the mood toward official police business, and she appreciated his discretion. Now she wondered if his departure hadn't been misinterpreted.

Helene glanced out the window to the dark lawn. "Meaning the law."

"I'd hope so." Agnes paused. "Is there something you're worried about? Something you didn't say earlier?" She kept her eyes off the door that Bernard had passed through.

The headmistress stood abruptly, her crutches banging the floor. "You think I'm worried about something Bernard has done?

You've misinterpreted my remarks. I simply wondered why Monsieur Vallotton is here, now. He's like the other directors. Comes only when it's convenient. Stays the minimum amount of time. Too busy to care most days, and now, when there is trouble, he is here. Interested. Why?"

"Officer Boschung called him."

"Not to bring him here, to inform him. Sometimes I think they work for the Vallottons and not for us."

"Boschung works for neither. He works for the *canton*."

Madame Fontenay arched an eyebrow. "Thank you for that civics lesson."

"Monsieur Vallotton is concerned about Guy Chavanon's death. That's why he's here."

Helene stood in the doorway. "Look elsewhere then. Look among his friends and family. Isn't that where trouble usually comes from?"

"He was the father of a student here, and he died here."

"He was an annoying man who . . ."

Agnes stopped buttoning her coat.

Helene took a short, deep breath before continuing, "I'm tired this evening. I simply meant that he was a typical parent who always wanted to prove that he knew better. He was one of many hundreds that we meet in our role as caretakers of the children. He died and that is the end of the unfortunate story. There are many unexplained problems in the world. We cannot fix them all, no matter how we try."

"His death isn't going to remain unexplained. We owe it to Monsieur Chavanon. As a director, Julien Vallotton understands that."

Helene nodded toward the window. "Speaking of whom.

He's waiting for you. Outside." She leveled her gaze at Agnes. "You'd better run."

Agnes stepped out the front door of the chalet. The rain had stopped and the clouds had dispersed, leaving the moon exposed. She had been tempted to actually run, but thought Madame Fontenay might not appreciate the ironic gesture; she had an agenda Agnes didn't entirely understand.

Julien Vallotton was standing on the raked gravel drive beside his Rolls-Royce, as comfortable as if he were in his own living room. He'd pulled his tie off and looked as if he were waiting outside an upscale nightclub.

"What are you doing here?"

He glanced up from his phone screen. "Waiting for you. You didn't think I'd leave you here?"

"Three weeks ago you told me that you barely visit your family; that you'd been in Switzerland only a few times in the two years since your father died." She shoved her hands in her coat pockets. "What are you doing here? In Switzerland."

"I'll tell my aunt you enjoyed dinner." He stowed his phone in his jacket pocket.

Agnes took a deep breath. "I'm sorry. Please do tell her. But this is a real question. Your friends tonight want you back in London. They're surprised you've stayed away so long."

He opened the car door for her, then settled himself in the driver's seat. "I like London. I like the English. They celebrate failure. Think of Dunkirk. Failure? No, they made it a triumph." He turned onto the lane. "My family have been in Switzerland since before there was a confederation."

"Yet you live in London."

"A man can move. I do own a perfectly usable home here. More than one, in fact."

She didn't speak. Waiting him out. Relaxing into the supple comfort of the seat. The dashboard glowed, the dials sent out signals she was too tired to read. She shifted to watch him.

"Things changed three weeks ago and my future is different now. Or I hope it is."

She forced herself to not look away. He couldn't mean anything to do with her.

"And there are responsibilities that go with that. I think that you, of all people, would understand them."

Realization dawned. Mimi. Agnes felt like a fool. Of course Julien Vallotton wouldn't leave a six-year-old orphan alone in a vast château with only his aging aunt and a handful of servants. He wouldn't sidestep his obligations.

"As you pointed out, I had been living in London. For too long, it seems. I need to reacquaint myself with . . . with everything."

Agnes shifted her weight and faced forward.

Vallotton changed the subject. "Bernard will see things more clearly in the morning. He might even prove helpful. He's a good headmaster. He's young at his job."

"Do you always find an excuse for people? Bernard Fontenay's job is to run the school and to retain control of himself, not collapse in a heap of anxiety and blame."

"He has his strengths, and what was discovered tonight isn't part of a normal day's work. Not everyone is prepared—emotionally prepared—for all eventualities."

She suppressed a smile. "I suppose a few shots of brandy were deserved after the day he had."

"The blood in the shed could generate bad publicity, or at least bad feelings in the village. Rumors start. Fear spreads, a bad feeling you can't get rid of. Someone starts the stampede, then others withdraw because students are leaving, and next thing you have empty classrooms." Vallotton turned on his left signal light to urge a slow-moving car out of the way. "I won't let that happen."

She nearly protested, but one look at Vallotton told her it was useless. She wondered for a moment what it felt like to have that kind of certainty. How many generations did it take to feel absolute authority was a birthright? And absolute responsibility, she acknowledged, knowing that's where his statement sprang from. He would take care of those connected with his family, and the Institute was closely connected.

"There is a possible link to Koulsy, of course." She paused to frame her thoughts. "Meaning his family is an obvious link between ill will and action. Although I'm not sure what the action was precisely."

"Perhaps no one was meant to see the shed *yet* and the message wasn't complete."

"Possibly." She felt herself doze.

"If we're talking about rumors, then perhaps what we saw tonight is based on ill will toward the Institute in general," said Vallotton.

"Or meant to harm the Fontenays as the headmasters?"

"Right now it could mean anything or nothing; someone or no one." Vallotton gave a faint laugh. "You've an interesting job."

Seventeen

The village clock struck two when Agnes opened the door to her in-laws' chalet. Quietly, she hung her coat and hat in the front closet and slipped off her shoes. The house was never completely dark, and not until she was halfway across the living room did she realize Sybille was awake. The flicker from the fireplace glowed a warning. Footsteps rattled in the hall and Agnes braced for the welcome.

"A long dinner?" said Sybille neutrally.

It took Agnes a moment to understand what Sybille meant; dinner seemed days ago. She walked into the kitchen and filled a glass with water from the tap, drinking it down. Sybille followed her. The oven was on and the smell of baking bread assailed Agnes. Suddenly she was hungry.

Always a mind reader when it came to food, Sybille pulled a loaf near, sliced it, then placed cheese and honey on a dish. "They didn't feed you?"

Agnes slathered the bread with honey and laid the Gruyère

on top, biting in. "They fed me quite well, but that was hours ago. I was called to a crime scene." She paused. "Maybe it is a crime scene. Not a violent crime, unless you count the dead chicken."

Sybille laughed and it was infectious. Suddenly the two women were weeping with laughter. Sybille reached into the refrigerator and pulled out an uncorked bottle of white wine, pouring two glasses.

"It was too quiet tonight, and I started making bread, thinking to get ahead for the week." She gestured toward the neat loaves on the counter, and the final two in the oven. "Thought I'd take a few to neighbors tomorrow."

"That's nice." Agnes sliced off another piece. She told Sybille about the meal at Château Vallotton, answering her questions. Sybille's knowledge of food was exceptional, and she expected the daughter of a great chef to be able to detail a meal correctly.

"Must be nice to eat like that every day."

"We do pretty well here," Agnes said, meaning it.

"They must set a prettier table."

Reminded of the candles and silver and crystal and servants, Agnes started to giggle again, unsure if it was fatigue, the wine, or some other emotional trigger. "The dining table seats forty."

Sybille laughed with her and poured them each another glass of wine.

"He's not what I thought he'd be," said Sybille.

That brought Agnes's laughter to a cold stop. "Julien Vallotton is very nice, but the entire family, his aunt, everyone is—"

"You know what I mean."

"It's not like that."

"Maybe not, maybe not with him, but one day it will be with someone. Don't say anything. I'm a mother. George was my only son, my only child. With his death I'm not a mother anymore and won't be again. There is no replacing him for me." Sybille waved off any comfort. "I won't insult you by pretending that a daughter-in-law is the same. You know I love the boys, but they're yours. They're only a little bit mine. Maybe that's why I cling to them so much. I need that little bit more than you need it."

"I miss George, too, there's nothing—"

"I know there isn't, not now. But one day there will be."

Agnes felt the pain of the words like a fist on her chest. Sybille couldn't mean what she was saying. It was a lie told because it was expected. Agnes leaned against the kitchen counter. Like the lies she told. It was tempting to say, *But George is the one who left me. Who left me twice, once by choice and once through death.* But she didn't.

Eighteen

Christine Chavanon paced from living room to kitchen. In the hours since she'd returned home with her arm stinging from the stitches, she'd checked the door locks twice to make sure they were secure. Her father's satchel lay on the center of her dining table. Beside it, his notebook looked old and worn. It felt toxic.

She turned her coffee machine on and recrossed the room to look out the front window again. The main house was dark; the lawn was a pool of inky black. She wouldn't be able to tell if anyone was there. She closed the drapes, checking that they were a barrier to all unwelcome eyes. She turned the coffee machine off, changing her mind. She didn't need caffeine; her thoughts were already too wildly discordant. What she had discovered was inconceivable.

She went to a different window, this time turning the overhead light off before she looked out. She waited, allowing her eyes to adjust. There were too many clouds to see any detail.

Marie had gone to bed hours ago, turning out all the lights. Christine fidgeted. She should talk to Marie, shouldn't she?

Turning the light back on, she stood beside the table and opened the notebook again. Her finger traced the writing, line by line. She turned a page and continued. She'd done this a half dozen times already, at first afraid the pain medication was making her believe the impossible. By the third time she was stone sober and focused, and she believed.

She slipped the notebook back into the satchel and stowed it under the sofa cushion. The cushions were sold as casual chic, which meant they were unstructured and didn't reveal what was stuffed beneath. This felt better. Safer. Tomorrow she could read it all again with a clear head.

Satisfied, she walked to the bedroom and turned back the covers, reaching for a nightgown. On a chair across the room sat the Steiff bear her father had given her twenty years ago. The bear was worn from childhood adoration, his arms threadbare and one eye replaced with a button, but the sight of him brought back all those years, all that she owed her father. She should have paid more attention.

What she needed to do—to say—couldn't wait. She would wake Marie up.

Retrieving the satchel and notebook from underneath the sofa cushion, she slipped the strap over her shoulder, then covered up with a jacket. She turned off the lights and peered out between the living-room curtains.

It was too late for cars on their road. No one was about. She told herself that whoever had broken into the workshop wouldn't return, especially only hours after the police left.

Something in the landscape changed. She focused in the

distance and not on the workshop. A man was crossing the lawn.

She held her breath and pulled her mobile phone from her coat pocket.

Then she recognized him. Stephan Dupré.

Carefully she closed the curtains and went to bed, taking the satchel with her.

Nineteen

"Colic. That's what the doctor told us," Petit said, jamming his hands into the pockets of his overcoat, then hurriedly removing them. Agnes suspected the coat was new and he was afraid of damaging it. She wondered if dressing in civilian clothes after years in uniform was liberating or uncomfortable.

"You could have called me and taken the day off if the baby's sick," she said. "You worked late last night and weren't supposed to come off leave until tomorrow."

His already-bulging eyes nearly popped out of his skull. "I won't let Bardy or you down."

"Is the baby better?" They reached the porch to Guy Chavanon's workshop, and she pulled a set of keys from her handbag.

"He's much better, especially now that we have a name for the reason he cries all night."

Agnes laughed, surprised by Petit's observation. "How did you leave things with Boschung last night?"

"He likes to pick his solution and stay with it. But we hit it off and he's okay with not blasting the news across the *canton*. We formed a real bond because of my time with the local police."

Agnes shot Petit a look, searching for any element of sarcasm.

"He'll start an investigation," Petit continued. "They'll question some of the locals and talk to the kids who usually make trouble. See if one of them vandalized the shed. That's what we'd have done in Ville-sur-Lac when I was with the *gendarmerie*." He spoke as if it had been years and not a few weeks since he left them.

"Is Boschung still convinced he's looking for a mass murderer?"

Petit grinned. "Right now, he'll agree with anything we say. If we're wrong, we take the blame. Either way he wins. Safer."

Agnes turned the key in the door lock. Petit's height made the front porch seem more a dollhouse than a real house. "Is Madame Chavanon meeting us here?" he asked.

"No, we'll see her in the main house, but I wanted to have another look around first." Agnes ushered Petit in, shutting the door behind them.

"You weren't exaggerating when you said the place was tossed." Petit crossed the living room to look in the kitchen, nearly banging his head on the old-fashioned brass chandelier. "He wasn't the neatest person to begin with, was he?"

Agnes studied the room, comparing it to the photographs she'd taken with her phone the day before. "The local police left everything as close as possible to how they found it. What do you notice?"

He eyed the scene as if preparing for an exam. "Apart from

the mess? Hard to tell if anything's missing. No spot where a computer should be. No empty space at all. I can't even tell where Chavanon sat to work, much less what he was working on. If that window hadn't been broken out, and the door left open, I might think he'd tipped these boxes over himself. Maybe he was angry?"

"Notice the chair." It was old and heavy with broad wood arms. Agnes touched it and the castors rolled easily. Cushions were arranged on the seat and against the back. "The wheels have rolled back and forth, damaging the floor over time. The cushions are worn."

"But where'd he work? There's stacks of paper everywhere. My wife says I'm messy, she should see this."

Agnes sat in the chair and pulled it up to the edge of the table. "I think he was cleaning up."

"He'd need a couple of trash bins for that."

She surveyed the room. "Not cleaning out, but up. Organizing. At university, I used to take my notes and exams and put them together at the end of each term. I don't know why, they're stored in a box in the attic now, but I kept everything. Even the notes I knew I would never need again."

Petit fingered a few stacks of paper. "You mean he's grouping them in a system of some sort? But the mess . . ."

"That's a separate thing. I think you're right, someone was angry and dumped the boxes. Might have been Chavanon, more likely it was whoever broke in. But look at what was here before. See how this stack of paper is fanned out? Even spilled you can tell how the pages were ordered. Notice how the ones on top look fresh and clean while a section farther down has yellowed and the edges are frayed and ripped. The next stack is the same way. If the stacks sat here for a long time, the top page would have aged, and even when toppled over, there would only be one old sheet. Here, there are chunks of old sheets mixed in. I don't think a burglar did that."

Agnes turned on a lamp in the corner, bathing the longest wall in bright light. The entire length was covered in butcher paper. Even the windows. She gestured. "I think these walls are where he started his work. The paper is uniformly aged." She ran a hand across one section. Dust drifted away. "They haven't been touched in weeks or months.

"He started here." She tapped the paper. "Then moved on to other ways of working and left the pages on the wall. It doesn't look like he used a computer. That might account for the sheer volume of paperwork."

Petit rifled through a few stacks. "Look at the dates. Three years ago. Five years."

Agnes started her own quick search through the piles. "Some are older. Perhaps left over from earlier projects; notes that he consulted."

"Do you think he came up with some great invention?"

"Who knows. We certainly can't tell from this. At least not without a careful study. It's possible that he was in the process of cleaning up after reaching a dead end. Giving up. From what I can tell, Guy Chavanon had a history of false starts. Maybe he decided he was at the end of trying with this one."

"That doesn't explain why someone broke in."

"Doesn't it? If someone thought Chavanon had invented something valuable, they would want it." Agnes remembered what Stephan Dupré had said: that Guy chased dreams. "People believe what they want to. If enough people say someone is a

genius, then it's so. It would be possible to not know his ideas—
this idea—hadn't amounted to anything."

"You think that a burglar saw the inside of the workshop
and left without taking anything? Maybe they realized their
mistake?"

Agnes turned the lamp off. "Could be. It's also possible someone took a key element of what he was working on." She studied
the room. "Stephan Dupré said that Chavanon was secretive
and that he didn't use the business safe."

She moved to the long tables, inspecting the edges for any
hidden drawers. Petit followed her lead and looked in the other
room, opening and closing cabinets in the kitchen. Agnes finished
checking the tables. Nothing. She moved to the desk. Again,
nothing. She started on the various side tables left over from the
days when the workshop was a house. Running her fingers
under the lip of the top of the smallest one, she felt a slight give.
She moved the papers off the top and tilted the table up, discov-
ering a thin drawer. The local police hadn't noticed it because
there wasn't a knob. Only a slight groove on the lower edge. She
pulled it. Nothing. She took off a shoe and banged the bottom.
The wood shifted and she pulled again. This time it jerked open.

Her excitement quickly faded. There was no notebook or flash
drive or envelope labeled *Secret Discovery*, only scraps of paper.
She sifted through them, finding a few receipts, a list of supplies, random notes about everyday matters. She was nearly at
the bottom of the stack when she came across a business card
with the Omega logo. Underneath it read *Director of Research
Gianfranco Giberti*. A time was penciled in across the bottom. A
meeting time? She turned the card over. No date, no place. It
was reasonable that father, daughter, and boyfriend met, but

why would the time be written on a business card? Wouldn't Christine make the arrangements and, if necessary, remind her father? Agnes didn't think that a woman needed a time penciled on a card to remember to meet her lover.

Agnes flicked the card against her hand. Was this a meeting between the two men that didn't include Christine? The director of research for a major watch company and the owner of a small family-owned one. Was this the investor Dupré had learned about? Omega certainly had the resources to purchase an idea. Agnes took a photograph of the card, wondering what Christine Chavanon would do if her father sold his greatest idea to another brand without telling her.

At precisely the agreed-upon time, Marie Chavanon greeted them on the front steps of her home. She was dressed for work, with her hands in the pockets of her suit coat as if protecting them from the morning chill. Ushering Agnes and Petit into the living room, she didn't offer any refreshment, and Agnes felt her colleague's disappointment. Petit was likely depending on a string of espressos to compensate for a night short on sleep.

Marie seated herself on a long stiff leather sofa in the living room, gesturing for her guests to choose from the chairs. "These photographs were delivered early this morning," she said without preamble, indicating a large envelope on the table in front of her.

Agnes removed her coat and laid it across the back of a chrome-and-leather chair before being seated. Petit chose its twin, keeping his coat on. She wondered if he'd judged the climate more accurately than she had. Madame Chavanon didn't look to be in the mood for a long chat.

"Nothing in the photographs, nothing about the workshop, spoke to you?" Agnes asked.

"What do you mean, spoke to me? It was a mess. Nothing like Guy before . . ." Marie swallowed to control her emotions.

Agnes had to prompt her. "Before what?"

"He became fixated, Inspector. Distant. Guy had always used the workshop as a retreat. It was a place to think and explore, he would say. But he stopped talking about his work some time ago." Marie smiled up at them and Agnes saw tears. The woman's eyes were carefully made up to conceal dark circles. "He used to talk about his ideas. Most of them were over my head, but Leo and I liked to listen. Guy was excited about everything. That's one of the things that drew me to him at first. His enthusiasm. Boundless enthusiasm. Every project had potential in his eyes."

"What kind of things did he work on?" asked Petit. "My father was a bit of an inventor himself. Small stuff to help around the house. Mainly improvements on what we had."

Marie Chavanon warmed to his question. "That sounds like Guy, except his inventions were always about watches. A more elegant stem, a unique case. He worked on the metals themselves, and the finer points of the mechanism. His background was engineering and he never stopped learning." She pulled a handkerchief from her pocket. "When he was younger, he made elaborate mechanical cases with pulleys and clocks and sundials. They were like miniature fun houses."

"I've seen things like that in the watch museum here in La Chaux-de-Fonds," said Petit. "School trip," he murmured in an aside to Agnes. She was reminded that he'd not been out of school that long himself.

"Yes, the cases are part of a long tradition of side hobbies, I suppose you could say, among watchmakers." Marie fingered a leather seam in the sofa. "These last months were different. He wouldn't speak of the project, except to say that he was working. He stopped paying attention to anything else. I was thankful Leo was away at school, otherwise he would have noticed something was wrong. Guy wasn't sleeping, he would pace or go down to the workshop at all hours."

"Are some of the pieces he created part of the collection?" said Agnes. "I'd hoped to see it yesterday when Christine gave me a tour of the factory."

Marie bunched a fist in her lap. "The collection. They always made too much of it, and it was gathering dust. None of Guy's creations are there; it was all old watches, a few desk clocks."

"That's disappointing. It sounded interesting." Agnes paused, but Marie Chavanon didn't add anything. "Have you remembered anything that might help us with the note your husband left?"

"You saw his workshop. Isn't that evidence of his state of mind? Doesn't anyone understand what I've been through these last months? These conversations only add to the trauma of losing him. Why can't everyone leave us in peace?" Marie Chavanon pressed her fingertips to her pursed lips. "Christine put you up to this, didn't she? These questions. I don't know how she got the idea of Guy's being murdered in her head. She's always been overly emotional. The fuss she made over that note, and yesterday, with her arm. Typical."

"Madame Chavanon, someone broke into your husband's workshop. There is more to what happened than an accident. It's too much of a coincidence."

"I've told you everything I know."

Petit disguised a snicker as a cough. Agnes kept her focus on Marie. "The last time it rained here was the day before your husband's funeral. The area around the broken window was dry, meaning the workshop was burglarized after the rain. Have you been near the building since then, or have you seen anyone near it?"

Marie placed her hands flat on either side of her as if balancing. "Christine. Ask Christine. She left him. She wanted more. More of what I do not know, but she left him. He never got over it. Did she tell you that? That she hurt him and didn't care, and now that he's gone, she's trying to make amends. Stirring up trouble, asking questions. Wanting to be part of everything now when it's too late. You need to tell her that. She made her choice and left us. She has to live with herself."

"You saw her enter the workshop?"

Marie gazed into the distance. "No, I didn't see anyone go inside. Christine and Stephan are the only two people I've seen cross the lawn at all." Marie shrugged slightly, an elegant gesture. "Others were here for the funeral, they wandered everywhere. It was a sunny day and they were on the veranda, maybe on the lawn. I don't know, I didn't pay close attention. It was too overwhelming."

"And you don't remember anything unusual about your husband in the days leading up to his death?"

"It was more of the same. He was more excited. Less able to sleep. I'd hoped seeing Narendra would help."

"Did you say something to Monsieur Patel? Ask him to speak with your husband?"

Marie recoiled. "Oh, no, I would never." She stopped. "There is a pattern to our days, and seeing someone you know well, but don't see often, can shift your thinking. The last few years Narendra and Guy would have time for dinner before Baselworld began. I had hoped Narendra would notice Guy's odd behavior and say something that might help."

"His change in behavior must have been obvious for a friend to notice it over dinner."

"They were close." Marie passed a hand over her forehead and smiled weakly. "There wasn't enough time for that, was there?"

"Did you ever think that your husband's behavior was the result of something going well with his work?"

"No." Marie half laughed. "You saw what he was when you walked into his workshop. He'd grown more disconnected, more abstracted in his thinking. I was worried." Her voice dropped to a near whisper. "About his mental health."

Agnes let the words hang in the air. They felt like bait without a hook.

"Your daughter shared that the financial situation hasn't been easy in recent years."

"She talks about family honor and tradition but isn't willing to sacrifice for it." Marie fisted her hands in her lap. "I'm sorry, I'm not myself today. It's the usual ups and downs of business. Christine isn't old enough to understand."

Petit shifted in his chair and his long legs struck the coffee table. Marie Chavanon glared.

"Was she angry with her father?" Agnes asked.

"Christine is young, still a child in many ways. She wasn't angry, disappointed perhaps."

"What about the company's new investor?"

"I don't know what you're talking about."

Agnes heard anger, but not surprise. "Monsieur Dupré mentioned it."

Marie picked up the envelope from the coffee table, toying with the clasp. "He must have misunderstood or been misled. Or perhaps you misunderstood. There wasn't an investor." She handed the envelope to Agnes. "Please take these, I don't want them around."

"There was nothing in the photographs that suggested why someone broke in? Nothing missing or disturbed?" Agnes asked.

"Who could tell what was disturbed?"

Petit shifted uncomfortably. "Your husband didn't use a computer?"

"No, he didn't like them. If something had to be done on a computer, he asked one of us to do it. Gisele has a monitor at her desk for the design programs. I have a laptop for the business accounts."

"He didn't own a device at all?" said Agnes.

"No."

"You're sure?"

"Ask Christine, she'll confirm that he never did."

"Things might have changed in the time since she left the company."

Marie stood. "I have to leave for work now."

Agnes gathered her coat. Petit took a final look around the room.

"There have been record crowds at Baselworld," said Agnes. "You must be pleased."

"That's why I must go. They're overwhelmed. So many people." Marie exhaled the last word and her fatigue seemed to deepen.

"One last thing," said Agnes. "Would you have time for me to show Officer Petit the factory? We would be very quick."

Marie hesitated, then pulled a piece of paper from a nearby notepad and wrote a number down. "Use this code. It's the one used by the cleaning service."

They waited until Marie drove off, waving to her from the sidewalk. Then Agnes led Petit to the rear door of the factory.

"Did you think she'd let us in here alone?" Petit asked.

"No. I thought she'd insist we come back later. And I believe she's hiding something about the collection. Christine expected to find it in the glass case and all of the pieces have been removed with no explanation." Agnes pulled the door shut behind them and heard the latch close. She gestured ahead. "That's the factory floor if you want to take a look."

Petit loped across the lobby and stuck his head into the large room. "Wow, like a place out of time."

Agnes led the way upstairs. The broken glass was still on the office floor. Petit studied it, then nosed around while Agnes located the latch mechanism that secured the wall panels. She found what she was looking for in the third concealed cabinet.

"Notebooks?" said Petit, peering over her shoulder.

"When Christine Chavanon showed me the family archive, she said that the owners have always kept a notebook of their designs and ideas. Anyone as proud of his heritage as Guy Chavanon would have maintained the tradition."

Nearly identical leather notebooks filled the entire cabinet from floor to near the ceiling. Agnes ran her finger down the rows. The red leather spines were stamped with the company logo and a set of initials. She opened a few. "These were his. See the GLC initials? The last one stops nearly a year ago, which means the current one is missing. I didn't see anything like this in his workshop, did you?"

Petit shook his head, "But it could have been buried under something. Or maybe he stopped using a notebook when he was working on a big project."

"I don't think so. Every year is accounted for until this one, and according to his friends and the family, he was always working on the next great idea. This wouldn't have started any different, regardless of outcome." She closed the cabinet. "It's possible that the current one is sitting on his nightstand. I'll ask."

"Or it's where his most important ideas were and it's been stolen?"

"That's what I'm afraid of."

Twenty

Gianfranco Giberti walked up the steps to the restaurant at a brisk clip. Agnes could easily picture him heading toward an assignation with a glamorous dark-haired beauty. Perhaps a visiting model from Japan. He was a man who always looked as if he were heading to or from a tryst. The deliberately rough shave, the well-tailored robin's-egg-blue suit worn a little too casually, the Ferragamo shoes, and the slightly loosened knot of his tie. His hair was dark and worn long to his collar, swept back from his face in a wave and held in a low ponytail. She hesitated for a moment, then followed him.

She was shocked to find that he was eating alone at a table for two. The other place setting had been cleared, and Agnes slid into the vacant chair. He half rose, his expression quizzical. When she introduced herself, his manner turned somber.

"Of course, I had met Monsieur Chavanon and was very sorry to learn about his death." Giberti motioned for a waiter to bring another menu. Agnes declined, requesting a small bottle of San Pellegrino.

"*Had met* sounds a bit formal for the father of your former girlfriend. Surely you knew him better than that?"

"Christine and I went out a few times. I date a lot of women. It's impossible to be serious with anyone given my work schedule."

A waiter brought a plate of steak tartare for Giberti and asked Agnes if she had changed her mind about ordering. She waved the waiter off, although the meal looked appetizing. Giberti mixed the chopped onion, capers, and raw egg into the minced meat, then took a bite.

"Despite this casual relationship, you were watching Christine closely the day before yesterday."

Giberti's fork stopped in midair. "That's where I recognize you from. She was crying, of course I noticed."

Agnes sipped sparkling water, eyeing the crowds passing back and forth across the Baselworld plaza. The enormous open circle in the center of the canopy looked like a giant metal web pulled open to the sky.

"When was the last time you saw Monsieur Chavanon?"

"Why are you asking these questions? Has something happened? Something else, I mean."

"His workshop was burglarized. I found your business card there with an appointment marked on it and wondered how that meeting went, and if you had something to contribute to our investigation based on your conversation."

"Appointment?" Giberti set his fork down with exaggerated care. "What has Christine told you about us, about me?"

172   Tracee de Hahn

"That you dated. She also mentioned your relationship with her father."

"She wouldn't have said I had a relationship with Monsieur Chavanon. He was clear that he didn't want to know me better." Giberti toyed with his silverware. "You're sure the appointment was with me?"

"The time was marked on your card. Why did Monsieur Chavanon object to your dating his daughter?"

A laugh escaped Giberti. "No man wants his daughter to date, not really. At least in my experience."

Agnes wondered if it was because fathers recognized the danger Giberti represented. Men might dream of being play-boys, but they wanted their daughters to marry stolid, respect-able bureaucrats. Giberti looked like a lifetime of despair dressed in a fine suit.

"When did you stop seeing Christine?"

"Three months ago this weekend."

Agnes blinked. "Are you always so precise with dates?"

"I am in a precise business, Inspector."

"And yet you don't remember the appointment?"

"I can't remember something that didn't happen."

Agnes stood, placing a ten-franc note on the table for her water. She was a half dozen steps away when Giberti called to her.

"Inspector, how is Christine? It's hard to lose a parent and I should have called her."

"You still can." Agnes turned deliberately. "They've dusted the workshop for fingerprints. It may take a few days, but we'll identify them all. And I may be back in touch."

Outside the restaurant, she could see Giberti through the

glass façade. He was on his telephone and it didn't look like a business call.

"Step farther out," Antoine Mercier said, beckoning toward the rail. The air high above the showroom floor was warm and stale, and the view through the open weave of the metal floor made Agnes uneasy. Mercier understood the power of place.

"Do they serve coffee and chocolates up here?" she asked, aiming for a light tone and failing. She took a final hesitant step to reach the rail.

"I thought you would appreciate the view." Mercier leaned forward, waving one arm expansively. "The big picture for the police."

"I'm more interested in details right now." Agnes gripped the rail. She'd never been afraid of heights, but then she'd never stood on an open walkway before. She felt the pull, the sickening sense of tipping. All she could think of was the Pont Bessières and George. She longed for solid earth.

"Why didn't you tell me that you were at the Institute the day before Guy Chavanon died?" She fixed her gaze on Mercier, trying to forget where they were.

"If I had been present when he died, I would have told you. The day before?" Mercier shrugged. "I hadn't seen Guy in months, not since our chance encounter in Genève."

"Which restaurant did you see him in?"

"How should I remember? I dine out frequently."

"You had such a clear memory of the meeting."

"Why does the restaurant name matter?"

"It is an open question, and I don't like those. Guy Chavanon didn't go to Genève often. It is unlikely he was there without a purpose. I haven't found out why, and if I knew which restaurant, they might locate his reservation—if there was one—and we might learn who he dined with. Unless you remember."

"Perhaps he was alone?"

"His family say that he didn't like to eat in restaurants by himself and that he wouldn't have."

"Well, I don't remember. I'm sorry, Inspector, unlike Guy, I eat out both by myself and in company frequently. It is impossible to remember each instance. I only remember seeing Guy because it was so unusual, and as you know, I felt that he was particularly buoyant. That's what I remember."

"And that it was several months ago."

"Yes, well, that, too." Mercier kept his eyes fixed on the ground far beneath them.

Agnes followed his gaze, concentrating. Most of the people were a blur of anonymous black, tan, and dark blue clothing. Studying the patterns, she thought about the Roach. She imagined this was the kind of view he would have appreciated. He could stand here, high in the air, secure in the knowledge that while the tiny figures went about their business—buying, selling, entertaining, amusing—he was silently draining their bank accounts.

She turned to Mercier. "You're not only the face, you are the eyes and ears of the Swiss watch industry."

"You flatter me."

"No, that's the assessment of my colleagues in Financial Crimes."

"You are now investigating *me*?" Mercier said sharply. "I have made it a personal mission to eliminate the sale and import of fakes to this country, and your colleagues have been my allies. The damage done to our national brand by counterfeit goods is inestimable—"

During their brief phone conversation Agnes had been warned by Aubry: once Mercier started on this topic, he wouldn't stop until his audience died from boredom.

"Beyond that," she interrupted. "You hear things, you know what is coming in the next years. People confide in you."

"You are mistaken. You've not listened to me. Secrecy underpins what is done here. Each company keeps their own counsel. I manage trends and assist with legislation. I am a liaison. I am a voice."

"I think you are more than that. Every industry needs their consigliere. Someone who keeps the secrets and advises."

"Now, you are flattering me, Inspector." Mercier appeared to relax. "I can assure you that I don't play that role. The federation is composed of many companies, each operating independently, much like our *cantons* and the federal government. We work together for mutual benefit and protection."

"Let's not exaggerate. Many of the companies operate under larger parent names. How much of the industry does Swatch control?"

"That's different. They may share internally, they certainly manage their brands in a tandem of development." Mercier stopped short. "What is this interest in me, and in who confides in me?"

"I think Guy Chavanon recently—in the past months or weeks—shared or let slip an idea that he was working on. You are right about secrecy, and by all accounts he was a cautious man. That's why I don't think he would have talked to just anyone.

He might have trusted you. Needed your advice." Agnes glanced down and felt that heady sense of tipping again. She drew a short breath. "Perrault et Chavanon is smaller now than in Chavanon's youth. After his daughter left he wouldn't have had a natural confidant within the company."

"His wife is—"

"Not a confidant who loves the industry and who could advise him on a special idea, particularly one that is innovative or revolutionary."

"This has gone into the realm of the absurd. I've told you that I haven't spoken with Guy in months, and on that occasion it was in a public restaurant for the duration of an aperitif. Hardly the time or place for the serious—clandestine—conversation you are suggesting."

"Yet you don't remember where you saw him or exactly when?"

"We have reached a stalemate, Inspector, where my memory is concerned."

"But not where your knowledge is concerned. You warned me about Copernicus because he was a revolutionary. Are you afraid of leaps forward in the watch industry? That is what you meant, isn't it?"

"Slow and steady is my mantra. That's what brought us back from near devastation."

"I understand that and applaud your work, but would you prevent a revolutionary idea? Shut it down?"

"You're putting words in my mouth."

"So if Guy Chavanon had a revolutionary idea—"

"Enough. Inspector Lüthi, I have known Guy for decades, an entire lifetime really, and do not like saying these things so soon after his death. He was a dreamer. An excitable dreamer.

He was innovative, yes, with the innovations that we all develop to keep the industry alive and competitive. He had skills and a brain and a depth and breadth of knowledge and made good watches. That is all."

"Sounds to me like it is possible he used all of those attributes to create something entirely new." Agnes remembered something Christine had said. "I don't expect a significant invention to pop out every year, but there can be one at the end of a lifetime of trying."

"You have insinuated that he confided in me, and now you criticize me because I do not believe in him. I was a friend of Guy's and resent being cornered into speaking ill of him, but he was not likely to develop anything of the magnitude of which you speak. He didn't have the staying power. He never did." Mercier glanced at his watch. "Now, if you will forgive me, I have other appointments. This is a busy week."

They shook hands at the bottom of the stair, and Mercier walked away, leaving Agnes to wonder why he had lied. His assistant had been clear that Mercier's calendar was open for another hour. And she wondered why he had been so interested in the movements of Gianfranco Giberti, whose bright blue jacket made him visible from the walkway.

Twenty-one

Narendra Patel wore a simple dark linen Nehru jacket, a sharp contrast to the brilliant fabric of the several dozen people circulating in his booth. The crowd lent the space a partylike atmosphere.

"Inspector!" Patel greeted Agnes warmly, shaking her hand as if greeting an old friend.

"A celebration?"

"Not at all, simply an invitation to gather for our many clients and good customers. It is an auspicious day when my uncle honors us with his presence to show his believing in this branch of the house."

Agnes looked around with interest. She'd not before been inside a booth in the Stones & Pearls pavilion. Plexiglas boxes were filled with loose stones. Each box was large enough to hold a pair of men's shoes and was tilted forward to display the gems by type and size: diamonds, emeralds, rubies, sapphires, and other stones she couldn't name. Along the walls, cabinets were filled with jewelry: antique and modern necklaces, bracelets, and earrings interspersed with tribal objet d'art. All of the pieces were set with precious stones. Many looked too heavy to wear. Some of the loose stones were as large as a bird's egg.

A flick of Patel's hand stirred a young assistant into action. He pulled jewels from the cases and laid them in front of Agnes. She admired the heavy earrings and thick bracelets and listened to a brief lecture on tribal boxes, daggers, and belts before thanking the young man and assuring him that he had done everything possible to entice her, but she wasn't prepared to make a purchase. Clearly dismayed, he had closed the cabinets when a handsome elderly man wearing a heavy silk Nehru jacket and kurta-pajama approached Narendra with a question.

"Yes, Uncle," Narendra responded deferentially. He introduced Agnes, then stepped away, leaving her with the billionaire head of one of India's most diverse and influential companies. Despite being small, the elder Patel had the gift of making everyone he spoke with feel that he or she was the only reason Patel was in the room.

"My nephew," Guru said, gesturing toward Narendra, "has proven himself this week."

Agnes glanced around the bustling booth. "Appears so. It's quite the gathering."

"Narendra is coming into his own with this company. He did very well for me in pharma, but I see him flourish here. Even the tiny setbacks he moves forward with. This is very important, as no business is a steady ride. It is the fortitude to navigate the disappointments that have made the Patel Group what it is today."

"Hopefully no big disappointment this week." Agnes caught

herself. "I meant business-wise. I was very sorry to learn of the death of Monsieur Patel's friend."

Guru made a tiny gesture with his hand. "I had only memory of Monsieur Chavanon from time he was at university and visited my family. His death was a great blow for Narendra. Very great. He has dealt with it admirably, keeping his focus with us."

"This is my first time at Baselworld. Do you always attend?"

"I am very old now and rarely travel. The younger members of my family handle the various international duties. Narendra asked me to come this year, and for him, I agreed. He is the son of my most favored younger brother."

"Are you planning to grow the watch and jewelry division of the Patel Group?"

"My nephew is the new generation. He will set the path."

"Did he and Guy Chavanon ever consider going into business together?"

Guru Patel flipped his fingers into the air in a gesture of dismissal. "They were old school friends, but I do not think that Chavanon could have been a business partner for our group."

"Why not?"

Out of the corner of her eye Agnes saw Antoine Mercier enter the hall. He worked his way past several booths until he reached the Patel Group. He stopped to greet a customer, and Narendra cut through the crowd to speak with him. Agnes watched the exchange of flattery, wondering if Mercier was looking for her.

"We operate at a scale very different from that of Guy Chavanon's company," Guru Patel said. "We are not artisans who run willy-nilly after ideas and then change our minds when the sun sets. We are an industry. It is a special blend of talent and creativity that results in entrepreneurship. That is what Narendra will need in a partner for expansion."

Mercier moved on to the next booth, and Narendra cut through the crowd to rejoin them. He looked flush with the success of the gathering. Guru Patel made his excuses and left to speak with others.

"You are certain you would not care for a small pair of earrings?" Narendra said to Agnes when they were alone. "I can show you something for everyday." He opened a case and removed a flat velvet tray of emerald earrings.

"Unfortunately, I'm not here for any stones, or watches for that matter."

"They are very flattering to the skin," he said, and selected a pair that Agnes could imagine wearing if she were here to shop, and if she were prepared to splurge.

"I have other interests today."

Patel stopped fiddling with the jewelry. "You are speaking of Guy's death? Of the obsession of Christine? It was a shock of the most troubling kind. But not a true shocking. Guy knew the dangers of his condition." Patel searched his pockets for a handkerchief to dab his eyes. "I cannot think of it even now. You saw me with Marie at the school. I tried to stay strong in front of her, but it is not possible to suppress the loss of a lifelong friend. Only a moment ago, when Monsieur Mercier mentioned Guy, I had difficulty controlling my emotions."

"You administered the shot that day."

Patel dropped his handkerchief and stooped to pick it up. "I hope that the police are not placing any blame on me. Yes, I administered the shot, against all my hatred of needles, and it is my thinking that it should have worked."

"It seems that Monsieur Chavanon needed more than the usual dosage. The"—she nearly said *coroner*—"doctor on the case isn't sure anything would have saved him due to the speed and severity of the reaction." Narendra absorbed her every word. "I'm interested in what happened before Monsieur Chavanon took ill."

Patel motioned to his young assistant and spoke to him in rapid Hindi. The man pressed his palms together and bowed slightly. "My cousin can take over for a few minutes." Patel led Agnes out of the crowded showroom.

They walked down the center of the pavilion, picking their way through the crowd of customers until they reached the Hall of Elements café where Agnes had first met Christine. They sat at the bar and ordered espressos. Agnes decided that the food vendors also did quite well during the show.

"Was that your first visit to the Institute?" Agnes asked.

Patel relaxed slightly. "Yes, and if the circumstances had been different, I would have been very pleased to see the property. Such a fine facility. Leo is very fortunate boy."

"You come to Switzerland often?"

"Recently, yes. Before, I have been working for my uncle first in manufacturing of electrical components."

"Gemstones are a far cry from electronics."

"My uncle has interests in all business. He sees connections and opportunities everywhere. That is how my uncle teaches us to see life."

Agnes stirred sugar into her espresso, thinking she might not actually drink it. "You must be very proud to work for him."

"My uncle is an innovator, a business genius. It is with his industry that we advance. He carries not only our family, but the future of development in India. We owe him everything."

"Have you always known you would work for him?"

"It was not mandated. Uncle is very generous in that way, but I have worked for him since I was a boy. It was he who sent me to school at the EPFL."

"You shared that with Guy, the importance of a family business."

"It is more than business. We take this very seriously where I come from. It is everything. My uncle is not only my boss. He is someone I would sacrifice my life for."

"That's a bit more than we'd say here."

Patel leaned forward, his face intent. "Friendship is very important—what Guy and I shared—but family is everything in India."

"Did you and Monsieur Chavanon ever consider doing business together?"

Patel didn't answer for a moment. "Is this what Marie said to you?"

"No, but I've been told that the watch industry is poised to explode into China and your country. A partnership between you and Monsieur Chavanon seems logical given your history and friendship and your expansion into gemstones and the connection to watches."

"Guy would have liked to join my uncle's group. He was constantly tossing out ideas that he thought we would buy." Patel smiled sadly. "Guy was a dreamer. Very inventive and very much imagination, but it was not a good fit for my uncle's needs. It is a great trust my uncle has given me, and I must do everything I can to honor it. Family honor and business honor are all that we have." He looked at her carefully. "Have you been to India?"

"Yes, years ago when my father was an invited guest."

"Honor is essential for us. So many people depend on my uncle's work. The people in my mother's village depend on it. Our factories support cousins and aunts and uncles. A great web that depends on our uncle. He is a great man at our center."

"Because of this, you never discussed business with Monsieur Chavanon?"

"We were discussing all the time, but to no mutual gain. It was the discussing of ideas and foolishness." Patel paused. "I would be very uncomfortable if Marie and Christine thought that I had rejected my friend's interest in a partnership."

"They've not mentioned it to me. Could you tell me about that day, when he died. You drove separately?"

Patel looked startled.

"You took Leo home afterwards. And the Fontenays arranged for Monsieur Chavanon's car to be returned to his house later."

"Yes, I see. It was convenient. I have rental car, a very nice Mercedes, and the Institute is halfway between Basel and Guy's home. Once the show started, I would have had no time for a visit."

Agnes glanced around. The café was filled with people having casual conversations that had nothing to do with the sale of watches or jewels; friends greeting one another.

"I wanted to see Leo," Patel amended.

"Did you arrive before Monsieur Chavanon?"

"Our timings were perfect and I arrived immediately after him."

"Did you speak to him earlier in the day?"

Patel hesitated. "Yes, I am remembering that we spoke. Very briefly. I telephoned to firm up the details of my visit."

"You met inside?"

"No, we arrived at parking together. Him in front. Me next."

"Tell me what happened then."

Patel's cheeks sagged in dismay. "We spoke, it was the first time in person since my arrival in Switzerland. We were emotional as we always are upon first greetings. Then we went inside."

"But not together?"

"You are correct. I went inside immediately."

Agnes waited.

Patel filled the silence. "It was very cold, at least for me. I come from a warm climate, and the transition is hard every time, and more now that I am getting older. Guy wanted to take a walk. He pointed me in the direction of the doors and I went in. It was very informal gathering and I did not feel out of place or I would have returned outdoors and found him."

"Monsieur Chavanon suggested you go inside alone?"

"He knew that I was cold and uncomfortable. It was a matter of politeness."

"What do you think he wanted to see so badly that he left you—his recently arrived friend—alone?"

Patel wagged his head side to side. "I am not understanding these questions. Guy had an allergic reaction, and although I administered the EpiPen, he died. The dose was not enough."

"We are all in agreement about the inadequacy of the medicine." Agnes leaned forward. "I'm interested in what happened before. How did he seem to you? In good spirits?"

"Yes, it is as I told Christine. Her father was in very good spirits. He was happy to see Leo."

"Then what kept him outside that day? It must have been important to leave you and to delay seeing his son. Were there others in the parking lot?"

"There were many cars, but no people." Patel sat up straighter. "Maybe I know what Guy wanted to see. Why he went for a walk. There was helicopter landing in the field next to the school. He walked in that direction. Maybe he knew the person. Maybe it was an important customer for him? If that is the case, then he would have preferred to make the greeting alone."

Mentally Agnes collated what other information she had. Petit was in charge of interviewing more of the staff and faculty at the Institute, and he'd called her with an update after she spoke with Mercier. Madame Jomini had also emailed her an annotated list of the names of the guests at the reception.

"Do you recognize the name of Han?" she said. "Monsieur Han arrived by helicopter."

"I do not recall the name. In the short time I was at the reception I had a few words with a very nice woman from England. That is the only person I remember." Patel rubbed his forehead. "I went inside, walking fast to escape from the cold, and then quickly, too quickly after he arrived, Guy was dead. We did not have time to speak again."

Agnes toyed with her spoon to give Patel a moment to compose himself.

"How long do you think Monsieur Chavanon was outside after you left him?"

"This is impossible to know."

"Tell me what you did from the time you left him, to the time you saw him enter the reception. That will help gauge the time."

"I crossed the room, it was already crowded, and asked where to hang my coat. Then I went to the toilet to check my appearance after the drive."

"Maybe five minutes to this point?"

"I could not say. Next I went to the main room. I did not see Guy or Leo, and without knowing anyone else, I stood at the edge of the crowd for a time."

"Until Monsieur Chavanon arrived?"

"No, I had decided to see what food was on offer. A very nice buffet they served, with many veg choices. That is when I was speaking with the very nice English lady. I saw Leo come in and go straight to his father. That is when I noticed Guy had arrived. Unfortunately, before I could join them, I had an important phone call. I left the room for only a few minutes to speak in private, and when I returned . . ." Patel's voice broke. "He was already ill."

A small chocolate was served with the espresso. Agnes unwrapped it and placed it in her mouth, savoring the sweetness after the bitter coffee, thinking that this was one of the pleasures Guy Chavanon, Koulsy Haroun, and Rudolph Versteegh had to forgo. The threat of cross contamination could be life threatening.

Patel leaned close and lowered his voice. "I have worried this last week about Marie. How does my friend's company survive in the current climate? Big industry is the future, and Guy was not prepared for that path. Has she said anything to you?"

Agnes had forgotten how open Indians were to speaking about business. "Christine seems confident that the company will continue in the family's hands."

Patel sat back with a thud. "It is a relief to know that the complaints Guy had were perhaps just that. Complaints and not the indication of serious trouble."

"He'd told you he was struggling?"

"One moment he had big plans and the next he was in despair. You understand that I did not want to be asking him closely about the details. I have the backing of my uncle and we are a large company. We are the future. Guy was a very proud man. It was not polite to show up a friend who might be in trouble."

Agnes looked around the crowded café, one ear attuned to snippets of conversation. It was what she expected. Gossip about friends and colleagues. Complaints about tired feet and long hours. Discontent with pricing. Pleasure at a good deal made. Boredom with a show visited too many years in a row. She wondered what Mercier knew and how it was tied to Gianfranco Giberti. Maybe Chavanon hadn't spoken to Mercier but Giberti had? She was certain they were both lying to her.

"Thanks for your time, Monsieur Patel."

"I hope that you will soon be able to leave this sad topic behind. For the sake of Marie and Leo." They rose. "You have finished with questions at the Institute?"

The image of the blood smeared across the wall of the shed came to mind and Agnes shook her head. "No, I'm afraid not."

They neared his booth.

"If Madame has no further questions for me, I must see to my clients. It is an auspicious day, but they quickly move on to other merchandise if I am not there to supervise the buyings."

Twenty-two

"They're still looking," said Marcel Aubry. A uniformed officer was seated at a monitor to one side of the security booth, scrolling through footage from the day the Roach died.

"Inspector Lüthi, any other hints?" the officer called out, pausing the video. " 'The most beautiful woman in the world' isn't much to go on."

Agnes shook her head, laughing. "When you see her, you'll know who I'm talking about." She turned to Aubry. "I was walking through the crowd in the pavilion when it came to me. I saw her on the footage the other day and I remembered seeing her before, in Tokyo when we nearly caught the Roach three years ago."

"They're pulling up the Tokyo video at the station. When they find her on one or the other, we can do facial recognition."

Agnes studied the bank of monitors. "I remember that she turned and walked away from the camera. Before she moved, there was a man with a dark tie to her left. He wasn't with her, but very near. Perhaps she wanted to give the impression that they were together. He was talking on a mobile phone."

Aubry called over to the officer, "Got that?"

"*Absolument.*"

"You think she's an accomplice," Aubry said.

"I think it's an extraordinary coincidence if she's not connected with the Roach, and if you catch her, you'll have answers."

Agnes was still thinking about the Roach when she arrived at the Perrault et Chavanon booth in the Palace pavilion.

Gisele stepped away from a client to greet her. "She's here, in the back."

Agnes understood who *she* was. Marie Chavanon had returned to work.

"She should have stayed home," Gisele said. "Perhaps you can suggest she leave?"

"Aren't you happy to have the extra help?" The booth was even more crowded than the previous day.

"Not like this. Madame is in a furor. Now there's an *atmosphere* hanging over us."

"Is that an accusation?" a man's voice carried from the small back office. "Two days certainly makes a difference. Is there something else you'd like to ask?"

Gisele turned away, shrugging at Agnes, and fixing a smile on her face before circulating among the clients. Agnes didn't move. A minute passed. She couldn't hear Marie Chavanon's response. Finally, Stephan Dupré emerged from the back room, red faced. He stopped when he saw Agnes.

"She shouldn't be here." He jerked his head toward the back room. "Talk some sense into her."

He hastened toward the exit and Agnes followed.

"If you have a moment?" she said when she caught up to him.

He marched to the nearby café bar and ordered a whiskey. "Make it a double."

Agnes joined him and asked for a glass of tap water. "Tell me more about Guy Chavanon being followed."

Dupré downed his whiskey in a long swallow and set the glass on the counter. "You're not interested in what Marie and I are fighting about?"

"Right now, I'm interested in Guy Chavanon."

Dupré drew in a deep breath; his shoulders rose and fell. He looked away from Agnes. "I've always wondered what people will say when I'm dead. What they'll remember, what they'll exaggerate." He nodded toward his empty glass. "I've a few photographers who've traveled with me into rough places, and they'll probably talk about my ability to hold my liquor. There've been times when we've needed it to get through the work." He motioned to the bartender for a refill. "But you're here to talk about Guy. Even dead, everyone is interested in him." He planted both hands on the counter. Agnes wondered if he was meditating.

"What do you think of him?" Dupré finally said. "You must have a picture in your mind by now."

She took a moment to gather her thoughts. "It's incomplete. I can't decide if he was a complex man or a simple one. His life was clearly rooted in his work, yet from all appearances he was a family man. He seemed to live in a world of invention and dreams, distant from the world of business. He was perhaps volatile. He was a scientist and also had an artistic temperament."

Dupré gave her an appraising look. "You've nailed it. Guy was all those things. He was brilliant and he was a screwup."

"Do you think he invented something important at the end of his life?"

Dupré took a sip of whiskey, savoring it this time. "I don't know."

"Whoever broke into the workshop must have expected to find something. You said he was afraid he was being followed."

"Have you forgotten that I exaggerated?"

"But you didn't invent it. What did he tell you?"

"He talked about a car parked on the street. He saw it too many times, or at an odd time of the day. It stuck in his head and bothered him."

"Did he describe the car?"

"He must have, but I don't remember. I forgot about it."

"But you remembered at the funeral?"

"I had forgotten, but it came back to me. Don't know why. Maybe it was the atmosphere that day. The shock that Guy was dead. We look for answers even when we have them." Dupré rubbed his forehead. "There were days when I was convinced he'd finally done it, invented something meaningful. The other half of the time I knew he hadn't. We'd built him up as a great thinker. An inventor. But what did he ever create? Mechanical toys, small refinements, not the kind of thing we credited him with. Maybe he'd decided to believe his own myth. Maybe Marie's right and he was crazy."

"Did you see signs of mental instability?"

Dupré shook his head. "I don't know. Fixating on a car, maybe that's a sign? Guy was always different. Focused. What's the difference between focused and fixated? Between concern and paranoia?"

"Did Madame Chavanon talk to you about him?"

"I know that she'd given up."

"On Monsieur Chavanon or the company?"

"I thought both. But who knows."

Agnes took another sip of water. The Pavilion was crowded but there were few customers in the café bar. The show had a momentum and now was the time for serious purchasing, not chatting with friends and colleagues. "When was the last time you saw Monsieur Chavanon?"

"The day he died," Dupré said slowly.

"You saw him that day? And you never told anyone? Why?"

"To avoid questions." Dupré clinked his ice absently. "I saw Guy, but I didn't talk to him. I intended to. I was watching for him, hoping to pretend a chance encounter. I wanted to catch him alone and outside. Maybe invite him to my place."

"What happened?"

"Marie was gone for the afternoon. I can see the road from my front porch, and I waited there, bundled up like an old man. Guy drove up and parked near the factory."

"Do you know where'd he been?"

"No, only that he'd been gone a short while. I assumed he'd picked up a newspaper or concluded some other small errand. I could tell he was in a dark mood when he parked. He spun into the lot in a hurry and headed toward the workshop. I started out to intercept him."

Dupré seemed to consider what had happened that day. "Maybe if I had, he wouldn't have died."

"What stopped you?"

"He got halfway to the workshop, then turned around and walked to the factory. I watched, thinking he wouldn't spend much time there; it was a Saturday and he might only be picking up something. He stayed a few minutes, then ran back to his car and roared off."

This matched Ivo's account of Chavanon's arrival and departure.

"What were you going to discuss with your friend that day?"

"It was personal, not anything about what happened later."

"Something about his wife?"

Dupré swallowed and sat up a few inches straighter. "So what if it was?"

"Do you think Monsieur Chavanon would have been surprised?"

The whiskey glass spun on the napkin. The man didn't reply and Agnes thought she had her answer.

Before she could insist, her phone beeped. She glanced at the screen. The message was from Petit: *Blood is human.*

Agnes hoped it was a riddle. But she knew it wasn't. The bloody shed. Dupré's confessions would have to wait.

Twenty-three

Agnes made the familiar trek across the lawn behind the Institute. She slipped through the hedge, and Petit rushed to greet her. Officer Boschung and Bernard Fontenay were behind him, waiting in front of the shed. It wasn't raining, but they looked as despondent as if standing in a downpour. Hamel stood back from the group.

Petit looked uncertain. Hamel annoyed. Fontenay sick with worry. Agnes thought that summed it up for her.

"The other samples were animal?" Agnes directed her question to Petit, who'd filled her in on the telephone. "Only the two taken from the back wall were human blood?" She'd counted on the tests proving the blood was from an animal; this was bad news.

Fontenay gave a grunt and stepped away. "How could this happen here?"

"Let's take a breath before we panic half the *canton*," said

Agnes. "This could too easily escalate, and none of us want that."

She could tell from Boschung's expression that he agreed with her or, at a minimum, hoped she was right. She remembered what Petit had said, the blame would rest with them . . . with her. "Are you going to take new samples?" she asked. "You know there's a chance of a false positive."

Hamel stepped forward. "It's too late."

"We can test blood for years," she said. "Really for as long as it exists."

The groundskeeper motioned toward the interior of the shed, handing her a flashlight and pushing the heavy door open. Agnes didn't need the powerful beam to understand the problem. The back wall of the shed had been washed. It wasn't precisely clean, but the blood was gone, leaving streaks where the wood had been wetted. The dark substance on the stump had been thinned, and the floor around it was muddy.

"No one thought to mention this first?" She sniffed. "Water with detergent of some sort. Something strong. Wasn't the door padlocked? How did they get in?" She saw the answer to her question before Hamel pointed. A small panel near the base of the side wall had been pushed away. Perhaps at one time a door for chickens. It didn't matter now. Someone had gained access to the room and interfered with their evidence.

"That corner was covered by a stack of boards," said Hamel. "Someone shoved in and pushed them away."

"We'll never know who did this," said Fontenay.

"It must be whoever splattered the blood in the first place," said Agnes. "This means they came back. That indicates it's not someone passing through. I can't imagine a hardened criminal returning. It's amateurish, yet another reason to think it is someone here, at the school or in the village. Possibly someone young."

Boschung and Fontenay both objected. She silenced them. "Don't deny that there can be tensions between the two. It's not unusual."

She pulled out her phone and scrolled through the images from the previous night. "Look at the back wall. The blood was smeared in places like someone dragged their hand across the planks. The wood is rough and there are small nails. Even a couple of large ones. What if whoever did this cut themselves and left some blood? A good smear? That could have contaminated the samples. The residue on the floor and on the stump tested negative, correct?"

Boschung nodded. "I took five samples on the back wall, only two were human. I'd have to look at my documents to see where those two were. Might have been near a nail."

Fontenay sagged. "To think that one of our boys would do something like this. And cause so much trouble."

"I didn't say it was one of your boys," said Agnes.

"That opening is small," said Hamel.

It was. Too small for a full-grown man to crawl through. Agnes thought about her sons. They were well behaved, but she knew that they could be convinced to do stupid things. She only hoped that the trouble remained fixable until they were older and could exercise resistance to peer pressure.

"Let's keep an open mind. It might not be one of the students," she said. "A small man or woman could fit through. I think I could fit, if I didn't mind scraping my shoulders."

All four studied the opening, imagining lying on the ground and crawling through.

"You haven't heard anything in the village?" she asked Boschung.

"No, and we've started questioning the likely suspects. Low-key, like you suggested."

"Ask them again," said Fontenay. "It's too easy to point fingers here. The village children have as much access to this plot of land as anyone. Maybe more, since we keep an eye on our students. I can't say that about every child in town."

"I'm not denying it could be someone from the village," said Boschung, "but no one's talking about coming up here, and you know people. They like to talk. I'll grant you there can be meanness, call it jealousy, but I don't see a point in going to the trouble of making a statement like this one if no one sees it."

"I'll lay odds that someone did this to scare or impress their friends," said Agnes. "Maybe on a dare, maybe to get someone in trouble. Maybe we stumbled upon it before they were ready for a big reveal. After all, it was only Monsieur Hamel's careful attention to the property that brought it to our notice. Possibly they learned the police were investigating and realized they had created more trouble than they intended. They tried to clean it up to destroy the evidence. Boschung is right, people who take the trouble to make a statement want it acknowledged. They don't wash it away."

"You still might be wrong," said Boschung. "Something bad may have happened here."

"Keep asking questions and get to the bottom of it." Agnes turned up the collar of her coat, looking in the direction of the chalet, thinking. "Monsieur Fontenay, alone of all the boys, Leo Chavanon has an alibi because of the timing of his return to school. I'd like to speak with him."

"He went off campus for Sunday lunch," Fontenay said.

"I'll wait."

Boschung opened the flap of his satchel. "I'll see if I can find a spot that's not been treated with solvent and try for another sample."

Agnes left the men to coordinate their next steps and walked alone to the chalet. There, she headed downstairs. Chef Jean and his assistant were too intent on their work to notice her. For a moment, she imagined how easy it would be to step into the kitchen and scatter peanut dust on the tray of cooling butter cookies. Or drop ground peanuts into the enormous floor mixer while it pounded flour and eggs into pasta dough.

She slipped away, heading to the farthest corner of the basement. When she found the correct door, she reached inside for a light switch. The room was neatly organized: wooden easels, toboggans, a bin full of soccer balls, a stack of tennis rackets. What interested her was the back wall. It was filled with bows and arrows. The bows hung neatly on wall brackets. The arrows were stored point down in narrow tubes with leather handles, the feather fletchings exposed. There were dozens of arrows, and no one would notice if one was missing. Anyone could access this room unseen.

"Have you found what you're looking for?" Helene Fontenay said, startling her. The floor was coated with vinyl, an effective silence of the headmistress's crutches.

"Monsieur Hamel told me I would find the school's sporting equipment here."

"Looking for the arrow shot into the wall outside Leo and Koulsy's room?" Helene moved toward the nearest tube. "It was one of these."

"Meaning one of the school's?" Agnes studied the ten or twelve arrows slotted into the tube.

"It's the same type." Helene shrugged. "I was hardly going to waste time finding the owner. Or is that stealing?"

"No. Only I'm surprised you weren't more concerned about it."

"After seeing how easily someone could take an arrow from here? You know boys. They take things they shouldn't and mess around recklessly. What happens when one misfires? Do you think they're going to tell us? No one was hurt; there wasn't a reason to make an issue of it."

"I suppose not." Agnes lifted an arrow. It was impossible to tell precisely which one had ended up in the wall of the chalet, and it didn't matter. They were all the same style and type. She frowned. They looked exactly like the ones she'd seen at shooting ranges her entire life. Basic and generic. It might belong to someone in the village. "You're very calm in the face of trouble. Monsieur Chavanon's death—"

"I still believe it was an accident and has nothing to do with us."

"Koulsy's fears aren't based on accidents."

"Childhood trouble. We'll deal with it."

"Not everything is innocent trouble, Madame. His is a well-known name. People have strong feelings about his father. Maybe they think the death of a boy—as a message, a warning, revenge— is nothing compared to the thousands dead under the father's rule. Villagers talk, they know who's here."

"They have time for gossip, I suppose."

Agnes replaced the arrow in the tube. "Even Officer Boschung admitted that there can be jealousy between the locals and an enclave of foreigners, and Koulsy's father is an international figure."

Helene's fingers whitened on the grips of her crutches. "You think I'm not troubled? I have too many troubles to enumerate. I don't have the luxury of worrying about children's pranks. Or even those of the village. Everything here is my worry. The food on the table, the wages, the maintenance. Don't pretend that staff do everything without being reminded. And the teachers? Everyone has their own opinion, without a thought to rules and regulations. Then there's my husband. Where was he when Monsieur Chavanon died?"

"What do you suspect?"

The mask fell across Helene Fontenay's face. "There is nothing you can help us with. I'm simply tired."

She turned and left, and Agnes didn't try to stop her. Instead she took her time, glancing in again to the kitchen and exchanging pleasantries with the chef before walking past the dining room on her way upstairs. The sound of voices caught her attention. Tommy Scaglia was apologizing.

"I didn't mean anything—"

Accented French cut him off. Narendra Patel. "What were you doing watching me? Lurking in the corner like a thief."

"I was waiting for you to finish. I thought you were praying."

Agnes watched from the doorway. Scaglia was red faced. He saw her and took the opportunity to run out of the room. Patel was only a few steps behind him, muttering that he had dropped off a gift and needed to return to Baselworld. She briefly wondered what Tommy was up to now.

Looking across the tables and chairs, she imagined what Patel must feel. The suddenness of Chavanon's death. The finality.

She felt that places—rooms—could communicate an atmosphere. To her the dining room was full of optimism and hope. It was youthful. She suspected it felt very different to Guy Chavanon's family and friends. To them, it was a place of loss and despair.

She climbed the stairs to the third floor and found Tommy Scaglia in the corridor. He was standing in the middle of the hall.

"I expect you startled Monsieur Patel," she said when Scaglia spotted her.

"Yeah, I did. The visitors don't usually yell at us."

She laughed. "No, I suspect they don't. I wouldn't take it personally. Monsieur Patel lost his boyhood friend in that room. I think he feels guilty that he wasn't able to save him."

Scaglia shoved his hands in the pockets of his uniform, looking very much as Agnes imagined a nineteenth-century clerk would, minus the ink-stained hands.

"I came up for a book," Tommy said absently, apparently still bothered by Patel's words. To distract him, Agnes asked what he liked about the school. It turned out that outside his concerns for Koulsy, Tommy liked quite a lot. The quaint village, the snow in winter, the cat he'd made friends with and named Taylor. "After my best friend at home," he said.

"Glad to hear you've settled in to life in Switzerland," Agnes said when he paused for breath. "And don't worry about Koulsy. We'll find out what's going on. The police have all sorts of ways to uncover evidence. Do you watch American police shows?"

His face sank. "Yeah, I do."

Earlier, Agnes had asked Bernard Fontenay if she could look into the dorm rooms and he'd said they weren't locked. She knocked on the door to the room Koulsy Haroun shared with Leo Chavanon. It hadn't been properly closed and swung open. She walked in, amused to see a Rolling Stones poster on one wall. Some things never changed.

The room was large enough to accommodate a twin bed, clothes cupboard, and desk for each boy. The desks were pushed against the wall opposite the door, fitting in under the window-sills. To one side of the windows a narrow door led to the balcony. The room was neat, and Agnes imagined the strict rules in place to bring order to the natural inclination of the boys who lived here. A gift-wrapped box was on Leo Chavanon's bed. She read the tag. It was from Patel.

A narrow door led from each bedroom to the balcony, and she stepped outside to look for the hole made by the arrow. It was easy to find, a deep chink straight into the wood. Tommy was right. A half inch over and it would have struck glass or passed through an open window.

She returned inside and surveyed Koulsy's belongings. A slew of swimming medals hung from a hook. Otherwise his side of the room was bare to the point of austerity.

Leo's side was cluttered. There were family photographs and a row of odd-shaped boxes scattered on a low shelf. She picked up the largest one, weighing it in her hand. Maybe large enough to hold a pack of cards? The smallest was the size of a man's thumb. Setting them aside, Agnes ran her eye down the row of books on the short shelf: volumes on math, science, and history. Tucked in among them was an old book on astronomy. She pulled it out. The title was long, but the essence was that it contained an explanation into the construction and use of astrolabes. Inside were photographs of various astronomical and astrological devices including the astronomical observatories in Jaipur and Delhi. She flipped to the handwritten inscription: *For my son. Love, Father.*

No date. No names. From Guy to Leo? Christine had mentioned that her father dreamt of building a replica of the Jantar Mantar observatory in Jaipur. This was a book he would share with his son. The book next to it was titled *A Treatise on Codes and Puzzles.* There was a lengthy subtitle, and Agnes glanced at the date of publication: 1887. This book was signed in the same hand but a date had been added. A recent date.

Her phone buzzed in her pocket—a message delayed by poor reception—and she listened to Aubry's update while skimming the pages of the book, admiring the old-fashioned diagrams and illustrations. Nowadays people encrypted their secrets. The earlier need to build a hiding place had a certain beauty. She closed her eyes and pictured Guy Chavanon's workshop. Had they missed his hiding place?

Twenty-four

"What are you doing here?" a man's voice asked.

Agnes turned to find Julien Vallotton lounging against the doorframe of the dorm room.

He walked in and sat on Leo's bed, bouncing as if checking the springs. "More comfortable than when I was at school."

"I was waiting to speak with Leo."

"We had a long lunch. I thought he needed an afternoon away. I know what it's like to lose a parent at a young age." He picked up the wrapped box and gave it a little shake.

Agnes took it and set it aside. "Did Leo come back with you?"

"Yes, and Bernard said you wanted to talk to him. That's why I came up. Leo's waiting in the office."

Agnes liked the way the boy spoke. His voice was still sweet, his cadence soothing. Leo Chavanon liked school, liked living on the campus, and it made her happy to hear this, given the tough week he'd had.

They were seated in the headmaster's office, and Agnes was surprised by the boy's ease. He had chosen a bentwood chair, and she took its twin. Petit had joined her for the interview. He selected a more comfortable armchair, stretching his long legs in front of him.

"Leo, you've only been back a few nights and I—" She nodded toward Petit. "We know you've a lot to catch up on, but we need your help. This is important."

The relaxed pose vanished. Leo sat up straight, fingers clutching the sides of the chair.

Agnes smiled to allay his fears. Unwilling to share details that might end up feeding the chain of rumors, she described the shed in vague terms. Vandalism was how she summed it up.

"Leo," she continued, "the Fontenays don't want to punish anyone. They're simply worried. When property is damaged, it often means the person—the vandal—is hiding their own trouble. They want attention because they don't know how to fix what's bothering them."

"The cow shed?" Leo asked, as if she'd suggested a Mars space station. "The other side of the hedge?"

Agnes nodded.

"That's awful far away. We're not supposed to go on the other side of the hedge."

Petit snickered softly.

"I have a son about your age," Agnes said, "and he's always in fields he shouldn't be in. We're not angry about that."

"There's got to be somewhere off campus that you go?" said

Petit. "Somewhere you can have a little fun? Get away from all of them." He jerked his head toward the closed door.

Leo swallowed.

"Somewhere in the forest maybe? That's where I went when I was in school." Petit looked at Agnes. "We built a tree house with a secret rope ladder. No one knew about it. A true hideout."

"No," said Leo. "There are wild boars in the forest. A few years back a boy from the village was attacked, and no one goes there now."

Agnes and Petit let Leo wrestle with this conscience. He bounced up and down in his seat uncomfortably. Then he went still. "There's a place in one of the fields near an old watering trough. You can't see it from the chalet. It's near the forest, but not in it, and we used to go there. There's a kind of structure built into the side of a dip in the hill."

"You use it as a sort of club?" said Agnes.

"No, just a place to go. The older kids walk into town on their free afternoons. We can't. Not until we're fourteen." Leo shrugged. "Besides, it's a long way to walk and there's not much to do. There's a café. Sometimes they buy stuff at the store, but we're not allowed to keep food in our rooms so it's mainly a place to go."

"What about the other boys, those younger than your year? Or maybe some in your year who wanted their own private place to meet? Do you think they might have used the shed?"

"I don't know. Monsieur Fontenay gets really angry when we wander into the fields."

Petit scoffed. "My mom got angry about nearly everything I did when I was your age. Didn't stop me doing it."

"The place you mentioned, near the old watering trough, is that off-limits?" Agnes asked.

Leo nodded.

"Meaning it's possible that some of your classmates might have gone to the other side of the hedge?" said Agnes.

"Why don't you ask Tommy?" Leo's face brightened.

"You think he goes there?" Agnes wasn't surprised. Tommy Scaglia struck her as a child who balanced ideal behavior with recklessness.

"No, but he knows everything. Knows who's going to get in trouble. Whose rooms are going to be searched for contraband." Leo shrugged.

"That's a gift, to know everything that's going to happen," said Agnes.

"He tells people. Warns them." Leo flushed. "I shouldn't have said that. There's nothing wrong with what he tells us."

"Is it a certain circle of friends he helps?" she asked. "Is Koulsy Haroun one of the circle?"

"No, it depends on what he finds out. He wants to help."

Tommy Scaglia the Good Samaritan didn't sit easily with Agnes. "Do people pay him for the information?"

"Pay him? He's got more pocket money than all the rest of us."

Thinking this over, Agnes walked to the window behind the Fontenays' desk. There were three windows in the room with nice views onto the lawns, but this one was heavily curtained. She started to flick the drapes open.

Leo coughed. "I wouldn't do that."

"Why not?"

"Madame Fontenay doesn't like things touched. Not in here. And she never opens those curtains."

"Fair enough, I don't like things in my office touched either." She crossed to sit by Leo again. "All of Tommy's money is from his allowance?"

"Where else would he get it?"

Agnes and Petit shared a look. Blackmail? Money to keep small secrets safe? Agnes didn't believe Leo was misleading them. He simply might not know.

"I'm sorry about your father," Agnes continued. "My boys lost their father a few months ago. It is a difficult time. Loss is hard."

Leo nodded again. She could tell that he didn't fully comprehend the reality of his father's death yet. The idea of permanence was abstract and difficult to absorb, and being here, in a place where he wouldn't see his father daily, probably helped keep grief at bay.

"Monsieur Patel delivered a gift for you. It's good you have adults to rely on. You know that, don't you? Your father's friends will be there for you."

"Yeah, Monsieur Patel's cool. He brings these packages of hot snacks when he comes to our house. Hot *spicy*, not hot *hot*. My mom hates them. Made me eat them outside. Said we couldn't be sure they were safe for Dad even though he took some to a lab one time and they said no peanuts, but Mom said she wouldn't trust that every time, since it came from India."

"If you think about something, something one of the boys tells you or you overhear, if that happens and you want to talk it over with someone you know, perhaps Monsieur Patel would listen? Or Monsieur Vallotton?"

"Sure, but I don't know anything."

"Just in case." Agnes had the feeling that this was a long shot. A truly long shot.

She thanked Leo and escorted him from the office. Just inside the door she noticed the tabby sitting quietly, licking its paws. Taylor, she remembered. Tommy had named the cat Taylor.

Twenty-five

Petit still had a long list of faculty and staff to interview, and Agnes sent him back to the task and asked Vallotton to join her. Madame Fontenay showed them into a large dark room that she called the boardroom. Agnes would have preferred to remain in the headmaster's office. This room was stuffy. The wood-paneled walls were filled with portraits of long-dead academicians, and the velvet sofas and chairs were upholstered in dark red, reminding Agnes of dried blood. She suspected the décor had been chosen in a century long past. It didn't look like anything the very modern Fontenays would care for.

"Do you know Koulsy?" she asked Vallotton. She was seated on a sofa, sinking uncomfortably into the cushions. Vallotton crossed to study a portrait above the mantel.

"Of course I do. He's Leo's roommate. And when he applied, there was a long debate about whether or not to admit him. There's always the risk of bad publicity with a family like his. Guilt by association you might say. I cast the deciding vote. The child deserves a chance."

Agnes stuffed a needlepoint pillow behind her back in an attempt to sit upright. "Koulsy thinks he's at risk of being kidnapped. That's why I wanted to speak with him."

"Leaving Officer Petit to conduct the real interviews." Vallotton gave her an incredulous glance. "You can't believe Haroun. When I was at school, there was a fellow in my year who constantly made up stories of death-defying acts, threats, call it what you will. He sounded like James Bond every time we had a school holiday. Essentially trying to impress the rest of us."

"Were you? Impressed?"

"Absolutely." Vallotton flashed her a grin. "Gave him all my spare chocolate in case he only had a few more days of freedom. Really was a great extortion scheme now that I think about it."

She fidgeted with the cushions again; trying to find a comfortable and dignified position. So far it was a choice between her feet touching the floor or her skirt not hitching up. Vallotton stepped near a particularly dark and somber portrait and peered at it. Agnes detected a resemblance between the two men around the eyes. Perhaps this was the founding ancestor? Vallotton turned as if comparing his profile to the man in the painting.

"You can't think this threat to Koulsy is real," he said.

"He has a peanut allergy. Which makes him a definite link to Chavanon's death. And Koulsy's fears may be legitimate. I'm trying to get to the truth of what happened."

"I thought you'd be the first to say that there is no truth in anything, only perception."

"We stay away from philosophy in the police, or at least

we did in Financial Crimes." She pulled out her notebook and glanced through it. "You're right though, truth is not an absolute. Anyway, I'm afraid there might be something to the things happening around him. The arrow in the wall by his bedroom—"

"Which is also Leo's bedroom."

"Yes. And the amateur display of blood in the shed."

"Amateur? Don't let Boschung hear you say that."

"He's driven by perception. He has a firm sense of what is right and wrong, and what he sees fits into those slots. Perhaps unchangeably. Man dead from an allergy was a natural death. Vandalized shed in his perfect village must be violent outsiders. We'll see what comes of it."

"Your gut reactions are better than his?"

"Don't mock my instincts. They've served me well."

"They've never failed you?" He looked up sharply and she felt him regret his words. Idly spoken, they touched upon a truth. He knew that her instincts had failed her, one fatal time. He didn't know the entire story, but even part was enough.

She shook her head and smiled at him. Surprised by her own equanimity. "It's possible that you're bored and falling back on old school habits. Stirring up police interest for an afternoon's entertainment."

"Asking the students to invent threats?" Vallotton had a paperweight in his hand, a bronze cube. It had enough heft to make a good weapon. He placed it carefully on the table.

Footsteps sounded outside the door, followed by a hushed verbal exchange. Agnes stood, frustrated with the sagging cushions.

Koulsy entered alone, although Madame Fontenay made eye contact with Vallotton before shutting the door, and the clatter of metal on wood indicated the headmistress remained nearby in case the boy needed her. Without wasting any time, Agnes introduced herself. Vallotton extended a hand in greeting.

Koulsy was a handsome boy of nearly fourteen and he didn't appear nervous. His features were subtly shifting to manhood, and he had no baby fat or softness. His skin was dark ebony, and light shone where it struck his high cheekbones. He was tall with broad shoulders, and he had an aura, a combination of stillness and energy that felt like an adult's awareness. Agnes thought he was one of the most handsome youths she'd seen.

"Would you like something to eat?" She gestured to a small tray. "We have a nice selection of chocolate biscuits."

The boy looked as startled as if she'd offered him a cigarette, and she moved the tray to the side and asked him to be seated. She selected a chair opposite him and Vallotton chose one to their side, slightly back from them, as if to clarify his role as an observer.

Koulsy spoke without waiting. "They are trying to take me."

Agnes was startled by his forthrightness. "The *they* who are trying to take you. Do you know who they are?"

Koulsy lifted his shoulders fractionally. "It is difficult to know who is angry at any one time. My father has many enemies, and they will see his son as a means to an end."

Agnes hit upon what troubled her. His words sounded formulaic, as if he'd heard them somewhere and was repeating what others had said. Out of the corner of her eye Agnes saw Vallotton shake his head in disbelief. She ignored him.

Koulsy laced his fingers together and closed his eyes, as if thinking. "They issue threats. The usual things." Again, the slight shrug.

Vallotton shifted in his chair and Koulsy turned to him. Agnes didn't know how Vallotton did it; transitioning from invisible to the dominant force in a room without even speaking. "Were there warnings first?" Vallotton asked.

Koulsy shook his head slowly. "You have experience of this, Monsieur?"

"Family is a blessing and a burden. They test our loyalty, don't they? Especially our fathers."

"You understand," said Koulsy.

"I think I do, actually."

"Was it like this for you, with your father, finding the things that make you grow fearful, but that you cannot speak of?"

"No, my loyalty was tested in other ways, by other people. But that doesn't matter. A test is a test," said Vallotton.

The boy moved closer to Vallotton, so that their knees were nearly touching. Agnes looked at the two, boy and man. Both sons of powerful men. Men who made their mark on their respective countries, albeit in opposite ways.

"What happened is no longer a test," said Koulsy.

"How long ago did the threats start?" Agnes asked.

"I don't remember."

"Why didn't you report it right away?" she asked. The boy didn't respond and she was reminded of Guy Chavanon's not reporting his fear of being followed. She knew that no one in Switzerland liked to cause trouble, but the level of reticence was starting to annoy her.

"You've always lived with threats, haven't you? They"— Vallotton nodded toward Agnes—"they don't understand what it's like."

"Who would believe me that a twist of paper or a burned

stick is a threat? No one here understands the superstitions that exist where I am from."

"Are you afraid of the superstitions or of the reality?" asked Vallotton.

"Is there a difference?" said Koulsy.

Vallotton reflected for a moment. "No, I suppose there isn't. Not really."

"Yet you decided to tell Madame Fontenay about your concerns. What changed?" Agnes asked.

"I found this." Koulsy extended his hand and Agnes took the scrap of thick paper, careful not to touch more than the edge. It appeared to be torn from a sack. The message was scrawled in pencil, and she could barely read the crudely formed words. Was it the scribble of someone ill-used to writing, someone barely literate? Perhaps it was the age-old technique of writing wrong handed to disguise the identity of the author.

"I now think that when Leo's father died, they meant for it to be me. Two days later I was nearly killed when an arrow lodged beside my open window. With this note, I understand. This note is my father's name in our dialect. The rest you can read. It says that he will have to pay to see his son again."

Agnes studied the words, finally discerning the meaning. She turned the paper over. On the back was a palm print made with a deep reddish-black pigment. The color evoked blood. Was it blood? Possibly from the shed?

"May we keep this?" she asked.

"Of course."

Agnes believed that most children feared the threat of a stranger taking them. Being snatched away. But kidnapping of the sort Koulsy feared was different. It was not random or happenstance. It was planned and plotted. Emotionally, there was a fundamental difference. She couldn't tell if this strange boy fully understood what he was implying. She felt a jolt of concern. Was the shed a ritual he would understand? Perhaps one performed before a kidnapping, or worse?

"Where did you find the note?" Agnes asked.

"On the front of my locker."

"The locker in your room?"

"No, at the pool house. It was stuck under the vent on the front of my locker, the little slices bend in and there's room—"

"Yes, I know what a vent is. We'll walk over and see it together, but before we do that, is there a reason you think these threats are being made? At this time, I mean. The death of Leo's father was certainly stressful for everyone at the school, and perhaps that has something to do with it?"

Koulsy sat up straighter. "The Institute has nothing to do with my family. These are threats from the outside. People who do not understand the good work of my father. He is the only one who can keep our country together, and that is the cause of much jealousy."

This did sound like rhetoric, and Agnes wondered where it came from. She exchanged a glance with Vallotton.

"Have you spoken with your father recently or seen him?" she asked.

"My father travels among the people of our country tirelessly. It would not do for me to bother him. That is why I am at school here."

Evil travels across borders, Agnes thought. She kept her pen on her notebook for a moment after the boy stopped speaking. Then she looked at him. His gaze was completely open and honest. So full of trust that she was taken aback. "When was the last time you were home?"

"The Christmas break."

"You're well settled here, though?" Vallotton said. "I remember when you first arrived, about two years ago. I presented the writing prize your first term."

"*Oui,* monsieur, I remember. And I have been content. My first school was in England. A very nice place." He stopped. "But this is even nicer. This is a good change for me."

"Did you have any trouble of this sort while you were at your previous school?" Vallotton asked.

"*Non,* monsieur. But I am older now and it is more acceptable to lay the problems at my feet. When I was young, it would not have been so."

He was thirteen, Agnes remembered. Possibly the symbolic age of manhood in his native country. The practice of early adulthood was certainly discounted by modernizing leaders. However, from what she knew of the elder Haroun, his idea of modernizing was to keep to the old ways, especially if that meant leaving him in charge. Haroun controlled roaming armies, food supplies, roads. Everything that mattered.

"England and Switzerland are both far from home," she said.

"My father keeps me informed so that I may return after completing my education and help him."

"You plan to return?" The words were out quickly; she hoped he didn't hear her surprise. To return to a war-torn country would be difficult after becoming an adult in the land of calm perfection.

"My mother would like me to stay in Switzerland. However, a man must follow his father."

"You have many years to go before deciding," said Agnes, thinking that there were many years yet for his mother's wiser counsel to take hold.

"Oh, yes, my father expects me to go to Harvard in America. Business school is his dream for me."

Since Harvard likely didn't offer courses in arms trafficking or rape and pillage, Agnes thought that business school was as close as he would come to finding something to help with the elder Haroun's work.

Vallotton sat back in his chair, relaxed again yet alert. "You really think these threats are from someone outside the school who wants to attack your father through you?"

"Monsieur, why would someone here do this to me? Threaten me for entertainment?"

"I don't want to downplay your concerns," said Agnes, "but it's possible that they are pranks. I have sons and I know the kinds of things boys will do. Not always good things."

"A prank would be a chocolate bar in my bed at night or putting my hand in warm water so I have an accident. That is what occurs here. This comes from outside." Koulsy hesitated. "Do you know what it is to have someone die because of you? Because of who you are? I know this emotion. Now, others, my friends here, might be in danger because of me, and that is why I went to Madame Fontenay. After Monsieur Chavanon died, with what followed this week I must acknowledge the connection."

"Koulsy, you aren't responsible for Monsieur Chavanon's death," said Agnes.

"From a poison that should have killed me. Poisoners can be devious. In my father's village they know how to make a thousand different poisons. All from plants. And so many ways to administer them. Secret ways. Ways that you will never discover."

Vallotton stood and walked to the window. Agnes wondered if he could see the poison garden from where he stood. This conversation would certainly make Jorge Navarro nervous.

They were interrupted by a knock on the door, and she called for the person to enter. The door flung open and Tommy Scaglia stepped in. He caught sight of Koulsy and grinned at him before turning to the adults.

"Chef Jean wonders if you'll stay for dinner. He could serve you in the lounge off the dining room downstairs. You wouldn't have to eat with the rest of us."

Agnes rose. "No need for that trouble, Tommy. We're finished here. Koulsy, if you'll get your coat, we'll go to the pool house now."

Koulsy rose and with a few long strides crossed the room. At the door, he gave a backward glance to Tommy, then left.

When Koulsy was out of sight, Tommy sighed elaborately. "I'm the one who made him talk to Madame Fontenay. My dad told me to look out for him. He's not quite tuned in to reality like the rest of us."

"You mean he's not bright?" Vallotton said.

Agnes thought that Koulsy had an unusual speech pattern, but if you listened, most people had distinctive habits; his were simply more than usually interesting.

"Smartest kid in my year, probably in the whole school. Speaks like five languages, can quote Shakespeare. Course that's because he was in England for a couple years. No, the problem is that his dad tells him all the things he sees on the news are made up. Did you see the movie *Lord of War*? I saw it last

Christmas on cable and Nick Cage was amazing. Have you met Cage?"

"No, I've not even been to Hollywood," said Vallotton. "Although the inspector probably has, her parents are American." He darted a quick look at Agnes.

"I've not met the actor either. It's a big country." She wanted to add, *And I was born in Lausanne.*

Tommy frowned as if truly dismayed. "That movie, that's Koulsy's world. It's sick when you think about it, and his dad tells him that what he's seen isn't the truth. And he's seen some stuff, let me tell you. No wonder his parents sent him to a place this isolated. Now, my dad tells me that everything I see on the news about him is true, and that there's worse stuff that they haven't found out about." Tommy laughed and eyed them when they didn't join in. "That's the reason Koulsy is here and not in England; the reality of what's going on in his country and how he needs my dad . . . well, me . . . to keep an eye on him. I mean his dad's a warlord. He needs a friend he can trust."

"Your fathers are close?" Agnes asked.

"Oh, yeah." Tommy crossed his fingers. "Like this. My dad knows how to protect people."

Agnes shifted so she couldn't see Vallotton over Tommy's shoulder. Julien's eyebrow was arched at an angle that nearly made her laugh out loud. "What exactly is their relationship?"

"You don't know my dad? Martin Scaglia, attorney-at-law? Criminal defense. Best in the business."

Agnes almost expected Tommy to pull out a business card and hand it to her. She also doubted General Haroun had much need for an attorney. He was unlikely to even nod to the law, much less fight it. Automatic weapons were more his style.

"Your father is Monsieur Haroun's attorney?"

"Yeah, and it's going to be a career achievement for him. Defending someone in front of the UN tribunal for High Crimes."

"Has Monsieur Haroun been charged by the International Criminal Court?" Vallotton asked.

"Not yet, but he will be."

Agnes wondered what the elder Scaglia's real connection was to Haroun. Probably something his son shouldn't know about.

"Let's get back to Koulsy," she said. "If you convinced him to talk to Madame Fontenay, what do you know about the threats against him?"

"I've seen the other notes and the arrow. That was scary. Could have killed him. Could have killed me."

"You saw it hit?" Agnes asked.

"Yeah. Well, I didn't see it. It was dark out, but I heard the thunk. We ran out to the balcony. and, wow, it was dug in right beside the window frame." He held his thumb and index finger out, slightly apart. "This close to coming inside."

"Who do you think is threatening Koulsy?" she asked.

"There's just so many bad people out there, it's hard to say." Tommy crossed his arms and pondered. "Really all people are bad, just give them the right reason to take action. Find the thing that undermines their world. It's not often you find a ready-made monster. Something creates it."

Agnes suspected this speech was poached from Scaglia senior to get a reduced sentence for a client, although she couldn't dispute the reasoning. "One more question. Earlier you said that at the reception Monsieur Chavanon looked better, and then everyone started screaming. What did you mean by that? Had you noticed him falling ill?"

"I saw him from upstairs, before I came down to the dining room. He was walking back from the classroom building and he looked like my dad sometimes. All red faced. When I saw him at the reception, he looked better. Until that whole attack thing. I mean, it was like something out of a movie, his body flinging around—"

"I understand," she interrupted. "Was someone outside with him?"

Tommy didn't answer right away. "No, he was alone."

Agnes could see the wheels churning in his head and decided that if he knew more, he would be eager to talk about it. She suspected he wouldn't hesitate to make up details to please her if encouraged.

"Thank you," she said. "If you could tell Koulsy we'll find him in the student lounge in a few minutes, I'd appreciate it."

"Sure thing. And let me know how I can help. We want Koulsy safe, and it's looking harder and harder to keep him that way."

Twenty-six

When Tommy Scaglia left the boardroom, it drained of life and energy. Even the portraits of the dusty old men seemed to darken. Agnes looked around for another lamp to turn on, but there wasn't one. Julien Vallotton shook his head and she held up a hand to stop him from speaking.

"He's young."

"He's American, is what you don't want me to say," said Vallotton. "His view of life is like a bad television program."

"The thousand poisons of the village? I don't believe in the myth of a secret deadly poison, but whatever is smeared on the back of his note looks suspiciously like blood, and to me right now that means the shed. I can't overlook the possibility that someone means to harm Koulsy."

She stood and walked around the room. Her leg hurt suddenly. The onset was always a surprise despite its regularity. "I visited Monsieur Navarro's garden yesterday."

"Do you think that's why Koulsy is thinking of poison? Navarro modeled the garden after the one at Alnwick in England."

"An odd hobby. I wonder what Guy Chavanon was doing outside the day of the reception? Why was he wandering around?"

"Parents like to take a tour. They like to know that their tuition is providing a perfect setting. Are you okay? You're limping."

She stopped pacing. "Sitting too long."

"I'm glad I stayed today. Hearing Koulsy takes me back to my own school years. What tales we must have told. My brother in particular."

"You were convincing. You don't believe Koulsy's concerns?"

"If Koulsy's correct and Chavanon died because of a poisoned dart, then I'll give you the land the school sits on."

The door opened and Bernard Fontenay strode into the room, looking as fresh as if it were the morning after a good night's sleep. "What's this, Vallotton, giving away our land?"

"The inspector has . . . No matter. We're going out to the pool. Is it locked?"

"Is Koulsy showing you where his note was tacked? Helene told me about that. He has a key to the pool house, so he can let you in." Fontenay stopped short. "Should I have confiscated the note? I thought it was boys being boys. Did much worse when I was a student."

Agnes was starting to feel some sympathy for Helene Fontenay. Bernard likely encouraged the boys' antics with his breezy manner.

"Vallotton, if you aren't needed, I have a question about fees next year and the school trip. Thinking about expanding. We need to get the kids out and about. More than Paris and London. Maybe a week in Hong Kong?"

Walking to the pool with Koulsy, Agnes was reminded of her oldest son. When seen from the back, Vincent was tall enough to look like a young man. Koulsy was even taller and she had to walk briskly to match his long strides. He didn't speak, but that didn't trouble her. Her boys vied between chatter and silence with little room in between for normal conversation. She wanted Koulsy to feel comfortable. They could talk about the note at the pool.

Up close, the building was as attractive as the other facilities on the campus. Although large, it seemed to grow organically from the land around it. Agnes didn't pretend to be an expert on architecture, but her eye told her this was well designed. Traditional wood was used in a way that felt modern. The doors were steel plates coated in something to give them a high gloss. Koulsy unlocked the door and pushed it open with a welcoming gesture.

Inside, the quality and size of the facility reinforced Agnes's ideas about the advantages of an elite education. The remains of daylight filtered in through the rows of skylights. Underwater lighting illuminated the pool. She felt Koulsy relax, and she started down the length of the pool deck to give him time to collect himself.

"Do you think they broke in through the drains?" Koulsy's voice echoed across the water. The strange blue glow from the underwater lights reflected up and onto his face. "When I was a tiny boy, my father had the drains screwed down on our property; he was afraid of vandals coming in from underground."

"No. No fear of things coming up the drains here. I was simply admiring the tilework." She pulled her notebook from her handbag. "When you found the note, you were the first one in that morning and the last one out the day before? No one was with you?"

"I was in a hurry and left the water on in the foot bath. Anyone entering after me would have turned it off. It was still on when I arrived the next morning."

They met at the far end of the pool.

"Here?" Agnes pointed to a knob that when turned created a mist across a three-inch-deep trench of water near the swimming pool. The small pool of water would cleanse feet of dirt before the swimmer stepped into the main body of water. "Maybe someone came in after you and they forgot as well?"

"We're pretty well trained to turn it on and off without thinking."

"You forgot."

"I was afraid I was going to be kidnapped once I left the building. I was preoccupied."

Agnes couldn't fault that logic. She also couldn't find a parallel between her sons or their friends and this boy. He was childish in his acceptance of his father's word, yet, at the same time, he was vigilant and suspicious. As if fate really existed and he could only sidestep it.

"Was there anything else unusual about the day you found it?"

"We'd all gone to a special service for Monsieur Chavanon. I thought it was supposed to be me dead."

He slid effortlessly between the threat of kidnapping and

death, and she didn't point out that it was unlikely he was in danger of both. It was usually one or the other. His odd maturity was mixed with naïveté, and if his trouble hadn't started prior to Chavanon's death, she would have thought that triggered the boy's fears.

"Could you show me the locker where you found the note?"

Koulsy led the way around a tile wall into a room that smelled so distinctly of pool locker that Agnes was taken back to her own childhood. He flicked a switch and lights illuminated the space. The front part of the room was lined with sinks and mirrors. Behind that, the room split into a wet side and dry side: toilet and showers together through one opening, and rows of lockers and benches through the other. Not surprisingly, the lockers were a superb example of Swiss craftsmanship. They were beautifully finished in light wood with rows of slashes on the faces creating vents top and bottom. It would have been easy to shove a piece of paper between two slits and have it hold. No need to access his locker, only the need to know which one it was. And, of course, you had to be in the pool house to begin with.

"You left after everyone the night before. Why so late?"

"I love swimming. Always have. I'm thinking about trying for the Olympics next go-round. It would be great to represent my country. Represent my father and the country."

Agnes could imagine the sportscasters having a field day with that combination; at least in America, where they had round-the-clock coverage to fill. The political side of Koulsy's story would make for exciting special reports on cable news stations. Maybe a remote Swiss boarding school was the best answer for Koulsy. Perhaps it demonstrated that someone in his life was capable of authentic love, and that love kept him isolated from the world. He could make the swim team, travel to the Olympics, and, if handled correctly, never see the media storm. If someone on the team didn't kill him, she added to herself, suddenly reminded that his father was truly a terrible man and many people wanted him dead.

Was that the answer here? Was someone using the son to reach the father? The larger question was, would the father love the son enough to sacrifice himself if he had to? If the boy was kidnapped, she doubted the kidnappers would want only money. A swap—father for son—made more sense to her. Then she remembered the horrifying images of the ongoing civil war and wondered if, when made to choose, the father might conveniently forget that he had a son. It was impossible to judge honor in a man such as General Haroun.

She led Koulsy out of the locker room. He doused the lights. "So you're a good swimmer?"

He spouted off times and distances, pointing to a board overhead. His name and those times and distances were written over and over. . . . Records broken. Excellence proven.

"Which means you are often the last one here and the first to arrive?"

"Yes, I have to keep an alarm button on me. It's sewn into my swimsuit and I can press it if I get a cramp or something. Otherwise, no swimming alone. But I am here for hours, there is no way someone could always be with me. They found a solution. A very nice solution."

"I'll look for you in the Olympics. I think you'll make it there."

Agnes took another look around. There were emergency

exits, but those doors opened from the inside. The only way into the building was through the main door. The other end of the structure could slide open in good weather, but the heavy mechanical device couldn't be operated without fanfare. There were no windows. During the day, the pool was lit by the many skylights.

They closed the outer door. She pulled the neck of her coat close. It was still winter, no matter how near spring they were, and darkness had fallen.

The boy pulled his hood over his head and hunched his shoulders. "It's always colder after the pool because the pool house is so warm."

"You don't mind making this walk alone after dark?" They were at the farthest corner of the lawn, slightly hidden from the chalet by the newer classrooms.

He shrugged.

"Places like this, with open fields and a forest all around, unsettle me even when I know it's safe," Agnes said. At that moment, the heel of her shoe hit a hole and her ankle went sideways. She reached for the boy's arm without thinking. His reflexes were faster and he had her elbow. "Maybe not safe." She moved her ankle carefully, testing it. "It's not the most even ground."

"Rabbit burrows. They fix it now and then. It's not a big worry."

Not for young boys wearing big tennis shoes, she thought, stepping more carefully. In the distance, lights were on in every window of the chalet, and to the side, the smaller dormitory was equally bright. The classroom buildings were dark shapes in even darker shadows. She looked over her shoulder toward the pool house. It seemed farther away than it had earlier.

"What's that?" She pointed toward the rise in the hill. Small lights were in the distance. They flickered.

Koulsy followed the line of her finger. "Nothing."

"It's something. I don't remember a building out there."

"It's an empty field."

She squinted. "Not fire, but lights." Exactly the same as the previous night. "Have you seen them before?"

"Yes, Madame, I have seen them."

"And you don't know where they come from?"

"I have asked. I was told they don't exist."

She remembered that he grew up in a place where it was likely one didn't ask a question twice. "Go ahead. I'm going to look and see what it is."

He hesitated, then turned toward the chalet. Agnes walked in the opposite direction. She had reached the far side of the new dormitory when the flickering lights went out. She waited, watching. Nothing. No sign of anything, and no way to tell where they had been.

She aimed the light of her phone and walked as swiftly as she dared over the uneven ground. The beam created a cone of light three meters ahead; beyond that was darkness. Even the sliver of moon was behind clouds now, and she felt rain was on the way.

When she reached the field north of the Institute, she paused, sweeping her gaze 180 degrees. Nothing stirred. Nothing that she could see. No buildings were in the field, that she knew for certain. Beyond the field was forest, and the lights might have come from there. She wouldn't have seen a building hidden in the growth of trees, yet lights would be visible for hundreds of meters in the dark. She had read that in complete darkness the human eye could see a candle flame thirty miles away. Perhaps that was all it was. Lights from a forest dwelling. She crossed the field, stumbling on the hard clods of earth. Ahead, in the distance, was a crack, like a branch snapping. She stopped and called out. No one answered and she waited, listening. The noise could have been a branch falling. She reached the far edge of the field and shone her light in both directions along the tree line. The trees were thin and tall, but the forest was dense. Signs warned of *sangliers* and she hesitated. The wild boars were large and fast and, if disturbed, dangerous. She couldn't risk walking into the forest at night.

She waited. Now all she could hear were the night sounds of small animals and rustling limbs. She tried to judge the distance back to the chalet, wondering how far away the lights had been when they flashed on and off. It was impossible to tell, and nothing more could be done here tonight.

She was twenty meters from the chalet when a man's voice called out. She recognized Bernard Fontenay the second time he said her name. He stepped from the shadows near the corner of the building. "What were you doing, wandering around alone at night?"

"Walking Koulsy back from the pool. He returned before me."

"Not wandering the fields, I hope. It's easy to turn an ankle or run into a wild boar. We wouldn't have known to look for you."

"There were lights in the distance. Over there." She pointed.

"Probably a farmer crossing to a neighbor."

"Is that a usual path?"

Fontenay hesitated. "No, I can't say it is. But that doesn't rule out an exception."

"Did you see anything, or anyone, out here?"

"Me? No, I just stepped outside. I was on my way to the classroom building to check on one of the whiteboards. Hamel says it needs replacing and I forgot to look today. But since you're here, let's go inside. I'll tend to it in the morning."

Agnes followed him. Glancing over her shoulder, she saw the faint glow of the pool house shining up through the skylights. Perfect for drowning a boy swimming alone. She shivered. She thought about Guy Chavanon and the spectacular—and public—manner of his death. About Koulsy and the notes and the arrow.

Too much was beneath the surface here, and someone needed to uncover the truth.

She stopped and suppressed a smile. She was that person.

Twenty-seven

Stephan Dupré reached out to turn on the bedside light. Marie threw the covers over her face, pretending to shield herself from the glow.

"No smoking," she said.

"You don't mind it in my house."

The covers quivered but she didn't respond.

"The lights are out at Christine's."

"It's late, of course they are," came Marie's muffled voice.

"He's still there."

The covers flopped back, exposing Marie's bare breasts. "How do you know?"

"A sneak can always sort out another sneak." Dupré leaned out of bed, reaching for his trousers, pulling cigarettes and a lighter from the pocket.

"No," she repeated.

He put a cigarette to his lips and clicked the lighter a few inches away, sighing as if it were lit. "At least let me go through the motions."

She punched him playfully and adjusted the covers across her shoulders. "Is he really there?"

"I think so. Gianfranco used to park beyond my house and walk over. The shrubs are a good screen in that direction, and it's only a short part where he'd be visible to anyone watching from here. I saw his car when I walked over."

"It could be someone else's. The same model but a different owner."

"It's his plate. I saw it enough those few months they were together."

Marie sat up, her face pinched with concern. "I don't understand why he's here. She wouldn't want to see him after how he treated her." Marie fingered the blanket. "When he left her, she was more upset than now, after her father's death. Sick with it. Why would she see him when she's already so fragile?"

"Maybe that's why. Her guard's down, he calls, wants just one night of—"

"How can you say that? I don't think he was such a terrible young man. Surely he has some feeling."

"He's a young man, they're all hormones."

Marie considered. "He's not that young. Thirty-two I think. Old enough to act like a man, not a child."

"As good-looking as he is, he'll never have to act like a man."

"Then he doesn't need to be here with Christine. There are plenty of available women. Women who aren't red eyed with grief."

Stephan lay his unlit cigarette on the nightstand. "You suspect something other than romance?"

Marie picked at the cover. "She was always a secretive child. She and her father were a little club of two."

"She left him."

"You make it sound like divorce."

"It was in a way," said Dupré. "It was the end of a business arrangement."

Marie sat up. "Did you know that when she left, Guy made her sign away all rights to the company?"

Dupré's head thumped against the headboard. "She agreed?"

"Oh, yes, she was that angry." Marie sighed.

"You think my seeing Gianfranco has something to do with Guy?" Dupré turned to face her and found her hand. "What have you been thinking? Something you didn't want to say this morning."

"It's the break-in. That inspector was right, it has to be tied to Guy's death. But why?"

Twenty-eight

It was early morning and both women looked tired. Marie Chavanon wore a flowing silk dressing gown, but the elegance didn't diminish the lines of fatigue on her face. Christine was dressed in jeans and a sweater. She sat across from her stepmother cradling a cup of coffee, watchful.

"Scribbles. A dream. That's all it is." Marie thrust the notebook away, sliding it across the polished dining-room table. "I've never seen this notebook before."

Christine caught it and moved her chair nearer her stepmother. "It's his." She opened the cover and pointed to a diagram before turning a few more pages. "You know this is his handwriting and I know Father's work. Look at the annotations. Look at the dates. This is what he was working on when he died."

"Where did you get it?"

Christine didn't respond immediately. "I found it in his car."

"Why were you looking in his car?"

Christine lifted her chin defiantly. "It was before we went in the workshop. I came in the house. I wanted to see his things." She paused. "I called out."

Softly, thought Marie, if at all.

"I thought you were napping in your dressing room and I didn't want to disturb you. I went into Father's closet. I wanted to see his clothes, get the scent of him. That cologne I hated."

"You gave it to him," Marie said not unkindly.

"When I was ten. He didn't need to keep buying it."

Both women wrinkled their noses.

"I looked for his satchel," Christine said.

"That was a much better gift."

"It was." Christine grinned. "I can still picture the market in Santorini. That was my first school trip. I thought it was a perfect size, small, just right for him to carry a notebook."

"You were ahead of the times; it was probably designed for a woman, but he loved it. He's had the strap replaced twice from wear." Marie traced a finger on the table.

Christine turned a few more pages of the notebook. "When the satchel wasn't in the bedroom, I looked in the trunk of his car. I realized that he would have left it there during the reception." She looked out the window toward the driveway. The lawn leading away from the house was empty, and the morning was only beginning to lighten. A few outdoor lights illuminated the factory. In the distance, her own house was a spot of shadow. The workshop was a dark hole sheltered by shrubbery.

"Did they find anything?" she asked, gesturing to the workshop.

"No. They showed me photographs and wanted to know if something was stolen. I can't tell. I don't know." Carefully Marie fingered the leather cover of the notebook. "You think this was the reason someone broke into the workshop? To steal what Guy had written here?"

"Yes."

"Why didn't you tell the inspector you'd taken it?"

"You're accusing me? You think I *took* something? I thought it was Father's stuff. The ordinary stuff he carried around. It was only after Inspector Lüthi left, and I went home, and my arm stopped hurting that I looked inside and saw the notebook. I wasn't hiding it from you. You know about his notebook. Why hadn't you looked for it? You aren't interested. You never really cared."

Marie jumped to her feet. "Don't say I never cared. All I've ever done since marrying your father is care. I learned the business from the ground up, kept it going when he stopped paying attention to how the bills were paid. Do you think this was my choice?"

Christine gasped, wide-eyed, and Marie heaved a sigh and sat down, pressing her palms to the table. "I thought I married a man. Instead, I married his work. I'd have been better off signing on as the manager and having my free time to myself."

Christine's look changed from alarm to horror.

"I didn't mean that." Marie raked a hand across her eyes. "I'm scared and angry and sad, and so many other things. You have to know that I've done my best. I don't feel about the company like you do. Or like your father did. But I've tried. I've done what I could to keep it intact." She stretched out her hand to reach Christine's. "I did love your father very much."

The younger woman allowed their hands to touch, but only for a moment. She swallowed and blinked back tears.

"Besides, I don't recognize this notebook. I wouldn't have known to look for it." Marie pushed back from the dining-room table and looked around. "Guy loved this house."

Christine accepted the truce as an apology. "Remember how he hated when anyone thought the architect was French and not Swiss?" She managed a smile. "When I was little, I loved visiting my grandparents here. It felt special. Futuristic. I guess it was."

Marie walked to the window and looked out.

"You never liked it, did you? Will you sell?"

"Help me open the drapes." Marie walked into the long gallery.

Christine walked the perimeter of the dining room, pulling cords until the early-morning light was uniform.

Marie returned. "No, I never liked the house. But I won't sell unless I have to. This house is about more than one person. It's part of the family. It should be yours or Leo's. We'll see what works best for the two of you."

Marie sat again at the dining-room table and pulled the notebook near, flipping through the pages slowly this time, peering through her reading glasses. "You didn't answer me. You think this means something. Something real. Of value?" She looked at Christine. "Your father was a visionary—"

"But he stayed trapped in the vision?" Christine completed the thought. "This is different, this is . . . more. It is . . ." She searched for a word.

"Revolutionary." "Transformative." The two women spoke at the same time. They looked at each other. Startled.

"I had all day yesterday to study it," said Christine. "The principle behind his idea is related to his thesis at university. I studied enough engineering to see that. And here"—she pointed to notations at the bottom of each page—"this is what he's always done to key his notes to electronic files."

"How could he have electronic files? He didn't have a computer."

"He could use one, he just didn't like to. He'd rather Gisele draw up his sketches." Christine reached for the carafe and poured another cup of coffee. "I'll check her computer. He could have used it when no one was there. You said that he'd been up early and late and acting erratically."

"She would have noticed."

Christine lowered her head into her hands. She took a few deep breaths. "Father was careful."

"He was paranoid."

"Which now looks like good sense. He always liked puzzles and complicated things. It would have been natural for him to guard his most precious secret with a system that kept the project in two places. You could have one-half and use it to develop the other, but it would take time. Months or years, even if you had the skills. If someone stole the other half, I don't think they can produce any product right away."

"Meaning if there is an electronic file and someone stole it, they're in the same situation we are?"

"Yes." Christine pulled the notebook near and thumbed through it. "He had this with him the day he died. He didn't expect to die. It was in his safekeeping. We don't know where he was going after the reception or who he planned to meet."

"If anyone. Maybe he stored notes in the company safe?"

"I'll look again, but did he ever keep anything there?" Christine returned the notebook carefully to her handbag. "I will look everywhere I can think of."

"Why didn't he tell us?"

"You know how angry I was when I left. I wanted to work for a company where craft was everything. I think he thought I wouldn't approve."

"You believe it's possible? Achieving his dream?"

"Yes. Based on what I see here, I think that Father had created something that will overshadow the quartz revolution. I think this will put watches—Swiss watches—back on the world stage for a long time."

"And put Perrault et Chavanon on sound financial footing."

"That is an understatement."

Marie folded her arms over her chest. "If only he'd said something."

"I think he tried to. At least with me. I ignored him, and I've always been willing to listen to the crazy ideas. If I didn't listen, he knew you wouldn't. Sorry." Christine touched Marie on the arm.

They sat in silence for a few minutes.

"Do you think anyone else listened to him?"

Christine considered. "Like Stephan Dupré?"

"Yes, like Stephan."

Twenty-nine

"I'm officially well enough to be back at work." Agnes dropped her handbag on the kitchen counter.

"Did you pay off the doctor?" her youngest son said, only to be smacked on the head by his older sibling.

"Hardly, although for a moment I thought I might have to. You've all finished eating?"

The boys were picking up their coats and heading for the door. "Can't be late to school, *mère*."

She said goodbye to a closed door. "Did you have a chance to eat?" she asked André Petit, noting his empty plate.

"Enough for three men. Sybille was insistent. I told her I'd wait here—keep an eye on the boys—so she could go ahead to the butcher. Something about a cut of meat he's ordered for her. Might be that she wanted me to get a dose of what it'll be like when my boy is older. I've never heard such complaining."

"Anything serious?"

He laughed. "No, complaining to complain."

"If you're on a first-name basis with my mother-in-law, you must have made a good impression."

Agnes took a forkful of risotto from the serving bowl. "She really is a good cook. So what did you find at the Institute yesterday?"

"It's worse than the scene of a traffic accident. I've talked to most of the teachers and staff, and they don't remember anything about the day Chavanon died. Or anything that matters. I've a few more to go before I'll call it quits. Maybe Boschung knew the man was killed but realized he couldn't figure it out and so called it a natural death."

"That's unfair."

Petit followed Agnes's lead and moved his plate to the counter beside the sink. "You're right. But they're all vague, and what they're not vague about conflicts with every other person's account. I don't know why they have these receptions if no one pays attention to what goes on."

"I'm not sure that's the purpose of a school reception. They're meant to be forgettable, a pleasant memory."

"It's a strange world, a boarding school. Superstitious lot."

"Why do you say that?" Agnes studied a chocolate cake under a glass dome. She gestured toward it.

"No thanks, I don't have a sweet teeth." He sat down on a stool. "I asked about the lights like you told me to. Got the stiff eye. A couple of them said they'd reported it to Monsieur Fontenay and got told off for not concentrating on their studies. I stopped asking since it's nothing to do with Chavanon dying and it was making them go quiet."

"You said you had something important to tell me?"

"Yes, the best is for last. I have two names I think you'll be interested in calling. They are parents at the reception." He passed a sheet of paper to her. She glanced at the notes and nodded.

"That's not all," Petit said a little proudly.

When he finished his report, Agnes thumped him on the shoulder. "I knew Mercier was hiding something. You earned your lunch today. Well done."

"You'll follow up on this?"

"Oh, yes, right away."

Despite Petit's revelation, Agnes was still thinking about the lights at the school when she walked into the security room at Baselworld.

"Found her," said Aubry.

"I got your message yesterday." Agnes shook hands with the officer who manned the monitor. He handed her a printed image taken from the video. "Was I right?"

"*Incroyable,*" he said. "She is beautiful."

"We used the software and found her on the Tokyo tapes as well," said Aubry. "We've got everyone on it. She won't elude us."

"She's probably on another continent by now," said Agnes.

"How would she know we're looking for her?"

Agnes glanced around. "Has Monsieur Mercier come by? I was supposed to meet him, and his assistant didn't know where he was. She thought he was here looking for me."

"No, but if he does show up, we'll call."

"Don't bother being nice to him; he's probably avoiding me on purpose."

•   •   •

A few minutes later Agnes checked an image in her stored photographs, then tapped a number on her phone screen. Gianfranco Giberti answered on the second ring. His voice over the phone was smooth as velvet.

"I don't have a great amount of time," he said in response to her request.

"Monsieur Giberti, I'm standing outside the Omega pavilion and see you. You don't look busy to me. Ten minutes is all I need."

When he joined her, she sensed the change in his manner. He was on edge. The Baselworld crowd flowed around them, but Giberti wasn't interested. He was entirely focused on Agnes.

"This shouldn't take long," she said. "I'm due to meet with Antoine Mercier. Do you know him?"

"We all know him. And I saw you holding the *Daily News* where we were photographed together."

"Of course. Shows how making a pleasantry can sound inane. Have you had a chance to think again about anything you know or have heard about Monsieur Chavanon? I'm certain there is gossip at the show."

"The police rely on gossip?"

"We rely on whatever it takes. Gossip isn't necessarily untrue, it's simply without purpose other than to pass on details of some happening."

"I know nothing."

"Is Mademoiselle Chavanon at work today?"

"Of course not."

"I'm surprised you know offhand. I thought that you had no contact now that you aren't a couple."

"I could hardly not notice her in the pavilion. It is large, but not that large."

Agnes shifted as if to shield her words from anyone passing by. "We know that there was truth to the rumor that Monsieur Chavanon had invented something important."

Giberti paled beneath his tan. "Do you have the invention? Did the police find it amongst his things in the workshop?"

Agnes shrugged noncommittally, hating to fuel the fire with nonsense but needing to shake answers from these closemouthed people.

"Are the family in danger?" Giberti added. "You would tell them if they were?"

"What makes you think they're in danger?"

"Monsieur Chavanon is dead, and you think someone stole something from him." Giberti's phone rang, and instinctively he pulled it from his pocket and glanced at the screen. Christine Chavanon's photograph and name flashed across the glass.

"Answer it," said Agnes, noting the alarm on Giberti's face. "What if there is a problem?"

"Christine," he said into the phone. "I'm surprised by the call, but hope I can help you."

Agnes couldn't hear the woman's voice, but she didn't speak long, for Giberti quickly replied, "I am being interviewed by Inspector Lüthi." He held out the phone to Agnes. "She's upset and dialed my number by mistake. Meant to get her supervisor. She'd like to speak with you."

"Why are you talking to Gianfranco?" Christine demanded once Agnes was on the phone.

"I happened to see him."

"I'm at Leo's school. Why don't you come here and we can talk more. I understand now what happened to my father."

Thirty

"I'm afraid I can't let you visit the workshop yet," Agnes said to Christine, surprised by the request. They were in Leo Chavanon's dorm room. The young woman was seated on her half brother's bed, holding the gift Narendra Patel had left for him. The silver frame was new and highly polished and contained a photograph of Guy and Narendra. In it, the two men were much younger and smiling broadly for the camera. Agnes pulled a chair from the desk and sat facing Christine.

"I thought you weren't comfortable in your father's workshop because of intellectual property. Surely those concerns still exist—his work is his company's work."

Christine placed the photograph on the nightstand. She closed her eyes, and Agnes wondered if Christine was trying not to cry. A bell rang in the distance, and a minute later voices floated up from the lawn. Agnes glanced outside and saw boys walking between the classroom buildings; a soccer ball materialized and an impromptu game was afoot. Bernard Fontenay crossed from the chalet to the science classroom; Navarro met him halfway. She recognized a few of the other boys. Koulsy Haroun was standing in a clump of kids who looked like school athletes. Tommy Scaglia was sitting on a bench, flipping through the pages of a textbook so quickly Agnes thought he was cramming for an exam. The tabby slinked across the lawn and sat next to him.

"I wanted to talk to you today, in person," said Christine, "because I don't think Father's work amounted to anything."

To conceal her surprise, Agnes picked up one of the small boxes she'd seen the day before and turned it, admiring the craftsmanship. "What changed?"

"What we saw in the workshop was unnerving." Christine spoke firmly. "It wasn't the place I remembered, and I thought maybe if I was wrong about that, then I was wrong about Father's accomplishments." She sat up straighter, on the edge of the bed. "It was wishful thinking. Trying to make something, to invent a legacy. But it's not right for Leo. We need to accept the past and not pretend." Christine reached her hand out for the box. "He doesn't keep anything in these."

Agnes handed it to her.

"They pull apart." Christine demonstrated. The box worked like a puzzle. "Father made them for us when we were growing up. I always kept treasures in them. Earrings, a bit of ribbon." She put the box down. "Do you remember the notebooks in Marie's office? The ones I showed you behind the panels? You asked if my father kept one."

"Yes." Agnes didn't mention that she'd returned to look for it.

"I have Father's here with me. It was at the house and I

thought you'd want it, since it is what he was working on when he died. After the break-in I wondered where it was." Christine held out an embossed notebook matching the ones in the factory office. It was stamped with Guy Chavanon's initials. Agnes flipped through the pages. The first date was seven months ago, the last two weeks before Chavanon's death. There were sketches of watch designs, notes about product updates, jottings about order quantities.

"There's nothing in there. Nothing exceptional." Christine shrugged. "I was wrong. I was wrong about everything. Who knows how he was exposed to the peanuts, it was always a risk. I'd become so accustomed to nothing happening that I'd forgotten. Once the funeral was over, I knew that he was truly gone and I panicked. There were things I regretted, and I wanted him back. Since that was impossible, the next best thing was to fight his death. To believe that it wasn't an accident. I was wrong. I need to accept the truth."

Agnes flipped through the notebook again. If it hadn't matched the series in the factory office and contained Chavanon's handwriting, she wouldn't believe it was his. Where were the notes to match the intellect she'd seen in the formulas in his workshop?

"You can return it to Marie when you're finished. I told her I'd give it to you. I needed to show you and apologize in person."

"I've lost loved ones and know how difficult it is to come to terms with sudden death. Regrets are normal. We all have regrets." Agnes stood and looked around the bedroom. "Have you seen Leo today?"

"No, I timed it badly and he's in class. I don't want to bother him. It was stupid to come here, but when we spoke, I thought

I might as well wait and talk to you." Christine stood. "Did Gianfranco tell you that I meant to call my supervisor?" She grimaced. "He must have been surprised. I was calling to say that I'm coming in to work today. Late, obviously, but they need me, and I'm ready to get back to normal life."

Agnes walked Christine to her car before returning to the Institute and the small room the receptionist had opened for her use. She thumbed through Guy Chavanon's notebook again. These were not the scribblings of a genius. They weren't even the scribblings of an inventor.

After assembling several explanations in her head, she stowed the notebook in her handbag, then pulled out her phone along with the names Petit had given her.

It took a few seconds for the call to connect. She took a seat in a comfortable chintz chair. Sunlight struck the carpet in a sharp blade through the open curtains. The yellow-and-blue wallpaper glowed good cheer.

Louise Kelly answered on the fifth ring and didn't express any objection to speaking with the police. Madame Kelly was the British lady Narendra Patel was speaking with when Guy Chavanon entered the reception. Agnes hoped she remembered something Patel had missed. That wasn't the only reason for the phone call, but it served as the excuse. Louise Kelly should be an acute observer.

"You understand that I am not, myself, the parent of a student," Madame Kelly said. "I was there to visit my nephew. My brother's child. My favorite nephew, although that shouldn't be noted."

Along with her phone number, Petit had provided an old black-and-white head shot of the woman on the other end of the line. Not elderly, but no longer young. Her nephew was possibly the child of a much younger brother. The voice on the phone conjured the image of someone white headed wearing a pastel sweater set. Or was that the wrong generation? Maybe a tweed jacket. Agnes was afraid her image of the Brits was based on television dramas.

"Michael, my nephew, had brought me a plate from the buffet," Madame Kelly said. "Then he went to his room to deposit a small gift I'd brought him. To store it away. I don't know any of the other parents, and since it will likely be my only visit, there wasn't a reason to meet them. I like to watch people, so I waited quite contently, enjoying my food. The quality of the selection was surprising."

"Did you speak with Monsieur Chavanon?"

"No, and of course I didn't know who he was until afterwards. Quite shocking, not at all what you expect at a . . . well, what you expect anywhere. I felt quite sorry for his son. They should have got him away sooner. Of course, I didn't know it was his son, or I would have done something myself. Can't blame the others, likely the same story. I don't think I've ever been dumbstruck before, but that's what I was. Dumbstruck. Just stood there for what felt like a quarter hour, although I realized later it was only minutes. Very long minutes, while the poor man struggled."

"What do you remember before that moment?"

"I was speaking with a nice man, an Indian. My father and mother were in India in the early days of their marriage, and the country has a special place in our memories. I have a photograph of them riding the most amazing elephant. Monsieur Patel and I were discussing the food at the reception. As I said, quite good. I can see where some of the tuition fees go, not like in England when I was at school. There, they still think cold water and boiled chops are character building."

"Was this about the time Monsieur Chavanon fell ill?"

"A few minutes earlier. I was alone when that happened. Monsieur Patel left to take a phone call and I was looking around for Michael, thinking he should have returned. I was wondering if he'd dodged out with his friends, although he is a nice boy and I think he enjoys seeing me. I was perhaps too preoccupied to really pay attention to what was happening until it was quite out of control. I remember that I was also thinking that I hoped to get away without catching someone's cold or flu. Recently, I've had a little health flutter, and I was reminded of the winter germs. But one can't stay home all the time, and my brother and his wife are in Antarctica on a scientific mission. I promised to check on Michael in person." Madame Kelly paused. "I'm not sure how this is helpful?"

"Did you meet Koulsy Haroun? He's a student in your nephew's year."

There was a slight hesitation. "Why the interest in him?"

"He had the same allergy as Monsieur Chavanon. But you probably knew that."

The line fell silent, and for a moment Agnes thought the call had dropped. When Louise Kelly spoke again, it was in a firmer tone. "I understand now why you called. I met Koulsy when he was a toddler. He won't remember me. We were in Africa. It was a long time ago and I had forgotten there was a man from your government at that meeting. An unsuccessful meeting. You've done your homework."

"We can't overlook the coincidence of his allergy."

There was a long pause.

"I was at the school because of my nephew. I'm long since retired from the foreign service."

Voices called down the corridor, boys returning from lunch off campus. Madame Jomini shushed them.

"Inspector, do you think Koulsy was the intended victim?" Madame Kelly asked.

"Everything is a possibility."

After final pleasantries Agnes hung up, reasonably certain that Louise Kelly was—at least in the context of the Institute—as she presented herself. A visiting aunt. It was only coincidence that she was also a retired member of the British Intelligence Service.

Agnes called the other name on Petit's list of coincidences. Gustav Schwartz had a pleasant voice, and a relaxed manner that indicated everything revolved around his schedule. Agnes introduced herself and restated what she had told his secretary earlier. There was activity in the background and she sensed a hand being placed over the phone.

"Sorry about that," Schwartz said. "They're putting *The Endeavor* in the water and it looked like things weren't going well."

Agnes could hear multiple voices in the background. It sounded as if the man was at a party, which she supposed he was if they were launching his yacht.

"You had a question about that day at the Institute," Schwartz said in her ear. "That's what I love about the Swiss. Keep great records. Dot all the i's and cross all the t's." His voice raised again. "Tell them I'll be right there. And not that bottle. That's for us to drink later. The other one is for Mariam to use on the hull." His voice shifted again and lowered. "Sorry, Inspector, you were asking about Chavanon. What I remember is straightforward enough. My wife and I were there. It was fortunate that I needed to be in Zürich on business. We came early and saw our boy's bedroom. Dinky thing, and he has to share, but I suppose that's part of the experience I'm paying for. Character building or something. Mariam's the one who thinks it's a good idea. Anyway, we went down to the party. Fontenay serves a decent wine—some local label—and I was having a glass near the window. I'll tell you now that I was preoccupied. I was in the middle of important negotiations, and there we were at an afternoon school party."

Agnes mumbled appropriate understanding and urged him to continue.

"My wife and son were outside. Monsieur Chavanon was nearby and we started talking. Then that math instructor came over and I headed out. Wicht thinks my son needs to be able to do calculations like an astronaut without a computer. He doesn't understand that we've got people who do that. Alfred can supervise someone doing the math for him. Anyway, I pretended I needed the toilet and left. That's it."

"Did anything stand out as unusual?"

"Except for Chavanon dying? It was the usual boring rigmarole. Don't know why they have these receptions. It's not like I need to meet more people."

Agnes was reminded of something Julien Vallotton had said to her when they first met. New people meant new problems, or something like that. In her line of work, it couldn't be avoided, but she was beginning to see his point. "What about Monsieur Chavanon? How did he look?"

"Damn cold was how he looked," said Schwartz. "Which was the reason I didn't follow Mariam outside. Course my wife was wearing mink from her ears to her heels, and my boy's full of vigor. They didn't mind the weather."

"You saw Monsieur Chavanon enter the reception from the lawn?"

"Yes, I watched him walk in. He was all red faced. His cheeks were ruddy."

"Other than being cold, he appeared well and in good spirits?"

"How should I know? He wasn't clutching his neck like later. Sorry. That wasn't kind. I didn't know him; it would be hard to detect a difference without a baseline of knowledge. He seemed normal enough to me. As normal as anyone else at these parent events. Have you met the others? What about Monsieur Han? There's a man I wouldn't like to meet in a dark corridor."

Monsieur Han was the grandparent of a student. He lived on the Côte d'Azur and had arrived in a helicopter. Madame Jomini had noted that Han wasn't yet down to the reception when they closed off the room. Tommy Scaglia's account indicated that the two men hadn't seen each other outside either.

"Do you remember what you and Monsieur Chavanon spoke about? Did he say anything about what he'd done earlier in the day?" She shifted the phone to her other ear and flipped a page in her notebook.

"Inconsequential things. I might not remember him at all if he hadn't died fifteen minutes later, or if I hadn't told this story to the police that afternoon. Chavanon and I introduced ourselves and pretended to remember one another from an earlier event. He said something that made me think he comes all the time, and I said I was only there because of business in Zürich. He acted interested and I added a bit more. Usually it's the Americans who ask about business and I hate to bore people, but he inquired."

Agnes could imagine the conversation. Polite interest, polite questions to fill the silence and keep the other person talking, when really every parent was there with only one objective: to see their own son.

"Seemed like a nice man. Said he was a watchmaker, but you know that."

There were shouts in the background and Agnes hoped the yacht hadn't sunk. Schwartz didn't speak for a minute, his attention diverted.

"Anyway," he finally said, "I'm not a collector, although I do own a few nice timepieces. Chavanon and I talked business a few minutes. It was a whole scale of enterprise that I'm unfamiliar with. I've been in multinational negotiations since I was in short pants, and we talked about that for a minute. I'm afraid I might have complained about the Swiss. He was going on about regulations governing the Swiss Made label as if they were more important than any multinational deal I could make. Full of national pride and put me in my place." Schwartz laughed and Agnes imagined he rarely had anyone disagree with him.

"I should have remembered where I was. Love doing business with the Swiss, but you're an insular group and I was a bit off the whole country at the moment. You don't have any raw materials, yet still manage to make me feel you have the upper hand. Next day we got our negotiations back on track and it all worked out."

Schwartz's voice dropped out for a few seconds and Agnes wondered if he'd turned into the wind. "My wife loves the place. People, climate, food. She would live there if I'd let her, but I'm not spending time anywhere with that much snow and cold. My father moved his business from Berlin to Argentina before I was born, and I'm not going back."

"What kind of business are you in?"

"The kind that governments need, but won't admit to. You Swiss smooth the gears. You're like a comfortable meeting room where we can gather."

"Monsieur Chavanon's work must have sounded quite tame by comparison to yours."

"We may have a more obvious global objective, but the watch industry? Cutthroat, don't fool yourself. All those tiny moving parts." Schwartz laughed.

Before Agnes could reply there was a loud crash outside and a scream reverberated. She hung up quickly, already running for the back door.

Thirty-one

Agnes arrived first. The shattered remains of a long flower box lay a few meters beyond the rear door of the chalet. Nearby, Tommy Scaglia struggled to his feet, dazed and pale. She ran to help him, then saw a foot sticking out from the debris of wood and earth. Whoever was trapped was moaning and trying to shift loose.

"Don't move," she cried, reaching for a board and shoving it away, exposing Koulsy's head and shoulders. He lay on his side, blood running from a cut to his scalp.

"Tommy, help me," she said. Scaglia didn't move. He stared at his injured friend. She grabbed Tommy's arm and shook him slightly. "I need your help." He blinked and started forward, his legs uncoordinated.

"Get over here." She was unable to lift the longer boards on her own. "Tommy!"

He stumbled forward.

"Lift there." Agnes motioned to a board pressed onto Koulsy's shoulder and hips. It was two meters long, as thick as two fingers, and heavy. Tommy grasped it, and she counted one, two, three, then they lifted. Koulsy let out a cry of relief. Agnes glanced up, wondering why no one had come to help, then realized that the teachers and other students were in class across the lawn. No one was near.

Tommy was breathing hard. He leaned over and put his hands on his knees like a runner at the end of a race. Agnes gave him a sharp once-over. He was scraped and bruised by his fall, but not seriously injured. Right now, Koulsy needed their help.

"Again," she said sharply.

Tommy flinched and straightened.

"Careful," she said as they lifted another board.

It took a few minutes to remove the pieces covering Koulsy. When he was free, Agnes knelt beside him. His eyes fluttered open and shut a few times. He grimaced. She yanked a handkerchief from her pocket and pressed it to the cut on his head. Koulsy rolled onto his back and blinked as if he were surprised to be alive.

The flower box had fallen from an upper-balcony balustrade. Constructed of heavy timber and filled with earth, it would have killed the boy if one end hadn't landed on the decorative concrete ball that marked the edge of the sidewalk. It had created a pocket of space for his head.

"Take your time. We'll get help," she said, looking him up and down. Despite his cuts and scrapes, Koulsy didn't appear to be seriously injured. "Tommy, go get the nurse."

"Is he going to die?" Tommy whispered.

"No, but he's injured. Go get help."

Tommy didn't move. She stood and looked in his eyes. They

weren't dilated and there were no other signs of trauma. "Did you hit your head?" She shook him slightly.

He blinked as if he were waking up. "It just happened. I was waiting and it all happened so fast. I thought he was dead."

"Tommy, you need to focus." Agnes gripped his shoulders. "Go get the nurse."

He wiped sweat from his forehead and started to speak again, but no sound came from his mouth. She was about to go for the nurse herself when he nodded over and over and turned toward the infirmary. Agnes watched him until she was sure he would make it. Then she knelt by Koulsy.

"I didn't see anything. If Tommy hadn't pushed me out of the way, it would have hit me on the head. He saved my life."

Koulsy was holding the handkerchief to his forehead, and she adjusted it to better cover the wound. Blood dripped down his temple, across his cheekbone to his chin.

"It fell. I didn't hear it. I was walking from the pool and had my head down." He looked up as if to judge the impact of the falling box. "I was standing right there."

Bernard Fontenay raced up, out of breath. "I saw Tommy . . . he was barely coherent. What happened?" Fontenay glanced at Agnes, eyes panicked, then quickly gathered himself. "How are you, son?"

Koulsy sat up slowly and used his free hand to brush gravel from his arms and legs. Fontenay helped him stand. Koulsy winced when his right foot touched the ground. He touched his ankle and groaned.

Fontenay looked up. "Hamel will be distraught when he sees this. He takes good care of the place, but you can't prevent everything."

Koulsy seemed steadier now, and Fontenay looped the boy's arm around his own shoulder to take the weight off the injured leg. Thanking Agnes for her help, Fontenay started toward the infirmary. She felt her heart slow with relief. The accident could have been a tragedy. She walked inside and headed up the stairs, curious to see where the box had fallen from.

The upper dormitory floor was empty, and she walked through the nearest bedroom to the balcony. It was narrow, just wide enough for two people to pass. A solid wood rail rested on sturdy carved spindles. The flower boxes were butted against one another the entire length.

Agnes looked down from the place the box had fallen. The balcony on the floor below was damaged as the box had twisted and hit before landing on the ground and splintering. Koulsy had been covered with debris after the box impacted. A direct hit would have killed him.

She studied the bare balustrade. The metal brackets that held the box in place were missing. All that was left were the holes where they had been screwed in. She moved to the adjacent box. The brackets were custom-made and fitted the rail perfectly, running along the top, then down the outside and turning back to clamp into place. This way no one needed to lean out and over to screw the box into place. She pushed the box and it didn't move.

Returning to the empty space, she crouched to study the holes left by the missing straps. She eyed them carefully. Were the holes enlarged by the force of the screws pulling loose when the box tipped over? She had trouble imagining that. What was the likelihood of all six screw holes giving way at the same time?

A dark concern emerged. This wasn't an accident. Someone

had loosened the screws and pushed the box over; perhaps timing it for when Koulsy passed beneath. She looked down at the ground again. If true, then this was a vicious act. Or was she jumping to conclusions? Perhaps a bored kid sitting on the balcony had fiddled with the screws, not meaning any harm, but passing the time? She knew enough about boys to realize that was possible. One of her own sons had loosened the ladder leading to his grandfather's hayloft without thinking about what would happen the next time someone climbed up. He wanted to see if he was strong enough to do it, was the explanation.

She studied the whole assembly. Even with the brackets loosened, the weight of the flower box should have kept it in place until it was shoved or dislodged by a strong wind. If this was done on purpose, then someone must have been standing on the balcony when it fell. She looked out across the campus. Almost every building had a view of the chalet. Someone had to be watching.

She texted Petit to meet her and headed for the ground floor. Monsieur Hamel was standing by the debris when she emerged from the chalet.

"Walked through the infirmary and Madame Butty told me what happened." He studied the remains of the shattered box. He removed his hat and rubbed his head. "I'd have never forgiven myself if one of the boys was hurt."

"No one is blaming you."

Hamel shook his head, mumbling to himself, and walked toward the garden shed. In his absence Agnes sifted through the pile of wood and earth. The earth was loose, with old roots mixed in. There was a small amount of trash: cigarette butts, an old lighter, a length of fishing line, plastic bottle caps. She found a loose screw and scratched it against a plank. The screw barely made a dent. This was old hardwood. Tough as iron. That eliminated any chance of the screws pulling out on their own. Once Hamel recovered from his shock, he'd realize the same thing. This wasn't negligence.

Pushing bits of debris aside, she found what she wanted: one of the metal brackets. Both heads of the two screws were scratched as if turned by someone using the wrong tool. Amateur or hurried?

Petit ran up, breathless with worry. Agnes expanded on what she had included in her text message. Petit gave a low whistle. "That would have been murder, plain and simple. Premeditated and carried out in cold blood."

"Start asking questions. See if anyone is unaccounted for and might have been on that balcony."

He shoved his hands in his coat pockets. "How could the kid not see that big box falling?"

"Easily. When I walked to the pool with him, he studied his shoes the entire time." Agnes looked across the lawn. It was deceptively serene. "I'll visit the infirmary and see what I can learn from the boys." She gave Petit a plastic evidence bag for the bracket and screws and told him to take photographs of everything.

When Agnes reached the infirmary, Madame Butty was in her office, washing her hands. The door to the examination room was closed. "I hope the boys are recovering," Agnes said after introducing herself.

"Koulsy needs rest. He hit his head when he fell, and although he doesn't need a stitch, I'd like him to be quiet and under observation the rest of the day. He told me that Tommy

Scaglia saved his life. He didn't see a thing until he was pushed out of the way."

"How is Tommy?"

"I just finished cleaning his scratches. He's around the corner. I asked him to wait a few more minutes before standing up. I think he should be excused from class as well. His injuries are superficial, but he's shaken. He's more upset than Koulsy, poor boy."

Agnes found Tommy sitting on a plastic chair, staring down at his uniform pants. Or what was left of them. They been torn up by the gravel, and the nurse had simply cut them off above the knees to treat his cuts.

"Madame Butty said they were ruined anyway," he said when Agnes approached.

"Something to tell your friends about." She sat next to him. "You're a bit of a hero, the way Koulsy tells it. What do you remember?"

He slumped over until his head was nearly between his knees, and Agnes wondered if he was going to be sick.

"I don't remember anything." She gave him a moment and he kept talking. "I'd left my homework upstairs and went back to get it. That's why I was late going to class. I saw Koulsy walking back from the pool."

"He wasn't in class?"

"Koulsy got special permission to skip because a dude came today from a swimming organization to time him. Anyway, I saw him coming across the field, and I stopped to wait. I wanted to hear how it went. When he got close, there was a scraping sound over my head. I don't know if I looked up or just felt what was happening." Tommy's shoulders heaved.

Agnes put her hand lightly on his arm.

"I didn't think. I ran forward, right into him, then it slammed into the ground. Koulsy yelled and I thought he'd been hit. Next thing I remember, you were there." Tommy sat up straight and wiped sweat from his forehead. "I thought he was dead."

"How many people knew Koulsy was at the pool?"

"I don't know." Tommy leaned forward, clutching his stomach. "Everyone who noticed he wasn't in class. It's not a secret. It's kind of cool that he's that good a swimmer. I'd have told everyone." He looked at her. "I was scared."

She believed him. He still looked scared. Not something she would have imagined upon meeting him. His swagger had been crushed.

"Why didn't he go straight to class from the pool?"

"He never does."

"But he changes in the locker room. It would be quicker to go straight on to class. Why would he climb all the way up to his room?" While boys had enough energy to run up dozens of flights of stairs, she knew they also were lazy. They called it taking a shortcut.

"Ritual."

Agnes nearly laughed, but Tommy's expression was serious.

"He always does the same thing, in the same order. Since he doesn't always need to go to class after a swim, the ritual has to be to return to his room. He just stops and picks up his books or looks around. I don't know. But he likes the ritual. Same thing with meals. Never has snacks or late dessert."

Agnes remembered how Koulsy looked nearly frightened by the idea of a chocolate biscuit when she offered one to him. She'd thought it was because they weren't usually allowed, but this made sense. She understood, to a degree. On the shooting range she had her rituals, most of them insignificant, probably not noticeable to anyone else, but she wouldn't shoot without them. Even her mental process was a ritual when she was out there. Even when the ritual happened in a flash, it was there. That mental process was what had kept her focused when she had needed to make that one shot just three weeks ago. Koulsy was a serious sportsman. He would take his rituals seriously. It was unfortunate that they might be used against him.

She warned Tommy not to talk to the other boys about what had happened. She thought he took her caution seriously. Likely because his father was an American criminal defense attorney. Probably had visions of "the slammer" if he didn't behave.

Thirty-two

Agnes met Madame Fontenay inside the chalet.

"Ask Jean to send something up. Coffee and a sweet," Helene said as they passed the receptionist.

"Don't trouble him for me," said Agnes.

"It's not for you."

Agnes followed the headmistress into her office and chose a comfortable chair. She had confirmed a suspicion with a quick phone call earlier and looked forward to speaking with Helene.

"I'm sorry I didn't recognize you. I remember you as Helene Durand."

Helene's expression froze for a short second, then she smiled and Agnes saw a light spark in her eyes. "I never used my married name professionally; it was easier to keep a name that everyone knew. What made you think of it?"

"I remembered the photograph on the wall behind you. Your face isn't visible, but I remember that day. I saw you ski a few times. World Cup at St. Moritz and Wengen, and maybe one other time. We are a skiing family. Of course, none of us have your technique. Do you miss it?"

Helene went rigid, then laughed. "You're the first person to ask me. People here don't know, or if they do, they treat the subject as if it's taboo. Even my husband mentions ski weekend like it's an Ebola outbreak. It's difficult to have something that was your entire life become the thing no one will speak about."

"Have you considered skiing again?"

"When I say that I loved skiing, I don't mean the beauty of the landscape or the peace of the slopes or whatever it is that you feel. The kind of skiing that could be arranged for me now. I loved the speed. I loved being on the outer edge of control." Helene shrugged. "That's what got me in the end, didn't it? Speed on the wrong side of control. Did you know that I crashed with a training coach? It wasn't even during a race. I practically flew over the fencing. They clocked me at one hundred and forty kilometers an hour and gaining. With perfect aim, I slammed right into a tree. My pelvis was crushed, along with a few other important things. Bernard was there, waiting to take me to dinner after the run. He was there when I regained consciousness in the hospital." Helene stopped speaking; it seemed as if she'd slipped into a trance.

After a few seconds, she shook herself slightly. "You're a policewoman. You've surely seen people injured. People dying, perhaps. Have you ever told someone to be thankful they lived?"

Agnes shook her head.

"That's what Bernard said to me when I woke up. What the doctors said. The nurses. My parents. I wasn't thankful. I'm still not. I have a half life." Tears glinted in Helene's eyes. "Bernard thinks it's been long enough. Like there is a timeline for recovery. The pain is lessened, so you're nearly there! Start your new life. Every day is the start of a new journey. So many platitudes." She pressed the corners of her eyes. "Next time someone says to you that they wished they'd died, do them the courtesy of believing them."

Helene adjusted the front of her sweater. "I should thank you, though. I actually like to talk about skiing. Those were the happiest days of my life. Reliving them is reliving them, not reliving the fall, which is what people assume."

"It must have been traumatic for Monsieur Fontenay; maybe that's why he doesn't care to relive it."

Helene Fontenay slid her crutches to the side. "More traumatic than it was for me?"

"As you say, who gets to decide how long it takes to heal?" For a moment, Agnes thought she'd gone too far, but the headmistress relaxed her shoulders and nodded.

"I'd like to hear about your ski career."

Helene smiled and shook her head. "Not today. You're not here to talk about my past. Or my present. You have other questions. We should move on to those."

Agnes nearly asked about skiing again, but she felt that the mood had shifted and the topic was closed for now. She understood that memories and grief, even if unconsciously, had to be compartmentalized. Denial, anger, bargaining, depression, acceptance. She hoped that Helene would someday make it past anger to acceptance.

"I wanted to ask where you were when the flower box fell?"

"I was here, in the office." Helene was Headmistress Fontenay again.

"Madame Jomini said you weren't here."

"Are you accusing me?" Helene didn't blink. "Clearly I don't remember where I was at that exact moment and I didn't hear it fall. I've been in my office most of the day, that's what I meant. At some point, I went down to speak with Chef Jean about his food order. He would serve the boys filet and truffles every day if I didn't watch him. I was reviewing the menus in my office before that."

"Madame Jomini said she looked for you downstairs and didn't find you. In fact, she looked everywhere she could think of. There was a parent waiting on the phone."

"Well, I wasn't upstairs throwing boxes off balconies." Helene shifted a crutch.

"I didn't mean to sound accusatory. I wondered if you saw anyone else. My colleague will check alibis. So far, you, Tommy, and Koulsy are the only ones who couldn't have done it. If you saw someone else in the moments when the box fell, I could rule them out."

"I wouldn't count Tommy out. I wouldn't count any of them out. Their own parents don't want them. You do realize that? Where can we send our child so far away we won't have to see Tommy or Michael or Rudolph again? We have the leftovers from parents too busy with their own lives."

Agnes felt the woman's anger like a blast of wind. It nearly pressed Agnes back. She wondered why Bernard Fontenay thought it was a good idea to bring his wife to a place full of children she obviously didn't like. Agnes's gaze flicked downward. Broken pelvis. Helene Fontenay couldn't have children after the accident. Agnes wondered if she'd wanted to before.

"Tommy was on the ground and saved Koulsy, nearly getting himself crushed." Agnes paused. "You feel these boys aren't wanted at home and that's why they're here?"

"It's obvious. Troublemakers."

"They seem bright enough and well behaved. Monsieur Navarro was telling me about Rudolph Versteegh, how he excels in the classroom and is a potential champion skier."

"That boy will never have what it takes to be a champion. It takes mental strength and discipline. These boys don't have that. They dillydally. Finish their homework just in time. Play at sports. They don't have the drive."

"I have three boys at home, and the ones here seem much like them. My boys do well in school. Usually. There are bad days and good days, but I think they're pretty normal. I'm confident they'll turn out to be fine young men."

"Three boys at home with you." Madame Fontenay gripped the handle of her brace until her knuckles where white. "A nice picture. Loving family all together. Here, we're paid to pretend to be their parents."

A pain fixed in Agnes's chest. She stood, unable to continue. She could not explain to this angry woman what they missed at home, what her boys didn't have. Their father. Thanking Helene for her time, she left the room.

Halfway down the stairs, she stopped. No one was around. The building wasn't precisely quiet, but she knew she was alone. She leaned against the white plaster wall and held her head in her hands. The leftovers, Helene had said. Agnes wanted to call her sons and ask them if they felt that way. Father dead. Suicide. Mother at work. Did they feel they were the leftovers? Surely not. They knew they were surrounded by love. Perhaps too much love, although what did too much love feel like? She didn't know, but hoped they did. She remembered them earlier at lunch, gently harassing one another.

They knew that they belonged. They didn't need to be smothered.

Somewhere overhead a door shut, and she stood away from the wall. She checked that her eyes were dry; only in her mind were tears leaking down her face. She straightened her jacket. When she reached the bottom step, she took a deep cleansing breath and opened the door.

Thirty-three

It was evening when Agnes followed the school nurse out of the building. The woman seemed impervious to the chill in the air.

"If he weren't already asleep, I would have sent him back to his dorm room," the nurse said.

"It's better that Koulsy stays here tonight," said Agnes. "You'll remain with him? I don't want him disturbed."

"Too many accidents?" said the nurse knowingly. "The infirmary is its own little piece of the building, so it'll be only the two of us. I bring my knitting when I stay over. No use having a nurse if she's asleep. I'll make sure he has a peaceful night."

Agnes bade Madame Butty good night and started across the lawn toward the chalet. Through the trees at the edge of the property she saw car headlights and thought it was probably Petit heading home. Between the two of them, they'd spoken with every child, teacher, and member of the staff at the Institute. Most were in class or with a group of colleagues and couldn't have pushed the flower box off the balcony. A few were alone at the time and could only offer their word that they hadn't. Petit had proven to be a master at getting people to talk. He had a harmless air about him that let people forget he was police.

She smiled. All afternoon Petit's excitement had been palpable. Nearly as palpable as his devotion to Bardy. She supposed it wasn't every day that a legend plucked you from the relative obscurity of the local police force. She was surprised he hadn't named the new baby for Bardy, but supposed that the wiser counsel of a levelheaded wife had prevailed.

She almost didn't see Bernard Fontenay until he was directly in front of her. The headmaster was walking with his head down, well bundled against the chill, and seemed preoccupied.

"Are you on your way to check on Koulsy?" she asked.

He darted a look in the direction of the infirmary and shook his head. "I called over earlier. He's asleep now, I take it?"

"Yes, and I'm leaving for the night."

Fontenay turned in the direction of the chalet to accompany her.

"You don't need to walk with me."

"I saw Julien Vallotton to his car and was out for a bit of air. No purpose really, I don't mind."

Agnes felt her breath hitch at the mention of Vallotton.

A group of older boys ran ahead of them, laughing. They opened the back door to the chalet and dashed inside. In the split second of light, a small figure was illuminated. "What's he doing outside?" said Fontenay. "Tommy? Tommy!"

The boy stood and turned in their direction.

"Son, you should be in your room, resting. Chef Jean is sending a dinner tray up to you." Fontenay put a hand on the boy's shoulder. "Were you worried about Koulsy? We've just seen him and he's absolutely fine."

Tommy glanced up to the balcony. He looked worse now than in the minutes after the window box had fallen.

"Do you need to see the nurse?" Agnes asked. "Does something hurt?"

"No. I wanted to see where it happened again."

"It's all cleaned up," said Fontenay. "An unfortunate accident. Put it from your mind and give yourself credit for being so quick-witted."

Tommy started to shove his hands in his pockets.

"Here, give me that trash and I'll throw it away for you." Fontenay plucked the wad of fishing line out of Tommy's hand.

"Just found it here." The boy reached in his other pocket and pulled out a wadded scrap of paper. "Take this, too? Thanks."

Discreetly, Agnes took both pieces of trash from Fontenay. "Why don't you take Tommy upstairs, Monsieur Fontenay, and I'll take care of this. I'm headed home for the night. Good night, Tommy. Sleep well."

She waited until they were inside the building before she looked at the fishing line. It was tangled around an inexpensive ink pen. The piece of paper was a wrapper from a candy bar. A Mars bar. An American product. Probably brought from home, she thought.

A riot of voices erupted inside the building. The older boys were enjoying evening privileges in the game room. The evening was cool, but not overly cold, and it was peaceful outside. She fingered the ball of line. The Mars-bar wrapper reminded her that she had a coffee stain on her scarf that needed to be professionally cleaned. She pulled the scarf from under her coat collar and sniffed. The stain was on a dark brown part of the pattern, hard to see, and she kept forgetting about it. She sniffed again. The potency of the smell and its incongruity with the smell of wool struck her.

She rounded the corner of the building and saw Julien Vallotton's Rolls-Royce in the parking lot. The front door opened and he stepped out.

"I was just writing you a note."

"I have a phone, you could have called."

"You're at work, I didn't want to bother you." He tucked the note in the breast pocket of her coat. "Thanks for letting me know what happened today. I'm afraid Helene didn't like my showing up to inquire about the boys, but Bernard understands."

"She thinks you're here to spy on them."

"When I lived in London, I wasn't very present. Now that I'm here, I'm interested. I have a responsibility."

She smelled the faint trace of his cologne and wondered what it was. Leather and old books and spruce.

"Do you have time for dinner?" he asked.

Her mind was on smell and she didn't reply. Smell and coffee. The smell of alcohol. She tapped the roof of her car, excited. Were they all fools or were some accomplices?

She opened her car door. "I need your help with something, first. I'll drive."

This was one mystery that, with some luck, she could solve tonight.

Thirty-four

Agnes didn't answer Julien Vallotton's questions, amused that, for once, he wasn't in command. After exiting the Institute's drive, she drove a hundred meters, then pulled over onto the shoulder. The narrow two-lane road was partially canopied by trees and it was dark.

"I'd pictured dinner in a restaurant, but if you have a picnic hamper in the back, this could be nice. Rustic, although liable to get us ticketed by Officer Boschung if he drives by."

"Wait here," Agnes said, enjoying herself. After checking that her mobile phone was in her coat pocket, she deposited her handbag in the trunk of her car. She swapped her pumps for boots and slammed the lid down.

Vallotton had opened the passenger-side door, and she passed by, saying, "Follow me."

She jumped the small roadside creek without getting her boots wet and climbed up the other side without incident, barely favoring her leg. Vallotton followed easily.

Training her flashlight on the ground, she led the way out of the thin line of trees and straight up the middle of the pasture. The farmhouse was to their right and the Institute well beyond that. The ground was rough going, churned up by cow hooves. Thick mud, and some other dark material she didn't want to think about, stuck to her boots. She appreciated that Vallotton didn't complain, particularly since he was probably ruining shoes that cost a week of her salary.

"I cannot imagine where you are taking me," said Vallotton.

"Because you haven't been paying attention. Now be quiet. Sound carries."

When they reached higher ground, she turned her flashlight off to avoid being spotted from the Institute. From that point on, she used the glow from her phone screen to occasionally check the terrain. The lights of the chalet let her judge their direction; twisting her ankle in a hole was what worried her.

Reaching the hut Leo Chavanon and his friends used as a meeting place, she stopped.

"This is it? This is what you want to show me?" Vallotton whispered.

"No. This is where we wait and see what happens."

The hut was built into the rise of the hill, with the back wall only a few feet above the earth. The roof was more of an over-hang than real protection, but the three walls provided shelter from any wind. The site also allowed a nearly unobstructed view across the entirety of the Institute, the neighboring farmhouse, and the pastures leading toward town.

Vallotton righted a three-legged milking stool and offered it to her. "I take it we're here for a long spell? You can take the first seated watch."

She smiled. It wouldn't be a comfortable perch, but was better than leaning against the wall or sitting on the damp ground.

"What am I looking for?" He gazed out toward the forest through a gap between the boards in the back wall.

"Lights, what else?" He started to ask a question but she cut him off. "Be quiet, or we might miss our chance. I only want to do this once."

The darkness of early evening had turned to the blackness of a cloudy night, and Agnes adjusted her scarf, wishing she'd brought a hat. However, her coat was warm and she wasn't too uncomfortable. Vallotton turned up the collar of his long coat and adjusted his scarf. She scanned the view, taking in 180 degrees from the Institute all the way across the pasture toward town. Vallotton kept watch in the other direction. Occasionally, lights in the chalet clicked on and off as boys went to bed early or stayed up studying. Otherwise, the night was dark. There weren't even car headlights on the nearby road. Agnes hoped it wouldn't be too long before they saw movement.

They swapped positions twice before being rewarded. Vallotton nudged her. A light bobbed in the pasture at the edge of the forest. Then it disappeared. She joined him to watch between the broken planks as the light flashed on and off again, too rapid to indicate direction. They waited, carefully scanning the countryside.

The light flashed again. She grinned and pointed. Vallotton nodded his head. The destination was clear.

They waited five more minutes, but there was no more activity. She turned on her flashlight. "They're inside and can't see us."

"You don't think we need someone else? What do you call it, backup? You're not armed, are you?"

"I think you're all the backup this requires. Come on."

Up close, the farmhouse was tall and broad. The traditional combination of house and barn resulted in an enormous structure capped with a high, sweeping peaked roof. The house was on the downside of the hill, and the main entrance to the barn was reached via a sloped ramp. Agnes held the light, while Vallotton tried the main door to the house first. It was padlocked.

"Don't worry, it's supposed to be uninhabited," she said. "We'll find out where they're getting in."

The shutters were closed and they didn't bother trying to find a chink in the wood. Despite being vacant, the structure was in good shape, maintained in readiness for someone to move in.

They followed the wall and walked up the ramp to the barn entrance. It, too, was padlocked. Judging by the pile of leaves and small branches piled against the door, it hadn't been opened recently either.

Vallotton was turning away when Agnes spotted a small, almost half-size door at the edge of the ramp. It looked as if someone had cut an opening in the wall for a special purpose, or to avoid a great rush of wind into the barn during an especially cold winter. The door didn't reach the floor, resting on the bottom logs of the structure, and it was no taller than Agnes.

She turned the knob. There was no lock, and the door shifted on well-oiled hinges. They waited side by side, listening for any sounds. After a few minutes, she clicked off her light and carefully pushed the door open. She smiled at Vallotton. This was what she was looking for.

Once inside, she was struck by the pervasive smell of hay. Vallotton shut the door behind them. There were small noises, from either rodents or farm cats.

"They've gone farther inside," she whispered.

"There's a lower level, then a true cellar," Vallotton whispered back, motioning across the room.

Agnes clicked her light on for a brief moment. He was right, there was a heavy door on the opposite wall. Vallotton tested the handle and it also opened easily. Silently. Too easily for years of disuse.

A corridor lay before them. The walls were planked with heavy timber, and the earth floor sloped gently down. A light streamed under the door at the far end. Agnes led the way, walking quietly. In front of the door, she listened, heard voices, and shook her head. She felt Vallotton tense. Pushing the door open abruptly, she stepped into the room.

Bernard Fontenay stood, tipping his chair over backward. Jorge Navarro dropped a glass beaker, shattering it.

"I've always wanted to do that," Agnes said. "Burst into a room like in a movie."

"Inspector Lüthi," Fontenay said weakly. "Vallotton."

Julien Vallotton didn't speak, but Agnes could sense him absorbing the details of the room. She hoped he didn't mind her having a bit of fun with the discovery.

"Monsieur Fontenay, it was the smell on your coat when I sat near it in your office." She walked farther into the room. "I didn't think about it at the time, but I caught the scent of alcohol."

Navarro pulled a broom from a closet and started cleaning up the broken glass. "I told you we'd be found out."

Bottles and beakers were strewn across tables. Clay jugs and wine bottles filled the shelves of a tall cabinet. Various other bits of equipment littered the room. The most interesting feature was the small still.

"This isn't left over from Amman, is it?" Vallotton asked.

"No, we built it," said Fontenay.

"What made you so curious?" Navarro asked her.

"Was it the lights?" said Fontenay.

"Partly," she said. "I asked about them and realized that there was a pattern. At first, people remembered seeing lights in the general direction of the fields. It was only later that they reported lights in the forest. You started walking up there and turning back, hoping to avoid being seen. You took quite a risk going there at night simply to misdirect attention."

"If people saw strange lights in different places they talked about it, but didn't search," said Navarro.

Vallotton picked up an open bottle and sniffed. "Plums?"

Fontenay nodded.

"It's not all plum brandy," Navarro said. "We're experimenting with pear and some other fruits. A few blends."

"I also thought the headmaster would be more worried about strangers crossing the property," said Agnes. "What if it was vagrants—"

"Here?" said Fontenay, eyebrows raised.

"You weren't concerned at all, even when we found the shed had been vandalized. And neither was your wife. You told some of the boys that they hadn't seen anything. Koulsy, for example. He knew what he'd seen. That scared him more. You should have thought of that."

Agnes picked up a glass and sniffed. "And then there were your clothes. We met coming and going several times and you were always bundled up for harsh weather. I've noticed that most of the faculty make the dash from the chalet to the classrooms or the other dormitory without even bothering with an overcoat. Some throw on a scarf or hat, but you were always wearing full winter gear."

"Setting an example for the students?" Fontenay said, smiling gently. "Don't want them to get sick."

"It was as if you were going somewhere colder than the rest of us." She looked around the unheated room. "If that was the case, then you weren't slipping off to the local bar to slosh brandy on your sleeve. I think that's what your wife suspects. Or worse. That's why she ignores the lights and avoids talk about anything of concern that happens here. Her injury has isolated her and made her afraid. But I knew you weren't going into the village. Boschung barely knows you."

"I wouldn't say that. You could see for yourself that he's respectful and that I trust him."

"Boschung feels like he's the shepherd guiding the villagers through life. If the two of you had any sort of friendship, he would have a different attitude about the Institute. As it is, he's angry because he feels cut off. He used to play here as a boy, and now as a man he's no longer an insider. A few drinks together in town and he'd have a different attitude."

"I've never had a talent for village life," Fontenay said.

"Tonight, the smell of alcohol on your coat came back to me. I recognized what had been in the back of my mind all along. Fermentation. You weren't drinking alcohol, you were making it."

"Julien, I didn't mean to betray your trust," said Fontenay.

"It was my fault," interrupted Navarro. "I've always wanted to experiment. Comes with being a chemist, I suppose, and we got to talking last winter. It was a cold, dark spell and there wasn't much to do. The students were on break and we played around with the idea in the lab."

"It was my idea to continue," said Fontenay. "I love the Institute, don't mistake that, but I've always liked the idea of making something. Something real. A product. I thought of using this house. I knew the water was kept running."

"Why not tell people what you are doing?" Agnes asked.

"We'd broken in here and don't have a license. Once we started in secret, we couldn't stop."

"That's what you were worried about the night by the shed," said Agnes. "Monsieur Navarro was returning to the chalet and we saw the lights."

"Didn't seem like a good time to tell Boschung what we were doing," said Fontenay.

"He's a stickler for rules, isn't he?" said Agnes. "And that night he was looking for someone to blame. I smelled smoke nearby a few times. That was also you?"

"We dress warmly but the chill sets in. Plus, part of the process needs heat. Working here belowground we didn't have much of a problem because the temperature was stable, but a few things we had to do in the kitchen, and we'd light a fire. Only at night or on cloudy days when it wouldn't be visible."

Fontenay moved to a cabinet and removed a series of bottles. Three of the four had labels. "The competition," he said, motioning toward them. "Quality control." He pulled out a set of small glasses. "I'd like you to know that we at least didn't risk our jobs for poor quality. I'm not proud of what we did, but I am proud of what we produced."

He splashed liquid in the glasses, then opened a second bottle and repeated the motion. He ended with a splash from the unlabeled bottle. "Not a blind test, but I don't think you're here to falsely flatter. That is, if you want to try."

Vallotton took a sip from the first two glasses. Agnes stepped forward and put a glass to her lips.

"Amazing," said Vallotton after taking a drink from the last glass, the brandy that Fontenay and Navarro had produced.

"I'm happy that whatever happens, we did one good thing."

Vallotton set the glass on the table with a small thunk. "It is disappointing. So much will have to change now because of this."

Agnes shot him a dark look, surprised by his attitude. Fontenay might be a scholar, but he retained his streak of childhood mischief. Vallotton had made other allowances for him, why not this?

"I should have quit and had the courage to go into the business," said Fontenay, "but we'd put all our capital in the Institute. Helene had already suffered so much, I had to give her this."

"I have the impression that Madame Fontenay doesn't care for the work here," said Agnes, hoping to delay whatever bad news Vallotton seemed intent on delivering. She had misread him, forgetting that he, too, could be a stickler for behavior. They had broken into *his* property, abused their positions at *his* school. She regretted bringing him here. This wasn't the end she'd envisioned. She hadn't misread Fontenay's temperament; how had she misjudged Vallotton's?

"Until the accident," Bernard said, "Helene wanted a dozen kids. It was always a matter of waiting until she finished the last ski season. It was to be her last. Her dramatic finale. World Cup in hand, she'd retire and we'd start a family. Instead, she had a dramatic finale of another sort." He picked up one of the small cups and downed it in one go. "I'd planned to join the faculty and teach somewhere, England most likely, since that's where her family is, and she'd want the help with our children. Once she couldn't have children, she was devastated and I hit upon the idea of going all in. A change of scenery and a way to have a family that would be ours, even if they weren't really ours."

"It didn't work out like you hoped," said Agnes.

"Not at first, but recently I've had hopes. Of course, now I've ended all that. The board won't want a headmaster distilling alcohol in the basement."

Agnes started to speak but Vallotton interrupted her. "I think they might object to one who drinks too much, but making it? That's entrepreneurial. A selling point among the parents. You're a man with experience outside the school." Vallotton clapped Fontenay on the back.

Navarro grinned. "Inspector, when you first showed up the other day, I nearly died of fright."

"I thought it was because of the poison garden," said Agnes.

"And I thought you knew what we were doing here." Navarro's dark eyes twinkled.

"A chemistry professor who grows poisonous plants and makes good brandy. You shouldn't have trouble getting your students' attention," she said.

Navarro looked surprised. "When you put it that way, maybe not. Botany is not a subject most students care for, and even the parents aren't interested. Chemistry isn't glamorous. Monsieur Patel understood, he studied chemistry and said that he was lucky to have used the degree at all."

"I"—Fontenay glanced at Navarro—"we don't have the means to really go into business. It was a small project only. These are test batches."

"You need a partner," said Vallotton.

"Oh, dear Lord, run!" said Agnes. "He's a dilettante."

"I am not. I have experience. I own a vineyard in the United States, in Napa, and a domaine in France, near Champagne."

"Certainly bought for the architecture," said Agnes.

"Yes"—Vallotton eyed her archly—"but they are still vineyards and I've learned some about the production. I'm not merely a man with more money than he needs, looking for ways to occupy myself."

"Either way, we call that an investor," said Fontenay.

"I like the sound of that," said Vallotton. "I can lease back use of the house here from the Amman family. He only wants the pasture and will be only too happy to get a reduction in his terms. We can convert the cellar and first floor into what you need, including heat and electricity. And you'll be near enough to keep on at the school. Who knows, maybe Helene will take to the place if she's more in charge, less under your shadow."

"You'd really keep me?" said Fontenay.

"Oh, yes, as Inspector Lüthi knows, I don't care much for meeting new people."

"The ones he knows already upset him too much," she said, feeling a glow of delight at the outcome for Fontenay and Navarro.

"There's that, and I think we can do good things here. I think the village could use a new enterprise, and we'll surely need to hire a few people eventually, for trucking and other practicalities."

Agnes felt her phone vibrate. She took a step away from the men and answered. It was Aubry.

Vallotton lifted his glass. "To the company. What will you name it?"

Agnes walked across the room, seeking better reception near the wall. Finally she heard Aubry clearly.

"Bardy is handling it himself," Aubry repeated. "Top priority, of course, but as low-key as he can manage. This is a disaster."

Agnes leaned heavily against a worktable.

Antoine Mercier was dead.

Thirty-five

Fortunately the body was discovered after Baselworld closed for the day.

Agnes watched the officers photograph and document. She'd seen the corpse. Now she was standing where Mercier was killed. Exactly where they had met the day before, high above the showroom floor. Yesterday, the open webbing of the metal floor felt precarious; seeing his body here only reinforced her fears.

"We're done," the last of the crime-scene team said, picking up his bag and indicating she could walk about freely.

"This changes everything," Agnes said to Aubry, repeating what she'd already said to Bardy. "Both Mercier and Chavanon were closely associated to the watch industry. The connection to their deaths must be here."

Aubry shrugged. "Thousands of people walk through the show every day. Anyone who knew Mercier would know he was here this week. Easy enough to join the crowds, kill him, and vanish. Trust me, I know. We're still looking for the woman in the video."

"Maybe I was wrong and Chavanon ingested the peanuts earlier and the reaction was delayed. He might have vomited up the evidence and it was cleared away." She edged carefully to the spot where dried blood colored the metal floor grate. "Mercier was stabbed here?"

Aubry had been on the scene when the body was discovered. "The blood was on him and under him. Nowhere else. He hadn't been moved."

Agnes walked around the stain to peer over the railing, feeling her stomach sink. Blood had dripped through the grate to the roof of the pavilion below. Eventually it had drained to the edge and down the side of the building into a potted plant. Housekeeping noticed it after the show closed for the evening.

"The lady who found it was hysterical," said Aubry. "Probably still is. She saw 'sticky red stuff'—that's what she called it— then looked up and there he was, silhouetted by the lights. If she didn't have sharp eyes, we might not have found him until tomorrow when his staff sounded the alarm."

"They weren't worried today?"

"Too busy to be worried, and he lived alone. He didn't have anything on his schedule that was absolutely fixed, more like 'I'll stop by and try to get a photograph with you.' Everyone thought he'd gotten busy with something or someone else. Bardy is building a timeline."

"I thought Mercier was avoiding me," said Agnes. She shook her head. "He lied about Chavanon. I should have tracked him down and insisted we speak immediately."

"Would he have been honest with you even then?"

"I'll never know."

A powerful flash erupted beneath them. Men were standing on the roof of the pavilion, documenting the blood pattern. Agnes spotted Bardy; he looked up and gave a small salute. She liked watching the team at work, seeing the division—her division—in this light.

"Mercier met with Chavanon two days before he died and didn't tell me about it," she said.

"But he must not have been the man's killer, since he's dead now."

Agnes studied the dried blood. "A knife, you said?"

"Knife or sharp object. He was stabbed."

"And he died right here, looking down over the show." The showroom sprawled out in front of them, sections of it too far away to see in any detail. "Is there surveillance video of the entrance to the stair leading up here?"

"Not precisely. There is an angle that captures people moving through the area, which means any one of them could have gone up the stairs, but the door isn't visible, and the next set of cameras doesn't pick them up immediately after. Thousands of people walked by. Including, of course, Mercier. But he was alone at the time. That much they have reviewed."

"Someone could have arrived before him and waited." She moved nearer the rail and pointed. "Why is he here? I thought they'd cleared the exhibitors out?"

Aubry glanced down. "He's Mercier's nephew."

Agnes headed for the stairs. Now she would insist on speaking with Gianfranco Giberti.

•   •   •

Giberti was dry-eyed, but the undercurrent of emotion was evident in the set of his shoulders and grim line of his lips. Agnes thought he looked like a glamorous advertisement for grief.

"I wish your uncle had told me the truth," she said, offering her hand but skipping pleasantries.

"What truth?"

"He last spoke with Guy Chavanon a few days before the man's death, not a few months ago."

Giberti frowned. "Antoine met with Christine's father? Why?"

"I hoped you could tell me."

"I don't think they were friends, or even friendly. That doesn't sound right. I didn't mean to imply animosity, only that theirs was a purely professional relationship."

Agnes took Giberti's elbow and guided him away from the officials examining the planter where the blood was discovered.

"Monsieur Chavanon wouldn't have talked to your uncle about any innovations he was exploring?"

"Definitely not." Giberti looked round the exhibition hall as if seeking answers. "My uncle is not who Monsieur Chavanon would have confided in."

"Because they had a difficult history?"

"No." Giberti looked uncomfortable. "My uncle was an amazing person, dedicated, really the one who made me want to pursue watchmaking as a career."

"But?" Agnes prompted.

Giberti turned so his back was to the policemen documenting the crime scene. "Monsieur Chavanon was too . . . *eccentric,* is a good word. Antoine liked things to move in a set pattern. He

liked change to occur in a manageable way, a controlled way."
Giberti shrugged. "Very Swiss, I suppose."

"Which Monsieur Chavanon wasn't?"

"Oh, he was Swiss all right, but there was a streak of creativity in him that was like an explosion. He was silent until it released, then he'd settle back into himself for a while."

"It sounds like you knew Monsieur Chavanon better than you admitted the other day."

Giberti had the grace to look ashamed. "Of course I knew him well. I should have said so, but I didn't want it to become too personal. I knew Christine wouldn't want that, having me part of your investigation, the police asking me what I thought about her and her father. I truly don't know anything important. I'm sorry."

"Why did Monsieur Chavanon have your business card?"

"I've told you that I have no idea."

"Be careful, Monsieur Giberti, two men have died. Now isn't the time to keep small secrets."

An officer approached, "Monsieur Giberti, the chief has a few questions for you."

As he was led away, Giberti turned to Agnes. "We hadn't met."

She watched them for a few moments then silently added, *Yet*. Maybe they hadn't met *yet*.

Thirty-six

Marie Chavanon rapped her knuckles on the door of the cottage. She planned on the tap of a stepmother's authority, but it sounded more like a panicked neighbor. Christine opened the door, her expression startled.

"We have to go to the police," Marie said without a greeting.

"What time is it?" Christine stepped onto the porch, looking around to check the position of the sun.

"Not that early." Marie hesitated, unsure of her reception. "I waited as long as I could. I had to see you. May I come in?"

Christine waved her across the threshold and closed the door.

Marie was conscious that she'd not been in the cottage more than twice since her stepdaughter had moved in . . . how many years ago? She recognized the décor from Leo's descriptions. He liked visiting here, which was fortunate, because he didn't realize they thought of it as babysitting. Leo thought he was visiting his cool, older half sister. He was honored that she would have dinner with him and play games all evening. Marie sometimes wondered if he'd even noticed his parents were gone. When he was home from school, he still looked forward to those nights.

"I must have fallen asleep," said Christine, leading the way to the kitchen. She was wearing the same clothes she'd had on the day before, and Marie noticed a small blanket on the sofa. Beside it was a stack of paper and Guy's notebook. Christine detoured to pick up the leatherbound pages. "I need coffee," she said, rubbing her eyes.

"Antoine Mercier was killed yesterday at Baselworld."

Christine stopped in the doorway to the kitchen. There was a long second, then she clicked the light switch on and walked to the counter. Marie pulled a chair back from the kitchen table and watched Christine pull out cups and pour water into the coffee machine.

"It wasn't an accident. He was stabbed. Inspector Lüthi telephoned me late last night. She thinks his death is connected to your father's."

Frowning, Christine held out the bowl of Nespresso coffee pods.

"An orange or red one for me, nothing too strong. I don't think my stomach can handle it."

"Who do they suspect?" Christine hit the appropriate buttons and let the coffee flow into the clear designer cups. She handed Marie her coffee with milk and drank her own espresso in a swallow, inserting a new pod and hitting the button to make a second one.

"We have to tell the inspector what you found," Marie said.

"There's too much at risk."

"A man died. What if it's because of what Guy invented?"

"I can't imagine the connection." Christine picked up her second espresso and downed it, shaking her shoulders as if registering the heat and flavor.

"But this is information—"

"I'm the one who went to the police in the first place. I want to find my father's killer more than anyone, but right now it's possible for someone to claim his work. We need to find the rest of his notes."

Christine took Marie's hands in her own. Marie felt the warmth and realized how cold hers were. She'd always admired Christine's closeness to her father. Not even the divorce of her parents or his remarriage was an obstacle to their connection. Until that day . . . that awful day when she left the company, casting Guy adrift. Ending the dynasty. Marie had tried to make him feel that he still had Leo, and that the boy would grow up in the same tradition, but her words had fallen on deaf ears. For he knew that if Christine could leave Perrault et Chavanon, then Leo could as well. Everything seemed to lead from that day.

"Inspector Lüthi will want to talk to me again." Marie shivered.

Christine gripped Marie's hands more tightly. "What could you possibly know that would help? She won't ask about Father's notebook. I took care of that. Don't you understand? If we turn over *this* notebook, it will be placed into evidence and anyone could see it."

Marie disentangled her hands and wrapped her arms around herself. "Are you sure that we found"—involuntarily she leaned toward Christine and lowered her voice—"that we found what we did?"

"Yes. I am sure. There hasn't been an idea like this since people started carrying watches. When I think back to those days . . .

Can you imagine what it meant to carry a timepiece on your person? To regulate your life according to minutes or hours and not rely on the sun or a city tower clock? It changed the world. Hundreds of years later we are still slaves to that mechanism strapped to our wrist. Father's creation changes this."

"I don't know how you can be so sure when what we have is incomplete."

"I've had two days and was up all last night researching the formulas, corroborating. It's all there. Well, not all there. Not all of the precise calculations. Father had a knowledge of materials engineering and anatomy and physiology that I don't have, and he took precautions to protect his invention." Christine sat down opposite Marie. "Think of it like this. You write on one page of a notebook, then the next page is in another notebook. You need both to have the whole thing, but if you skim along with only one, you can see progress. It's not haphazard ranting. It is the documentation of a complex development."

"You've looked everywhere for the missing parts? For the rest of his work?"

"Yes. Everywhere I could think of."

"What about in his workshop?"

Christine gave Marie a dark look. "I started there."

Marie looked shocked. "The police said we couldn't enter, they left tape on the doors."

"I crawled in the bathroom window late last night. I know how to get in the cottage windows. It's not difficult."

Absently, Marie fiddled with her coffee. "I don't know if we're doing the right thing."

In the next room a radio alarm turned on, blaring the morning news. Christine rose as if to turn it off, then changed her mind.

"Do you want Father's work to be lost? Or worse, to be claimed by someone else? No patents have been filed. There's nothing to prove it's ours until we have everything and can go about it carefully." She knelt so her face was level with Marie's. "This is a once-in-a-lifetime—no, once-in-a-century chance. This will secure Leo's future. Don't you want that? Isn't that what Father would have wanted?"

"Yesterday Stephan asked me again if I'd found anything. I think he knows something." Marie closed her eyes and inhaled deeply. "Have you seen Gianfranco recently?"

Christine looked surprised. "In passing at the show. Why? Has he contacted you?"

"Of course not, I only thought that—" Marie brushed her hand across her brow. "It doesn't matter."

Christine gripped Marie by the shoulders. "Think about it. If you truly believe that Antoine Mercier's death is related to my father's and if someone was willing to kill them for this, then they will stop at nothing. They would come after us next. We can't tell anyone we have this notebook."

"I can't believe he actually created something important." Marie rubbed her eyes so hard it hurt. "The police have seen everything in the workshop, the papers, all those sheets tacked to the walls. Won't they know what he was working on?"

"That's another reason I broke in. I wanted to see what was there. If you know what you're looking for, then you see how his thought process evolved. Or at least where he started. But they don't know. His idea is so fantastical that they would never guess, and so the calculations and notes look exactly like what they are: random formulas and problem solving. Like a man dabbling in his love of science and numbers. I think that what is there—particularly on the walls—are the oldest notes. Father was toying with notions. A warm-up, you might call it."

"Why did someone break in if it's such a secret?"

"He has to have told someone. Not about the entire idea, but enough to interest them or to ask about a manufacturing process." Christine stood and placed another pod in the coffee machine.

Marie shook her head at the offer. She wondered if she had gotten an ulcer over the last two days. "Do you think he told Antoine Mercier? He didn't like the man, I can't see him as a confidant."

"I can't either. He hated Mercier. But Stephan," Christine hesitated. "He might have talked to him."

Marie sat silently, toying with her sleeve. "You heard what Stephan said. That Guy had hinted, but that was all."

"And you believe him? Completely?"

Marie inhaled sharply. "What about Gianfranco?"

"Father disliked Gianfranco. Said he was the face of commercialization." Christine gave a half smile.

"Your father disliked Gianfranco because he knew he would break your heart. And he was right."

Christen looked startled. "That's what you think? That he broke my heart?" She looked away. "Do you know why I left the company?"

"You said that we didn't have a future."

"I'd always wanted to go back to our roots. We can't compete with companies like Omega, so why try? Instead, be different, be like before. Small, with incredible craftsmanship. Just me and Father, a few watches a year. I could have done it. But he couldn't. He wanted the freedom to think and wander. The company was floundering and I left."

Marie tried a smile. "You both loved the traditions."

"But he didn't." Christine leaned against the kitchen cabinet. "I think he only said that he did. He loved the idea of the traditions, but that was really pride in a lineage. Deep down he wanted to innovate."

"We always talked about his inventions."

"Yes, but even in our wildest bragging we knew that it was incremental innovation, refinements. He meant it when he said big ideas. Father wanted to leave the past behind. He would have, if he'd lived." Christine fingered her espresso cup. "I think that's why he only hinted at what he was working on and wouldn't say any more. He was afraid of what I'd say, that I'd ridicule him for abandoning our long history. He knew that I wanted to manufacture purely mechanical watches. I like the *making* of it."

"It makes no sense that he wouldn't tell you. You weren't working in a small traditional workshop, you were with a large company."

"Only because as my father's daughter I couldn't apprentice to someone like Dufour. They would have been too suspicious of my motives. I chose the middle ground. Father thought I'd taken a stand. He was afraid to tell me the direction he'd gone."

"You think he told someone?"

"He couldn't have manufactured it. We may be an old firm, but we're small and have never dealt with this kind of technology." Christine smiled. "Well, I guess no one has. Father would have had questions. He wouldn't have wanted a repeat of the quartz debacle, when we had the technology in Switzerland but let the moment slip by and other countries made the real money. They got the market share that we should have kept. Father remembers this. Maybe he thought to partner with someone who already had a powerful manufacturing presence and would know how to make this leap?"

"He despised the large companies."

"Like Omega?" Christine smiled.

Marie shrugged an apology.

"This wasn't something he could do himself." Christine tore off a piece of croissant and ate it slowly. "I think he spoke with someone. It depends on who that someone was. I know what's it like to work for a large company. And we're part of an even larger one. The notion of crushing the competition exists. Depending on who he talked to, once they knew, anything is possible."

"But murder? Who would kill for an idea?"

Christine laughed. "That's all anyone does kill for. Wars are about ideas. Plenty of killing there. This is no different than fighting over physical territory. This is intellectual territory. The winner gets the spoils of war. The money. Let's say whoever he told simply wanted it for themselves, or maybe they had a deal and changed their minds. Or maybe Father held out or maybe they are greedy. Who knows? What I do know is that my father was on the brink of unimaginable success and he died. And around that same time someone broke into his workshop. We have his notebook as proof of his ideas."

"Not telling us, that would be like Guy. He liked to waltz in on a bed of glory." Marie smiled weakly.

"He would have been so proud."

The women sat silently for a moment.

"He didn't need to die." Marie heard herself. "The inspector would help us, you know. You were the one who contacted her in the first place. We could trust her."

"It's not about trusting Inspector Lüthi. It's about everyone else. Give me more time. Once we tell the police, there will be talk. Think about La Chaux-de-Fonds. Everyone knows everyone else, and there are relatives in the police and in the watchmaking companies. All it would take is someone processing the paperwork or having a coffee with a friend and the secret leaks. If someone stole the other part of Father's work, we don't want them to know we don't have a complete copy. Trust me, now that Mercier is dead, they will be paying attention. Listening and watching. If they think they can claim the work for themselves, they will. Right now, they'll assume we have everything and could prove that they are the thieves."

"I just don't know." Marie thought about Guy and his failures and how impossible this all sounded.

"Three more hours. Let me finish looking."

"Life changing," said Marie weakly.

"Revolutionary," Christine reminded her.

Thirty-seven

Complaining to complain was what Agnes thought upon waking. It was what Petit had said about her boys at lunch the day before. It was what all young people did.

She'd planned a stop on the way to Baselworld, knowing Bardy had the investigation into Mercier's death well in hand and didn't need her there. She arrived at the Institute after breakfast and went straight to see Koulsy in the infirmary. He looked alert, and his injured ankle was less swollen, which Agnes suspected Madame Butty hesitated to admit since she was enjoying having a patient under her care.

"I let him have a visitor this morning," the nurse said. "I thought Tommy deserved to see his friend, and I was right. He's still shaky, poor boy. Seeing his friend get hurt was hard on him. They are more sensitive than they let on at that age. Maybe I should have kept him here yesterday."

Reassured about Koulsy's recovery, Agnes walked to the chalet. Absently, she reached into her handbag and fingered the junk she'd collected the day before. Why was fishing line tied to a pen?

Across the lawn, Tommy Scaglia emerged from a classroom building and walked around it to the other side. She had woken in the night, thinking about him, and his fright after the flower box fell. Now she was standing exactly where he had been when the rush of wood and earth descended from the sky. She looked around. There was an anomalous column. Maybe at some point the balcony had started to sag and the owner had added the support? It was carved with the same elements found elsewhere on the building: birds, circles, and darts. A few hooks and nails were in it, mostly worn down and no longer used. Ignored, but there.

Agnes stepped back and looked high overhead to the empty spot left by the flower box. It was directly above her. From her handbag, she retrieved the fishing line and pen. She tossed it gently, thinking, feeling the slight weight. It fell.

Suddenly she knew. Complaining to complain. And boys never picked up trash voluntarily. She headed across the lawn.

Tommy wasn't behind the classroom building, but the tabby was slinking across the lawn in the direction of the farmhouse. She followed and slipped though the hedge. No one was in sight, which meant only one thing. She pulled the padlock key from her handbag. Standing in front of the shed she stopped to listen. An indistinct voice was audible through the thick door. She slid the key into the lock and turned it, silently thanking Hamel for keeping everything in such good working order. The padlock opened noiselessly. She slipped it off, then grasped the iron strap and, in one heave, opened the door.

Tommy gasped and leaped to his feet. She blocked the door

in case he tried to run. His shoulders slumped. They were dusted with dirt where he'd crawled through the chicken door. He looked down as if considering a dive back through the small opening and Agnes imagined she could hear his heart race.

"Tommy, what made you do it?" she asked without preamble.

"Do what?"

"This." She motioned toward the back wall and stump. "The notes, the arrow, the flower box. Everything."

"I didn't." His voice was firm, but his hands shook. "I only came here because I wanted to see where all that blood was. I'd heard everyone talking about it and wanted to see it for myself. . . ." His voice trailed off.

"Who has been talking? Your classmates don't know any details."

"Somebody found out, I don't know who. It's no use asking me, I don't remember. Just talk at lunch or dinner or something that I overheard."

Agnes dropped the padlock into her handbag. "Did you hear this from the Fontenays? You hide behind the curtain on the window seat in their office, don't you?"

He clenched his fists and at first she thought he was angry, then she realized he was afraid. "That's how you know things, isn't it? How you are able to warn the other students?"

She walked inside, no longer blocking the door; entering his space, but letting him know he could run out if he wanted. Light flooded the center of the room, and Tommy stepped deeper into the shadows. The cat walked through the small opening and made a circuit of the room. Disdainful of the smells.

"If they send me home, I'll tell my dad the other stuff. What Monsieur Fontenay does when he's not in class. I'll tell Dad how much Madame Fontenay hates being here. How she hates us all."

"Is that what you want, Tommy? To go home? Couldn't you talk to your parents and tell them you're not happy here?"

He hunched over as if he'd been hit.

"You're a long way from California. It's understandable."

"You can't expel me. I know too much."

"What did you say the day we met? That you thought there were scary things happening and your father would take you home? I think that you really meant that you *wanted* your father to take you home. Is that why you started the notes targeting Koulsy? So that your parents would think the Institute was unsafe and remove you?"

"I would never do anything to hurt Koulsy."

"I don't think you intended to hurt him." She took a few steps closer. "You picked Koulsy because he's not afraid, right? He only started to care when Monsieur Chavanon died and he wondered if someone else might get hurt. You wouldn't have done those things to scare someone."

"That wasn't me."

"I know Monsieur Chavanon's death wasn't your fault. But the rest was."

He was breathing rapidly, nearly hyperventilating. She moved toward him slowly. He didn't react when she placed her hands gently on his shoulders. His breathing slowed. She waited.

"How'd you know?" he finally asked.

"Are you on the archery team?"

He shrugged. "No."

"The hole made by the arrow was all wrong. It looked like someone had thrust it in by hand. The hole should have angled sharply. The arrow would have hit on an upward trajectory if shot from near the building or a downward trajectory if shot from farther away and striking on descent. You thrust it straight in." She reached into her pocket and pulled out the length of fishing line and the pen. "Yesterday evening you came outside to look for this. Monsieur Fontenay thought it was trash you had picked up."

He reached for the bundle, then stopped himself and slipped his hand back in his pocket.

"You loosened the screws on the flower-box bracket, then looped this around it or around the bracket, and dropped the line off the balcony. You knew the box was heavy enough to not fall unless pushed or pulled. You tied the line to the pen for weight before you dropped it over the edge, then you attached it to one of the hooks on the column. The line is nearly invisible and the column is a natural place to wait. You made sure you were there when Koulsy walked back from his swim trial, and you took a few steps forward to greet him and pulled the line with you. The box dislodged and fell."

"It nearly hit me, why would I do that?"

"The plan didn't work exactly as expected, did it? You miscalculated. The box hit the lower balcony and twisted. You had to save Koulsy by pushing him aside." She looked around the shed. "This is the only part that I don't understand."

"I didn't mean for anyone to come in here. . . ." His voice trailed off, the energy gone from his face. "They'll send me home, won't they?"

She studied him carefully. He wasn't hopeful, he was concerned. Complaining to complain. All kids did it, only Tommy Scaglia had created something to complain about.

"What made you orchestrate the mess in here? It was a chicken, right?"

"I saw it in a movie. There was a mob boss and he—"

Agnes held up a hand to stop him. "Maybe you should try your hand at writing movies." She led him outside into the sunlight. "Your parents will have to be told."

"Brenda's not my mom. She's my stepmom."

"Your father then." Agnes remembered Helene Fontenay's remarks about the unwanted children. Perhaps Tommy had been sent far away to school, out of the way of his stepmother. Or perhaps that was simply in his imagination. Certainly Leo Chavanon wasn't sent to the Institute as punishment. He was a cherished child and loved it here.

"Here's what we are going to do. You're going to tell Madame Fontenay what you've been doing and talk to her about going home. Or staying. Tell her that you need her help."

Tommy opened his mouth, then shut it. He did this a few times before speaking. "Do you think Koulsy's going to be very mad?"

Agnes took Tommy's hand and led him toward the hedge. "I think Koulsy, of all people, will understand."

Thirty-eight

Agnes took the highway south to Bienne. While driving, she spoke on the telephone with Petit, and he described the atmosphere at Baselworld.

"I can feel the tension. The exhibitors wonder if they will be next."

She hoped he was exaggerating. The deaths of Antoine Mercier and Guy Chavanon were certainly connected, but she didn't think they had a serial killer working his way through the watchmakers. She asked Petit to check on Gisele and Ivo at the Perrault et Chavanon booth.

When she reached Bienne, she parked on the street near Omega headquarters. Gianfranco Giberti wasn't there, something she had counted on.

"I was surprised Monsieur Chavanon wanted to meet with Monsieur Giberti," his assistant said after they'd exchanged greetings. The woman was clearly dazed by the news of Antoine Mercier's death and happy to talk to someone official about it. "That's one of the reasons I didn't mention it to Monsieur Giberti."

"You scheduled the appointment and didn't tell him? Was that unusual?"

"He doesn't like to be bothered with day-to-day things. I email a PDF of the next day's schedule the night before, and he follows it to the letter. I make all of his appointments."

"But you were surprised at Monsieur Chavanon's request? You thought he might create trouble for your boss?" Agnes pictured Guy's anger at the younger man's treatment of his daughter. Broken hearts were a serious offense.

"Oh, no, only it was sure to bring up bad memories. If Monsieur Giberti knew about it beforehand, he'd brood."

"Messieurs Chavanon and Giberti had a difficult past?"

"Only because of how she left him." Giberti's assistant leaned forward and lowered her voice. "I wasn't supposed to know. Monsieur Giberti never mentions his personal life, but I was in the office late one night—came back to get my gloves—and I heard him on the phone with Christine. She'd dropped him. No explanation. Nothing. He looked sick for a week, and I pretended I didn't know anything about it. I knew that seeing her father would bring it all up again. It's only been a few months."

"Three months," Agnes murmured, recalling what Gianfranco had said. No wonder he remembered exactly how long. He'd been devastated. Everything he had said to her was turned on end now. Giberti wasn't avoiding Christine, she was avoiding him.

"Did Monsieur Chavanon give a reason for the appointment?"

"No, and I didn't push him to. He's a well-known figure and

if he wanted to meet with Monsieur Giberti, then I couldn't refuse."

Agnes thanked her and drove the few blocks to Antoine Mercier's office. She greeted the police officers who were questioning the staff, explaining that she wanted a minute with his assistant. One of them made a crack about the wrecked Ferrari at Baselworld, saying it would have been better to let the man get away than have a fine machine damaged. His remarks reminded her that only five days had passed since the Roach's death; it felt like a month.

Mercier's assistant's eyes were red from crying, but she was calm and professional. Agnes thanked her for her help on the telephone over the last days.

"If I'd realized yesterday that something was wrong," Sara said. "My calls were going to voice mail and he didn't reply to any of my emails." Her voice broke. "He was probably already dead." Agnes patted Sara's arm and guided her to a comfortable chair.

"I'm interested in scheduling details," Agnes said. "Monsieur Mercier visited the Institut de Jeunes Gens in Rossemaison recently."

Sara wiped her nose with a handkerchief and nodded. "Yes, he went there once or twice a year. He liked being visible in the community."

"That was a Friday two weeks ago," Agnes said. "Monsieur Mercier was introduced to a boy named Chavanon that day. Upon learning it was Guy Chavanon's son, Monsieur Mercier commented that he'd seen Leo's father the day before. It was a comment made in passing, but I'd like to know more about that meeting." This was the important detail that Petit had uncovered and that Mercier had omitted to tell them.

Sara nodded slowly. "It wasn't a meeting." She glanced around the office. "I had the day off and saw them. They were standing on a sidewalk. They were angry."

"About what?"

"I didn't get close enough to hear. I didn't want Monsieur Mercier to see me."

Agnes wondered if Sara had claimed a sick day when she wasn't actually ill.

"I stepped into a café and waited until they left. I don't think they planned to see each other. They weren't near any place Monsieur Mercier took his guests, and it wasn't listed in his appointments. He's very meticulous."

"Can you tell me exactly where you saw them?"

Sara gave the name of the café she had ducked into. "They were just a few meters up the street."

"And you didn't hear any of what they were saying?"

"I may have heard something like 'your ideas.' Monsieur Mercier said something like that. But I can't be certain."

"You are positive he was speaking with Monsieur Chavanon?"

"Oh, yes, I know Monsieur Chavanon well. He goes to the candy store down the street about once a month and brings me a treat afterwards."

"Which means that he and Monsieur Mercier saw each other often?"

"No, Monsieur Chavanon would leave a packet of candies. Sometimes I'd find it on my desk. He didn't expect to see Monsieur Mercier and he never stayed to talk."

"You knew about Monsieur Chavanon's allergy to peanuts?"

"Of course. He explained it to me. That's why he came to Bienne, to get his special candies. I guess he'd been going to the same store for years and years, and they make sure the candy isn't cross-contaminated. They were sharp lemon with a sugar coating. He carried them with him everywhere. Must have been hard having to avoid everything else." She put her hand in her drawer and pulled out a small white sack twisted shut at the top. "He always left some of these for me. He remembered what I like because they're his daughter's favorite. Butterscotch."

Agnes thanked her, offering a few final words of condolence. She walked down the street from the office, looking for the café near where Mercier and Chavanon met. Today, the cybercafé was filled with young people sipping coffee and typing on their laptops. She couldn't imagine the man who took five minutes to order an espresso at Baselworld entering this café. And Sara was right, there wasn't an obvious place for Mercier and Chavanon to meet nearby.

With nothing more to be learned, Agnes walked to her car, calling first Marie Chavanon, then Christine Chavanon, on their mobile numbers. Neither answered. She turned onto the highway, placing the next call through the car speakers. Gisele answered at the Perrault et Chavanon booth at Baselworld. Agnes heard a murmur of voices in the background. They were busy. Tomorrow was the last day of the show.

"Did Monsieur Chavanon carry a special candy with him?" Agnes flicked on her turn signal to merge into traffic.

"How funny of you to think of that. Yes, little lemon things. I didn't care for them, but Ivo did."

"Did he keep them in the paper packet from the store?"

"No, he had a special box. It was small. About the size of a Ricola packet."

"Can I speak with Ivo?"

"Is it important? We are really busy."

Agnes assured her it was important, and momentarily Ivo was on the line.

"A quick question. Did Monsieur Chavanon have his candy with him when he came to the factory the day he died?"

"Of course."

"You're positive?"

"He offered me one."

"While he was angry, he offered you candy?"

"It was a habitual motion, almost like a handshake. He always offered me one when I saw him. I'm the only one here who likes them. He had the box in his hand when he saw what I was working on and, after that . . . well, you know what happened."

"It was definitely the box containing his candy?"

"Positive. I'd recognize it anywhere. It was a gift from Monsieur Patel. A very handsome thing from India. Good-quality silver with a ruby cabochon clasp. Very nice. He'd had it for years."

Agnes remembered Louise Kelly's worries about catching a germ at the reception. She had seen something that put that in her mind. Someone taking cough drops. Candies that might look like cough drops. Where were those candies?

Thirty-nine

Agnes stood and brushed her knees. She looked around the Institute's dining room. She'd checked under every piece of furniture and every cabinet. No silver box.

"You're certain I can't help you?" said Madame Jomini, who had followed Agnes down the stairs and into the room, perplexed.

"I'm looking for a small box. The size of a Ricola packet. Silver. It had candy in it."

"You don't think someone stole it?"

"No, but it might have slid under the buffet and wasn't noticed right away."

"I'll ask the maids."

"Find Tommy Scaglia. Tell him he's not in any trouble, but I have a question for him."

She revisited what she'd overheard two days day before. Tommy Scaglia had asked Narendra Patel if he was praying. She had assumed that Patel was standing in the room where his friend had died, closing his eyes to reflect. Or pray. But what if he was kneeling and looking for something? Tommy might have thought Patel was kneeling in prayer.

"Inspector," a voice said behind her. "If you're looking for Scaglia, he was out back with that friend of Leo's family." Agnes didn't recognize the student in the doorway. "I saw them when I came from class."

Agnes rushed toward the sliding doors and ran up the slope to the main lawn. Patel was here?

Dozens of students and teachers were walking back and forth. No sign of Scaglia or Patel. Her phone rang.

"Boschung, thanks for calling me back." She scanned the groups of passing students. "I'm at the Institute."

"I got your message. Why do you care who was parked on the side of the road the day of the reception?"

"Just answer the questions."

"Patel, Monsieur Chavanon's friend, was on the side of the road. He moved along nice enough, no trouble."

"The foreigner," said Agnes softly. That's what Boschung had said the first time, and it hadn't struck her as important because nearly all of the parents were foreign. Only some looked more foreign than others. She turned 360 degrees to scan the campus. Patel told her that he arrived immediately after Guy Chavanon, pulling into the drive after him. But he hadn't. Not exactly. He had arrived before Chavanon and waited on the side of the road. Why?

"What about the symptoms?" she prompted Boschung, reminding him of her second question.

"Monsieur Patel was ill after Chavanon died."

"His symptoms," she repeated.

"I called the medical-response team and got it precisely. They thought he was suffering a heart attack. He was pale and sweaty and had a significantly increased heart rate. Apparently it subsided, and they decided it was a panic attack brought about by witnessing his friend's death. Same symptoms as a heart attack."

"Same symptoms a healthy person would get if he stuck himself with an EpiPen. The adrenaline would simulate a heart attack." What if Patel hadn't met Chavanon at the reception but waited for him, making certain his friend pulled into the drive before following?

The tabby ran across the lawn toward the side of the chalet. Agnes turned in time to see a shadow pass along the side of the chalet toward the parking lot. She squinted. Tommy.

"Get over here," she said to Boschung, hanging up.

In the distance, she heard a car-door slam, then the roar of an engine.

Fourty

Dust and gravel spun from beneath the rented Mercedes's fender. Tommy Scaglia was in the passenger seat of the car, his face pressed to the window. Agnes jumped in her car and started the engine, swinging onto the lane a minute after Patel drove off. He was driving fast, too fast for safety, and she pressed her foot to the accelerator, confident her Peugeot could keep up with his heavier sedan. She pictured the web of roads. He'd avoided the route to the highway, which didn't bode well if she lost sight of him.

She used voice commands to telephone Boschung.

"I'm caught in traffic," he said.

She explained what had happened and gave her location. "We need roadblocks."

"I'm on it, but there are four roundabouts ahead of you; with turnoffs, that's twenty or more roads. I don't have that many men. Stay with him."

Agnes didn't need reminding of the difficulties. Patel roared around a car, cutting it off as he swept through the intersection.

Agnes hit her brakes to avoid an accident and fell behind. She honked and maneuvered around the traffic. The other cars honked back.

Her phone rang and she answered through the car's speakers.

It was Julien Vallotton. "Did I just see you leave the Institute? I'm here to talk to Bernard about a plan going forward. I think it's best to get everything settled."

She swerved around a truck, only to have to slam on her brakes to avoid hitting the next vehicle.

"Scaglia's been kidnapped—" she nearly shouted, honking at a passing car and wondering where the police were. "Patel has him." The call dropped.

The Mercedes accelerated around a line of cars and she raced to catch up. Ahead was yet another roundabout. More routes that could change the entire trajectory of Boschung's interception. All around was countryside; they were far from town and his base of men.

From the corner of her eye she saw a car on a parallel path. A red Ferrari Pininfarina Sergio. For an instant, she had a vision of the Roach bleeding on the road at Baselworld, then she remembered that Julien Vallotton had an identical car. He had followed her and turned onto a farm lane. A field separated them.

He accelerated. It was like a rocket taking off. His trajectory altered. He was on a path to intercept Patel.

She was trapped behind a truck and couldn't see ahead. There was a crash. A squeal of tires. The traffic stopped. She hit the gas and pulled into the oncoming lane where traffic should be. There weren't any cars; they were blocked by the wreck.

Her heart pounded. When she neared the collision, she gasped. Patel had slammed his car into the Ferrari without stopping. She tried to keep her eyes on the road and look for Vallotton at the same time, but the crowd gathered around the Ferrari blocked her view. Her foot shifted to the brake, but she corrected it, bypassing the accident. She had to find Tommy.

Beyond the final roundabout, the road was a narrow ribbon through the countryside. It was some minutes before she sighted the dark Mercedes in the distance. She knew radar boxes were clocking them and would send a speeding ticket to her home, but no policemen were in sight.

The Mercedes ate up the kilometers, lengthening the distance between the two cars. Near the crest of a small rise, Patel roared up behind a trio of slow-moving delivery trucks. He didn't hesitate, swinging out into the opposite lane to pass. Agnes held her breath, unable to see if there was oncoming traffic. Horns blared as Patel topped the hill and disappeared from sight.

She nearly swung out to follow him, but an oncoming car sped past. She took a deep breath and stayed in her lane. It was seconds, but felt like minutes, before she reached the top of the hill and could see her way clear to pass the trucks. She pressed her foot to the floor, feeling the Peugeot hit every minor bump on the country road. The pavement curved, heading higher into the hills, and she wondered where Patel was going. There were fewer and fewer turnoffs now.

The road bent in a gentle *S,* and at the end of the second loop she saw Patel's car, closer than she'd expected. She started to hit the gas, thinking she could finally close the gap, but what she saw on the side on the road made her slam on her brakes.

Tommy Scaglia was lying in a dry ditch.

She swerved to pull over, jumping from her car as it rolled to a stop.

He was clutching his elbow. Tears streamed down his face, mixing with blood.

"I didn't give it to him." He held out a clenched fist. Carefully, Agnes peeled his fingers back from a small box. It was heavy silver with a ruby cabochon clasp. Guy Chavanon's. Candies slid around inside it and her heart lifted. They were surely laced with peanut or Patel wouldn't have been so determined to find the box.

This was the evidence she needed. "You did good."

The angle of the boy's arm looked painful. "He threw me out of the car. I wouldn't help him. I wouldn't give it to him. I found it under the buffet in the dining room last week, and I swear I didn't know who it belonged to. I forgot about it until I saw him looking. He told me to eat them or he'd hurt me."

"Tommy, you've done an amazing thing." She took her coat off and laid it over him. He was shaking.

The delivery trucks lumbered to a stop. One of the driver's ran up. "Did he run out in front of you?"

"Call the police," she said.

The second driver was already setting out road flares. Agnes reached for Tommy's hand. They were close to the French border, and she wondered if Patel hoped to make it across. He might blend in with the larger population and evade capture. With his uncle's money behind him, the options were limitless.

"Tommy, we're getting help and you're going to be fine." His eyes were closed and she shook him slightly, not wanting him to pass out.

A hand touched her shoulder. She recognized the cologne before he spoke. Julien Vallotton. "Go. I'll stay with the boy."

She hesitated for only a moment, then ran to her car and roared off in pursuit of the Mercedes.

They had entered dense mountainous forest, and she gripped the steering wheel and leaned forward, concentrating, looking for Patel's car in the distance. She was so focused that she nearly missed the plume of gravel dust near the forest floor. She slammed on her brakes and reversed. Patel had turned onto a smaller road. She knew this place; this was where she and George had picnicked all those years before.

She skidded left, ignoring the ping of gravel stripping paint from her car. The road ascended steeply then curved. The Mercedes was only a few dozen meters in front of her. She pressed her horn, hoping Patel would realize the folly of his flight. He slammed on the brakes and jumped from his car. He ran deeper into the forest and she followed. She knew where he was going.

"Stop," she hollered. "Don't do this. We can talk."

She stopped, the pain in her leg a sharp spike. "Wait."

He didn't pause, his feet crashing against dry branches, and she took up the chase again.

She reached the small clearing a moment after him. Patel was standing on the edge of the gorge. The spot was well-known; it even had a name, but she couldn't remember it.

She stopped, not wanting to startle him. "I only want to talk."

Patel looked backward over his shoulder into the ravine. He was less than a meter from the edge. She could hear the rush of water below.

"Let's talk for a minute. Take our time."

"Guy lied to me. Humiliated me. What was I to do? My friend, the one I trust for these years and he comes to me with his great idea. What do I offer? Everything. The power of the Patel Group to manufacture and market. Our financing. Our ability to operate on a truly global scale." Patel glanced down again into the gorge.

Agnes took a few steps closer.

"Stay back," Patel rounded on her.

She slowed, holding out her hands, showing him that she meant no harm. "What happened?"

"My *friend* told me that he'd changed his mind. That he could not partner with a company that wasn't Swiss. He with his tiny family business and we are global concern—and now we are not good enough."

Agnes listened for sirens. "Was your uncle angry? I understand the pressures of family. We all understand."

Patel took a step back, nearer the edge. Agnes exhaled to calm herself.

"Do you think that I would shame my family? Tell my uncle that I have started negotiations with someone who now says we are beneath him? I tell my uncle that Guy has lied to us and has no invention. That it was all a figment of his imaginations. That he was chasing a dream. I will not have the Patel Group embarrassed. It is Guy who should be ashamed."

"You didn't have a choice, did you?"

"It was my duty."

Agnes heard faint sirens in the distance. She wished they'd turn them off and not frighten Patel.

"Is that why you broke into the workshop, to steal Guy's notes?"

"Maybe there is no invention is my thinking when I see what it is inside."

"You slipped in during the reception after the funeral?"

"Yes, and I am finding nothing. Maybe he has lied to me? Lied and betrayed me. All of us. Marie, Christine, Leo."

"Come to town with me and we'll talk."

He edged backward and she stopped speaking, holding out her hands in a gesture of supplication. There were multiple sirens now. She heard them pass on the main road and knew they had missed the turn into the forest. She needed more time. The longer Patel hesitated, the less likely he was to do anything rash.

"That horrible boy stole the candies." Patel glanced first left, then right, to look over his shoulders.

"Guy dropped them at the reception after eating one?"

"There was much commotion that day and I did not find the box. That boy saw what was dropped and claimed it. He had no right to take what was not his."

"That was clever of you. Peanut dust on his candies. Although I don't know you did it."

Patel offered a broad smile. "It was a masterful idea. Guy dead from something we had always known would kill him. It was easy to switch his box with my identical one. He is a man of habit and keeps it in the passenger seat of his car when he drives."

"You were waiting for him when he came to the Institute. He had already told you he had changed his mind about a business partnership. He didn't arrange to meet you, but you knew about the reception and went there. You got in the car with him."

"He called to tell me that he was looking for a partner in Switzerland. That week—when I am flying to Baselworld and all is to be a grand surprise celebration—he tells me that he cannot go through with his promise. He talks to me about pride. To *me* about pride. What of *my* pride? I have arranged for my uncle to be there and planned a party to announce the news of our joint venture. I am forced to lie to my uncle and conceal everything so he will not suffer humiliation. My uncle is a famous and respected man. What he does is reported in all the business journals. What they would not give to report this. That even my friend does not trust the Indian partnership. I could not bring this shame to my family."

Patel looked down toward the distant rushing creek. "I came to the school to give him one last chance. Guy would not speak to me; his mind was made up." Patel took a tiny step nearer the edge. "This made the decision very easy for me. I had prepared the duplicate box as insurance and carried out the switch as I sat down. We were only in the car for a second. He would not listen to my side of story. He was not even respecting me this much."

"You went inside to wait and see what happened," Agnes said, talking to buy more time. "Guy didn't walk across the campus to see something. He was avoiding you. He hoped you'd leave, that you'd give up. When he came inside, you noticed him take a candy. You recognized the gesture, maybe he was already returning the box to his pocket. It was something no one else paid attention to. You knew it would be a matter of minutes and faked a phone call so you wouldn't be in the room when his symptoms started."

She'd remembered the voice mail she had received from Aubry. The call hadn't gone through because she was in the dining room. Patel couldn't have received a call during the reception because there was no service in the basement.

Narendra stiffened. "He was no longer my friend. He had betrayed my trust. I would have been ruined, my family's honor destroyed."

"You could have saved him. You knew about the EpiPen.

Instead, you gave yourself the shot, didn't you? In the coat closet you discharged the EpiPen into your leg. You told me that you'd worked for your uncle in the electronics division, but he mentioned that you'd also worked in pharmaceuticals. You knew what would happen. Everyone thought you panicked and nearly had a heart attack, but it was the adrenaline from the shot. One dose might have saved him. It nearly killed you."

Agnes felt the breeze shift. Patel adjusted his weight. He looked over his shoulder. She had to keep him talking.

"Why kill Mercier?"

Patel looked at her and she relaxed. "I am most certain that he was the one who turned Guy against me. He made a point to visit me at the show and spoke only about Swiss Made. I knew then that he was to be Guy's new partner. I could not have him telling this tale, and others knowing what had happened to the Patel Group."

Patel took a great gulp of breath. He stared at his feet, clenching and unclenching his fists. Agnes could see his lips move. He edged backward until his heels were on the brink of the ravine.

"Ending your life won't help," she said softly.

Patel looked up and smiled at her, serene. "This is only the start of another life. I will be rewarded for my sacrifice. For what I have done for my family."

He stepped backward off the edge of the cliff and fell. Agnes ran forward. He screamed, the sound echoing in the cavern, the end abrupt. This was how she had imagined it. She fell to her knees.

Fourty-one

A dozen official vehicles were in the small clearing, lights flashing and sirens muted. Boschung sent climbers down the cliff to find the body, and Agnes shared the details of her exchange with Patel. She had finished when a bright red Ferrari drove up. The front bumper was crushed and the side panel destroyed. Vallotton leaped from the impossibly low seat, then stopped when he saw her standing among the uniformed officers.

She felt her heart flutter and excused herself to walk toward him.

"What were you thinking?" She gestured toward the smashed bumper and side panel. "You could have been killed."

"But I wasn't."

She pressed her hand to her throat as if to contain her fears. Her pulse beat beneath her fingers; it was comforting.

"I know the roads around here and knew I could cut across on the farm lane. I thought I'd block him. I thought he would stop. Never considered he'd bash his way past." Vallotton ran a hand along the crumpled fender. "I'll tell my brother you were driving."

"I thought it was your car?"

"Technically, legally, it is, but it's Daniel who bought it. He sent the bill to me."

Agnes laughed with relief at so many things. She slipped her hands into her pockets.

"You're not hurt?" He took a step nearer, then stopped as if remembering himself and where they were. He looked her up and down. She shook her head and explained what had happened after she left him on the roadside.

"Tommy's off to the hospital," he said. Agnes nodded. Boschung had told her.

"Broken arm, cuts and bruises, but in good spirits." Vallotton glanced at the officials milling around. "You don't need me. With my stunt, I've already created more trouble than help—"

She reached for his arm. "You did help. You slowed Patel and stopped the other traffic. I was afraid he'd disappear on a small road and we'd end up with a hostage situation."

"I was afraid for the boy. Afraid for you, Agnes."

Boschung called for her, and she said she needed another minute. A few of the police cars pulled out, but there was still a crowd. The body was carried away.

"When did you know it was Patel?" Vallotton asked.

"I think it was the phone call. When Chavanon entered the reception, Patel left to take a call. But when Aubry called me the other day, his call went to voice mail. It only came through when I left the basement. That, and Patel had a background in pharmaceuticals, which meant he understood how the EpiPen

worked and how to dose the candies with peanut. Guy Chavanon's candies were the missing link."

"Why didn't Marie or Christine think of them?"

"Those candies were so ubiquitous that no one who knew
him well thought about them. Plus, Marie Chavanon didn't
want to go through her husband's belongings. She hadn't realized the silver box wasn't with his personal effects."

"We still don't know if there was any legitimacy to Chavanon's
big invention."

"Certainly both Marie and Christine stopped believing in a
real invention years ago." Agnes remembered the notebook
Christine brought her. It was part of the series but it didn't seem
like Guy Chavanon. It was a pale imitation of him.

"If there was a great discovery it would be a shame to think
that Chavanon gave his life for something that was then lost."

"He was a paranoid man," Agnes said. "He liked hiding
things." Her thoughts drifted to the absence of a computer and
to the cybercafé. Was Chavanon using one of the café's public
computers? His work would be completely anonymous if the
data was stored on a flash drive. Maybe he took photographs of
notes and transferred them to a drive? Burn the notes and keep
the drive safe? Complicated, but for a man who liked complications, possible. But where would he have stored the flash drive?

"Did Patel also kill Mercier?" Vallotton asked.

"Yes. I think they'll find that the murder weapon is an antique from Patel's showroom. He had tribal pieces there, and
among them several daggers. Mercier was killed because Patel
thought he was Chavanon's new partner for his invention."

"That's unlikely. Mercier was a bureaucrat, not a watchmaker."

"Patel didn't know that. Mercier spoke with him about Swiss

Made, and Patel thought he was delivering a message. A reminder of why Chavanon backed out of a partnership with the Patel Group. The other federation members are with watch companies; Mercier is probably the only one who retired from active manufacturing and took on a purely advisory role. Patel didn't know them well enough to understand that Mercier was the last person who could have partnered with Chavanon." Just as Mercier didn't know how his warning to her about Copernicus would prove true. In some ways, he was killed by his fear of a radical idea.

"Marie and Christine will be grateful to know what really happened," Vallotton said.

"I'm not sure."

"Christine, at least, wanted the truth."

"Everyone wants the truth until they hear it. Guy backed out of an agreement with a friend. It doesn't justify what happened, but it wasn't the most honorable action."

Boschung called out to her again.

Vallotton gave her the smile she remembered from the first time she met him, when they'd stood on the top of his château and looked out across the frozen lake. It was a smile that held promise.

"Please tell your aunt that honor *is* as powerful as the seven deadly sins and that pride and honor aren't easily separated. She will know what I mean."

Boschung called out again.

Vallotton straightened her coat collar. "I'll let you get to work now that I know you're okay." He slipped into his car and lowered the window. Despite the cosmetic damage, the car roared to life. He backed up slowly.

"Call me for dinner," she said. But it was too late for him to hear.

Fourty-two

Agnes was waiting by the front door when Tommy arrived. She followed him into the chalet. He was grinning despite his bandages and cast. Clearly a night in the hospital had restored his spirits. He was holding Helene Fontenay's wrist and smiling. The headmistress said something to him in a low voice, and he headed toward the stairs.

"Chef Jean has set up a welcome-home party in the dining room," Helene said to Agnes. "Ice cream and cookies. Bernard dismissed classes for the rest of the afternoon."

"I called the hospital. They said you didn't leave Tommy's side all night, and that he will make a complete recovery."

Helene shrugged slightly. "He'll probably have some bad dreams. I know I did after my accident. Hopefully his will only last a few weeks. But we talked about it, and I think he will be fine."

"Are his parents coming to get him?"

"They're on their way, but only for a visit, I think." Helene looked around the entrance hall. "When we came here, I hadn't healed. I had too much pain, physical pain, and emotionally I wasn't ready. I'd never felt a physical limitation before, and to be trapped here." She shivered. "I hated the boys who were living far from home, having their own school adventure. Young, their entire lives in front of them. I hated the fact that they didn't understand how precious their time was. Why weren't they striving to excel; why didn't they want excellence in everything they did every day?" She glanced at Agnes. "You're kind not to laugh at me. I wasn't a perfect child, or even a perfect athlete. But it's easy to forget when you're on the other side."

"You'd suffered a terrible blow. Most people wouldn't be near your level of recovery."

"Bernard told me about his ridiculous distillery. Not that the project is ridiculous, but hiding it? You don't know what I'd imagined. It opened my eyes. I'd trapped myself in these walls. There's no reason I can't walk to the farmhouse and see what they are doing. Just like there's no reason I can't try skiing."

Agnes was surprised.

"It won't be the same. But nothing ever is, and maybe I'll learn to appreciate the beauty and serenity of the slopes. I'll take it easy on the speed. After a lifetime of triple black diamonds, I'll be a fixture on the blue slopes now."

"And Tommy, what about him?"

"We're going to give it the rest of the semester. That's what we decided." Helene adjusted her crutches, and Agnes could tell that she was exhausted from a night spent in a hospital chair. "He likes it here, but wants to be home. Wants to impress his father, but also find his own way. He's not so different from the rest of them, he simply decided to act out on his feelings. He's got a tendency toward the dramatic."

Agnes laughed. "Understatement."

She asked if she could go to the dormitory floors, and Helene waved her on before joining the party.

Standing in Leo's room, Agnes studied the shelves. There were five little boxes, not the four she remembered. She picked up the one she'd not seen before. It was the size of a man's palm, made of wood and fine strips of metal. She toyed with it for a moment, then pushed a faint recess. A tiny drawer opened. Hardly more than a sliver. She closed it and turned the box over again. This time she pulled. The box slid open, revealing a long, narrow hollow.

Downstairs she found the entire school gathered in the dining room. Tommy and Koulsy were sharing the glory due healing heroes. It took her a moment to find Leo Chavanon.

His eyes brightened when he saw the box in her hands. "That's my favorite, too."

"I didn't see it in your room before."

"Loaned it to Rudolph. He thought he could find all of the secret drawers. He only found three." Leo grinned. "My dad told me there are nine, but I've only found five. He gave it to me last term, and it's the most complicated one yet. He liked to play with it when he visited." His face clouded over. "Do you think I'll ever find them all now that dad's gone?"

"I suspect you will." She turned the box over and over in her hands. "Do you mind if I borrow this for a few days?"

He shrugged, "No, but if you find all the drawers, you have to show me, okay?"

She kissed him on the top of the head and said goodbye.

Fourty-three

"I heard that you left Omega," Agnes said to Christine. They met on the lawn in front of the Perrault et Chavanon factory, Agnes having called ahead.

"I couldn't leave Marie with all of this—" Christine waved her hand around the property. "Knowing that Father was killed has shaken her badly. And Leo. We tried to spare him the worst, but he knows. He liked Monsieur Patel. It was a shock."

"Particularly since Patel took great care to appear interested in Leo in the week after his father's death. Learning that he had an ulterior motive is traumatic." Agnes turned to look down the hill toward town. The sun was shining and it didn't look as gray as she remembered from previous visits.

"You've decided to rejoin Perrault et Chavanon? Carry on the tradition?"

Christine didn't speak for a minute. "Yes, the tradition. We will return to our roots and focus on the highest-quality pieces we can manufacture. It's what I always wanted to do."

"But not what your father wanted?"

"No, it wasn't. We just thought it was. Funny how a tradition can mean different things to different people."

A car pulled in and Christine flushed. Agnes watched a handsome man step out. Gianfranco Giberti. She stifled a smile. "You broke it off with him, not the other way around."

"I couldn't believe that he wanted to be with me." Christine waved and he waved back and gestured that he was going to the house. "He's been a real help these last days, after . . . everything."

"I hope you didn't mind me bringing Leo's box here and asking you to return it. He challenged me to the nine-drawer discovery. I didn't have time to find more than two." Agnes held Christine's gaze. "Were you more fortunate?"

Giberti called out and Christine said she'd be there in a moment. "Yes, Inspector, I was able to open all nine drawers."

"That's what you were looking for the day you visited Leo at the Institute?"

"I was convinced Father had saved an important part of his work electronically. He went to see Leo so often, almost too often, that I started to wonder if he was using the Institute as a place to keep something hidden. I knew Leo had a few of the boxes, just not how many. That day you saw me in Leo's room, I'd searched them all and decided I was wrong."

"It was only chance that Leo had loaned his newest box to a friend," Agnes reflected. "It was fortunate, actually. That's the day Monsieur Patel delivered the photograph to Leo. It was an odd thing for him to do, not in keeping with Indian tradition, and it bothered me later. If Leo hadn't loaned the box out, Patel would have found it before you."

"Would he have destroyed it?"

"I think so. He wanted to protect his uncle, which meant erasing all evidence of a business deal. I don't know that he wanted to steal the invention, only eliminate the connection."

"It was thanks to you we found it. I wouldn't have gone back to look. The flash drive was there." Christine gave a bright smile. "Finding all nine secret places was almost impossible. I nearly took a hammer to it."

"You didn't give me his real notebook, did you?"

Christine blushed. "It was Father's notebook, just not the one you wanted. He'd started keeping two. He loved a secret and kept making notes in the one that matched the series. I suppose he liked the idea of a decoy. The real one he kept with him at all times."

"This means his legacy isn't lost."

"No, Inspector, my father's legacy isn't lost. Although it won't be a Perrault et Chavanon legacy. Not exactly." Christine looked into the distance. "Marie made a decision when Leo asked why Monsieur Patel killed Father. She didn't want to tell him it was because Father backed out on an agreement with his friend. That's a hard thing to tell a boy."

Agnes nodded. This was a nuance that did not concern the police. Narendra Patel had killed two men to appease his own sense of betrayal. He had killed. End of story. Nothing would justify what he had done.

Christine wrapped her arms across her chest, but it didn't strike Agnes as the gesture of a woman protecting herself; it was the gesture of a woman content. "I don't object to the large brands. They have a role and I loved my time at Omega. But I have a chance now to make Perrault et Chavanon what it once was. A company that makes fine, exceptional, sometimes unique timepieces. That's my dream."

Agnes smiled at Christine. "Now you have a way to finance the company's future."

"It's like a miracle, isn't it?"

Agnes's phone rang.

It was Petit. "Are you finished there?" Before she could answer, he continued, "Because you're needed. They've arrested the woman you called the most beautiful woman in the world. She says she'll only speak with you."

Agnes grinned. Maybe they would find out where the Roach hid all that money after all.

After saying goodbye to Christine, she slid into her car. Something crinkled in her coat pocket. When she pulled it out, she remembered that Vallotton had put a note there the night she took him to the barn to uncover Fontenay's distillery. She'd forgotten about it until now.

She opened the note and read it. Then read it again. *I must go to Paris in a few days. Would you accompany me? We can stay at my house there, or I can put you up in a suite at the Meurice. Either way I promise you an adventure.*

Agnes grinned. Paris. What would Sybille think? Agnes was shocked by the realization that she didn't care. She would go.

Fourty-four

Six months later

The New York Times

GENEVA, Switzerland—International luxury manufacturer Omega will hold a press conference on the first of the month to announce the unveiling of a new line of timepieces. Industry insiders, who were given a preview of the technology after signing a nondisclosure clause, state that the innovation will have as much impact as the creation of the mechanical watch in the sixteenth century and the introduction of quartz technology in the 1970s. A member of the Swiss Federal Council, speaking on condition of anonymity, remarked, "What I was shown today is so far beyond what I imagined possible that I am unable as of yet to grasp the full range of implications."